IRISH CRYSTAL

A Nuala Anne McGrail Novel

Andrew M. Greeley

Thorndike Press • Waterville, Maine

Published in 2006 by arrangement with St. Martin's Press, LLC.

Thorndike Press® Large Print Mystery.

The tree indicium is a trademark of Thorndike Press.

The text of this Large Print edition is unabridged. Other aspects of the book may vary from the original edition.

Set in 16 pt. Plantin by Ramona Watson.

Printed in the United States on permanent paper.

Library of Congress Cataloging-in-Publication Data

Greeley, Andrew M., 1928–
    Irish crystal : a Nuala Anne McGrail novel / by Andrew M. Greeley.
        p. cm.
    ISBN 0-7862-8386-6 (lg. print : hc : alk. paper)
    1. McGrail, Nuala Anne (Fictitious character) — Fiction.
2. Women detectives — Illinois — Chicago — Fiction.
3. National security — Fiction.   4. Irish Americans — Fiction.   5. Chicago (Ill.) — Fiction.   6. Vehicle bombs — Fiction.   7. Psychics — Fiction.   8. Large type books.
I. Title.
PS3557.R358I735 2006b
    813′.54—dc22   2005032833

IRISH CRYSTAL

Also by Andrew M. Greeley in Large Print:

Irish Cream
Irish Stew!
Second Spring: A Love Story
The Bishop at Sea
Fall from Grace
Happy Are the Merciful
Happy Are the Poor in Spirit
Irish Eyes
Irish Gold
Irish Mist
Irish Whiskey
An Occasion of Sin
St. Valentine's Night
Wages of Sin

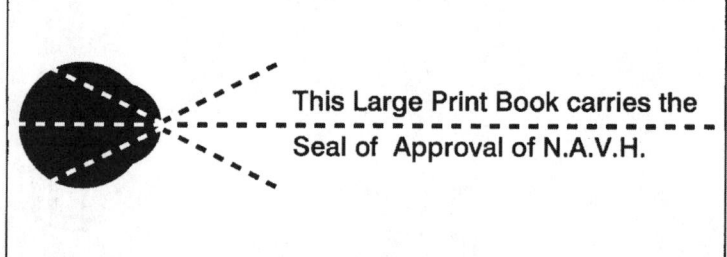

This Large Print Book carries the
Seal of Approval of N.A.V.H.

For John Schaefer and the search for
"Dark Matter"

As the Founder/CEO of NAVH, the only national health agency solely devoted to those who, although not totally blind, have an eye disease which could lead to serious visual impairment, I am pleased to recognize Thorndike Press* as one of the leading publishers in the large print field.

Founded in 1954 in San Francisco to prepare large print textbooks for partially seeing children, NAVH became the pioneer and standard setting agency in the preparation of large type.

Today, those publishers who meet our standards carry the prestigious "Seal of Approval" indicating high quality large print. We are delighted that Thorndike Press is one of the publishers whose titles meet these standards. We are also pleased to recognize the significant contribution Thorndike Press is making in this important and growing field.

Lorraine H. Marchi, L.H.D.
Founder/CEO
NAVH

* Thorndike Press encompasses the following imprints: Thorndike, Wheeler, Walker and Large Print Press.

— Author's Note —

This story is a work of fiction. All the characters — clerical and lay — and situations in Chicago are products of my imagination. There is a parish on Southport, but the one in the story is also a figment of my imagination. I have taken some liberties with the Lincoln Park West (or DePaul) area of Chicago between Clyborn and the River. There never was, as far as I know, a house like the Curran House. The unnamed priest who describes Ireland at the turn of the eighteenth century is also a product of my imagination. The conversations he reports are mostly fictional, though the conversation between General the Lord Cornwallis and George Washington actually happened. I will defer to the note at the end a discussion of the "Irish question." However, I do agree completely with Nuala Anne that if the English government had the sense not to postpone Home Rule till after the end of the Great War, none of the subsequent violence — even to the present — would have occurred.

My attempts at verisimilitude on the two Irish brogues in the story are intended to make fun of neither but rather to revel in the variety of ways English is spoken.

— 1 —

The woman in my bed woke up screaming. Hysterically.

Legions of demons with pitchforks were chasing her, I thought with some lack of sympathy. And herself believing that there were only good angels.

Strong, resourceful spear-carrier that I am, I struggled out of the depths of sleep and put my arm around her. She was as stiff as a redwood tree.

" 'Tis only a dream," I said bravely.

She continued to wail.

"They're all around us!"

" 'Tis only a dream," I insisted. "I'll turn on the lights."

"Don't!" she begged. "I don't want to see them."

"Who don't you want to see?"

"Whom," she sobbed and collapsed into my arms.

I felt the soaking-wet cotton of her Notre Dame sleep tee shirt with the word "Irish!" scrawled above her breasts in gold — a redundant label if there ever were one.

"Whom?" I corrected myself.

"The spies, you friggin' eejit!"

That was a new one. I didn't like it. Often her nightmares were a warning that we were about to embark on one of our mystery tours. There are costs in being married to a fey woman from the Gaeltacht.

"They're part of your nightmare. They're not real."

"They are too real!" She clung to me in desperation. "They're all around us."

Two other presences stumbled into the room, one large and canine, the other small and human.

"Are you all right, Ma?" Nelliecoyne, our seven-year-old daughter, asked.

A very large muzzle nudged around my arms — Fiona, our senior citizen wolfhound. Like the woman in my bed they were both fey. Three of the dark ones in my house — wife, older daughter, and hound.

She eased out of my arms so as to embrace the little girl and pat the big canine on her massive head.

" 'Tis only a nightmare, dear," she said to the little girl.

"Aren't they the terrible things altogether, Ma!"

10

Since she was speaking English with a brogue, Nelliecoyne pronounced the "th" words as though they began with a "d" as in "dey da terrible dings." She talks brogue only with her ma, and with me sometimes, when I'm around. Otherwise, she talks either Chicago English (with its flat "A") or Irish. Trilingual, like I say, just like her ma.

"Did I wake herself up?" The woman put aside her hysterical mask and became an anxious mother.

"Sure, Ma, don't you know that lightning could strike in the backyard and that one would sleep right through it?"

"That one" was her little sister, Socra Marie, a reformed two-year-old terrorist, doing her best to act like a three-year-old "big girl" and losing sometimes to her exuberance.

"I'm fine now, dear. You and Fiona can go back to sleep. Doesn't your da always take care of me when I have these nightmares?"

"Da says that creative people have them all the time."

"And isn't Da always right?" She sighed.

"And doesn't he always take good care of you?" Nellie replied with her own sigh.

"Always."

They both sighed together. These were West of Ireland sighs that sound like the advent of a serious attack of asthma.

As spear-carriers go, Da isn't the worst of them.

After hugs and kisses the dawn patrol departed. The woman reclaimed the protection of my arms. She was still trembling.

"Can I turn on the lights now, just to be sure?"

She huddled against me.

"All right," she said dubiously.

YOU JUST WANT TO SCREW HER.

She's my wife.

YOU'RE TAKING ADVANTAGE OF HER FRIGHT.

I turned on the lamp at the bedside. Cautiously the woman turned away from my chest and glanced around our bedroom.

"Well, they were here when I woke up."

Her long hair was in disarray. Her face red from tears. She was still shivering. Her sleep shirt was askew. Her eyes darted around, looking for monsters. She was nonetheless gorgeous.

As in all matters, the woman's collection of sleepwear was variable — from outrageously erotic to dull. Moreover, her choice in night garments was not an indicator of her interest in sex. So the blue-and-gold shirt was hardly a hint — not that I needed much of a hint to want her.

I am going to make love to her. She's in her shy West of Ireland mode. Can't beat that.

ONLY IF SHE ASKS YOU. DON'T BE A HORNY NOTRE DOMER ALL YOUR LIFE.

"It was just a dream, Nuala Anne."

"Sometimes dreams are true."

She disengaged from me and lay back on her pillow, still trembling.

"They're just reviews of the day, aided by that last drop of the creature you had at dinner."

"A lot you know."

"Cindasue talked about spies at dinner last night . . ."

"They're all around us, Dermot Michael. Won't we have to fight them!"

I didn't like that one bit.

"Well, we'd better get back to sleep."

She reached for a tissue on the nightstand and wiped away the tears. Almost nine years of marriage and a little gesture like that still destroyed me altogether, as she would have said.

"I'm sorry I woke you up," she said.

"No problem."

"I don't suppose, Dermot, you'd ever want a little ride now, would you?"

"I could be talked into it."

The result was marital sex — a gentle, tender, healing journey down a familiar path which was always new towards a sweetly explosive finale somewhere in a field of flowers. Perhaps, I thought as she slipped back into sleep, this is why God or evolution or someone created marriage.

I have been working, if that's what poets do, on a cycle of poems about marital love. I suspect that the reason God and the evolution process made men and women so much alike and yet so different was to provide surprises in the marriage union. If herself ever stops surprising me, I'll know that our marriage is in trouble.

Reversing the stereotypical expectations, I remained awake, wondering and worrying. Nuala Anne, my glorious and treasured wife, was in one of her labile moods, something that happens to your dark ones intermittently. The problem was that she wanted another child, a second son for the Mick (Micheal Dermod, our son and so far our middle child) to fight with, though there was no sign that our self-possessed five-year-old was looking for a fight with anyone. "Four is a nice number, isn't it now? A nice round number?"

Her first three pregnancies caused serious problems. Nelliecoyne proved difficult to carry and difficult to bring into the world. After the arrival of the Mick, my wife went into postpartum stress. Socra Marie showed up after twenty-five weeks, weighing eight hundred grams. I was uneasy about what might happen next, but I have enough sense not to argue. Then, despite considerable, and admittedly pleasant efforts, she did not conceive.

"Maybe someone is sending us a message," I had suggested very tentatively.

"Maybe," she admitted.

Earlier in the week we had our problems with the dogs — our large and amiable snow-white wolfhounds, Fiona and Maeve. On nice days, as Nuala determined them, they would accompany her and the kids across the street to the local Catholic school, where they perform for the entertainment of all parents and children present.

So on Monday evening I had received a call from the pastor of the parish, a humorless little man who considered our family one of the many burdens he must patiently bear.

"Mr. Coyne?"

"Yes, Father."

"I'm calling about your dogs."

"Yes, Father."

"They are very big dogs, Mr. Coyne."

"Yes, Father."

"And frightening."

"They're very gentle and loving."

Unless someone tried to harm Nuala Anne or her children. Her husband, the canines figured, could take care of himself.

"I have been receiving complaints, Mr. Coyne, about their presence in the school yard in the morning."

"How many complaints, Father?"

"That's not the issue. Parents are worried about the safety of their children. Would you tell Mrs. Coyne that I must insist that the dogs do not come to the school yard anymore."

"I will relay your concerns to Nuala Anne, Father. I never try to tell her anything."

"I would, Mr. Coyne, if it became necessary, request assistance from the police in this matter. I also wish she would stop bringing them into church. It is unseemly to have such large beasts in church."

"I'll inform my wife of your decision to ban her dogs from the parish."

Passive aggressive jerk!

Nuala's face, on her couch across the study, threatened explosion.

"Just one complaint," I had suggested.

She had risen from the couch to her full height without comment and strode down to the room where the kids were doing their homework under the supervision of Ethne, our nanny who was working on her doctorate in elementary education at nearby DePaul.

I had followed along wondering what would happen. All three of the children were engaged in creating crayon-colored designs on drawing paper.

"Is there anyone in the school yard," she had demanded, "who doesn't like the doggies?"

"Mrs. Carson." Nelliecoyne had not looked up from her art. "She says they're dangerous."

"She's a bitch," the Mick had added.

"Bitch, bitch, bitch!" the little one confirmed.

Ethne had giggled.

"Where did you learn those words?" my wife had demanded, her face turning a pleasing shade of crimson.

"From you, Ma." Nelliecoyne had continued to work on her color scheme.

"I don't ever want to hear it from you ever again! Do you understand!"

"Yes, Ma."

Their father, fearing for his life, kept his mouth shut, lest he erupt into laughter.

"You just keep your frigging mouth shut, Dermot Michael Coyne."

"Yes, ma'am."

Back in our study, she had picked up a phone and called the rectory. I lifted the one at my easy chair.

"Father, my husband tells me that you have banned my doggies from parish property."

"Ah . . ."

"I will bring the children to school tomorrow morning without the dogs and tell everyone there that you have banned them at Ms. Carson's request."

"Ah . . . I wish you wouldn't do that . . ."

"Nonetheless I will."

She was talking Chicago English with just a touch of Trinity College superiority.

"Well . . ."

"Well, what, Father?"

"That would be very embarrassing."

"I'm sure it would be."

"Uh, suppose you bring them over on a leash, a kind of compromise . . ."

Passive aggressive jerk.

"I will have to consult my husband about that."

Yeah, sure.

She had hung up the phone triumphantly and thrown herself into my arms.

"Showed that gobshite, didn't I, Dermot Michael Coyne!"

WHAT HAPPENS WHEN SHE GETS THAT ANGRY AT YOU?

I'll never suggest that her mutts are a threat to the common good.

The next afternoon we had our second crisis with the hounds.

It was a remarkably warm and sunny April day. We were outside superintending Socra Marie's first ventures on her Christmas present tricycle, accompanied by most of the children in the neighborhood and some of the mothers, including our friend from down the street, Cindasue McCloud Murphy of the Yewnited States Coast Guard and her daughter Katiesue, Socra Marie's inseparable friend — on her own brand-new tricycle.

Tone-deaf our small one might have been, but she has more than enough muscular coordination. She mastered the little vehicle with ease and to great applause from the spectators.

"She a being shunuff good, ain't she, Ma?" Katiesue said.

"Shunuff."

Then a large man with receding hair and

unshaven face lumbered down the street towards us. He was wearing a dirty white down coat, open to his potbelly — our neighbor Mr. Klein, owner of a small but apparently successful trucking company, allegedly "connected." I had never met him but he had a local reputation for irascibility.

I am a retired high school wrestler and linebacker in good shape and about six feet two and a half inches tall. Usually when other men size me up in a bar, for whatever reason, they figure I'm a pushover because of my light blue eyes and blond hair and innocent face. Fortunately for all concerned, this innocence is rarely challenged.

"You Coyne?" he demanded, his beery face two inches from mine.

The kids and their mothers stepped out of the way, save for my wife, now in the Gráinne O'Malley mode and doubtless wishing that she had her canogi stick handy.

"I think so," I said pleasantly.

For a pushover like this guy I didn't need any more testosterone than my normal supply.

"I have three young daughters," his nose almost touching mine.

"Congratulations," I said backing away from his body odor. "I have only two."

"I don't want that prevert who walks

20

your dogs talking to my daughters."

"Mr. Damian O'Sullivan is not a pervert, sir," I said mildly. "He is an artist and he owns a major electronic company."

Which he had inherited from his late father, who also thought he was a pervert because he was a painter of dogs and little children. He was also a "jularker," as Cindasue called swains, to our nanny.

"I don't care what the fuck he is." Klein sneered, once again enveloping me in his body odor. "He's a convicted felon."

"Watch your language around children, Mr. Klein," the virtuous Nuala Anne warned him, with perhaps a touch of hypocrisy.

"You a downright ole polecat, Mista Klein," Cindasue, arms around both our little girls, informed him.

"The next time I see that prevert with your dogs talking to my little girls, I'll beat the shit out of him."

He shoved me, perhaps a mistake.

"I'll advise Damian to avoid your corner, Mr. Klein. I should warn you, however, that our Irish wolfhounds might take some exception to that."

Canis Gaius Hibernicus is the technical name for our beasts.

"I'll shoot your goddamn dogs!"

He swung a fist at my jaw, missed, and

bounced ineffectually off my chest. I grabbed his arm, twisted it behind his back, and sent him sprawling on the newly emerging grass.

"That was a misdemeanor, sir. And you are engaging in disorderly conduct, which is another misdemeanor, and your threats may constitute a felony. All in the presence of witnesses. I suggest that it would not be good for your business if these charges should appear in public."

He struggled to his feet, considered charging me, then thought better of it.

"I have to protect my daughters," he said, tears pouring down his face. Then he turned and lumbered back towards his house a half block away.

"Show's over, folks," I said, inordinately proud of my masculine restraint. "Let's get back to tricycles . . . I have a phone call to make."

"Vermin!" Cindasue proclaimed.

"Shunuff," her daughter and ours agreed.

My wife squeezed my arm in approval and sighed loudly. Perhaps the contretemps had ended too quickly to suit her.

"Gobshite," she whispered softly, so as not to shock the children!

I called Mike Casey, superintendent

emeritus of the Chicago Police Department and head now of Reliable Security. I told him the story.

"Scott Klein is all right," Mike said, "till he starts on his afternoon beer, then he becomes a problem to everyone. His company does good specialty work, but they could lose some of their contracts pretty easily if he got his name in the papers. We'll have a talk with him. I suspect he may want to move out of the neighborhood. I'll have some of our off-duty cops keep an eye on him until then."

That was that. Unofficial power used quickly and sternly. What choice was there?

Peter Murphy, Cindasue's husband, came over after supper to make sure everything was all right. He is some kind of shirttail cousin of Mike the Cop, as they call the superintendent.

"If he had attacked you," Peter observed, "I know two Irishwomen who would have torn him to pieces."

"Even if one is Scotch Irish," I agreed.

"I've had dealings with both," he said with a laugh.

Nuala Anne was not amused. However.

"Dermot love." She hugged me. "There are people out there that don't like us."

A couple of nights later, after we had dinner with the Murphys, her dreams began.

— 2 —

The morning after her dream-induced hysteria. I turned off our alarm at 7:00 a.m., our normal school day beginning, and stole out of the bedroom to awaken the kids for breakfast.

"Gwasses," Socra Marie demanded as she did every morning. So far in her young life only her eyes showed any effect of her premature birth. Far from resisting the glasses when we put them on her, she reveled in them because they made the world "all pretty."

"MA!" she protested loudly. It was her mother's duty to affix the lenses.

"Ma is sleeping in," I said.

"She had a terrible dream," Nelliecoyne explained.

"Poor Ma," the tiny one said as she permitted me to equip her with the spectacles.

"So pretty!" she exclaimed.

They sighed in unison, Irish matriarchs in training.

"She just needs a little more sleep," I

said, leaving for the next room, where my namesake (ma-HALL DER-mud) was wide-awake and scrawling lines which may have represented a soccer team on a page torn out of a spiral notebook.

"Up and at 'em!"

"Where's MA?"

"Sleeping in."

"Why?" He frowned at me.

"Bad dreams!"

He nodded sympathetically and bounded out of bed.

"Poor Ma!"

No sympathy for poor Da, who had to do all Ma's chores and himself not good at them at all, at all.

So I got them dressed and fed and escorted them over to our parish school, which was just across Southport Avenue, all the time admiring meself for my adaptability. Finally we collected the two mutts who were standing at the doorway, panting eagerly.

Spring was pondering the wisdom of returning to Chicago in mid-April. In her wisdom she usually decided against it and withdrew to the south. April is the cruelest month of the year in Midwestern America for different reasons than in Mr. Eliot's England. Nature was not going through the cruel experience of birth. Rather, despite the technical arrival of spring at the vernal equinox, nature was determined to wait at least another six weeks. Winter, it seemed, would never end. Easter snow was not unheard of. Yet the sun shone brightly on the Southport Avenue homes, some of which had survived the Great Chicago Fire and others that had sprung up right after the Fire. The grass was becoming green, an occasional daffodil had imprudently appeared, and tiny buds were emerging on the trees. An early spring? No, another dirty trick.

The procession across the street to the school was part of our morning routine. The snow-white giants would accompany us to school and play with the children. Normally our babysitter Ethne or Damian, our protégé who runs the dogs and paints portraits of dogs and children, or my wife were responsible for this pilgrimage. But all our help had Monday off, so I was in charge. The canines like me — heck, they like everyone — but they did not respect me as they did the alpha person in the house. So I had to put them on expanding leashes.

The rest of the children milling around in the school yard shouted their joy as the two "Santa Claus" dogs approached. The huge white canines offered paws, sat up, rolled over, solicited belly scratching, barked loud but harmless warnings at other dogs, and worked the kids up to a fever of excitement that the poor teachers would need a half hour to calm down.

The bell rang, and just as in the old days in a Catholic school yard, solemn silence descended upon us, even on Maeve and Fiona. Then another bell rang, the children formed up ranks and marched quietly into the school.

Many things may change in Catholicism, but that will never change. The dogs and I watched forlornly as our threesome disappeared through the main door of the school.

Then they decided to pull me towards the church. If Nuala had been presiding, they would have entered the church for the Eucharist, much to the unease of the poor presiding priest — though the hounds were nothing if not reverent in the solemnity of the old church. Not having as much karma as my wife, I didn't trust them in church. The pastor thought our whole family was just a little mad and not without some reason. I didn't want to provide him with more data for this judgment.

"Let's run!"

The wolfhounds promptly forgot about the wonders of the church and dragged me to the Lincoln Park dog run. The welcome from the pooches there was much like the welcome in front of the school. The white hounds were big and scary and fun to play with.

As they scampered and frolicked, I replayed our dinner at the Kurdish restaurant on Clark Street the previous night with Peter Murphy and his wife, Cindasue McCloud, parents of Katiesue Murphy, and prospective parents of Johnpete, who would arrive very soon.

Johnpete would be named after his great uncle, the little Archbishop over at the Cathedral, and his father. "Even if that thar bishop a papist priest, he all right," Cindasue explained. "So we're a fixin' to name him after his great uncle and his father. Powerful name."

Cindasue, a small, sexy woman with large round eyes and a solemn face whose expression never changed, unlike my wife's, which was in constant flux, was allegedly from Stinking Creek, West Virginia.

"Happen I ever lose my mind and becoming one of you papists, need a powerful priest and myself a hard-shell Baptist from down to Stinkin' Crick."

Cindasue was Protestant Irish. Her family moved out to Stinkin' Crick fifty years before that thar "Dan'l Boone came through." My wife was Irish Catholic from Carraroe, an Irish-speaking community at the end of Galway Bay, and was still struggling with Homeland Security about her citizenship papers. They had bonded instantly — two Irish matriarchs. She was a lieutenant commander in the Yewnited States Coast Guard and acted as their occasional spokesperson because she was cute in her uniform ("pretty little girl in a sea scout dress," her mother-in-law, Dr. Mary Kathleen Ryan Murphy, had said when first meeting her) and could slip back and forth seamlessly from American Standard Bureaucratese and Appalachian Hill talk, both of which were admirably suited to confusing the media if that's what you wanted to do. Her husband, Peter Murphy, was an associate professor at Loyola whose doctoral dissertation at The University had been on a little-known tribe called "commodities traders." He had confided to us that his wife was some kind of gumshoe for the Treasury Department, who still worked for them, though the Coast Guard was now part of Homeland Security and not Treasury, where its origins as the Revenue Cutter Service had properly placed them.

"Sure," my own wife had said, "isn't it a case of the Lord made them and the divil matched them?"

I didn't ask her what Irish saying might apply to our marriage.

We had been talking about the owner of the restaurant, a Kurdish refugee and a superb cook, whom Homeland Security had incarcerated on the grounds that a few weeks in one of the Kurdist activist organization twenty years before made him a threat to the United States in the war on terrorism. He would be tried in administrative court, then shipped off to Turkey, where his life would be in serious danger.

"Them polecats are interested only in collecting another scalp. Makes them feel right proper. Useless varmints. They give themselves points for every innocent person with dark skin they can throw out of the country."

"Bureau?" I asked as I sopped up the last remnants of my kavurma with a hunk of Turkish bread, meaning the notoriously incompetent but arrogant Federal Bureau of Investigation. (As in, "we don't care whether Arabs are learning to fly airplanes out there in Minnesota.")

31

"Worse. One polecat comes into my office and says he want all my records. I tell him if he go sleep with a badger, I think about it. He say he send a memo to Mr. Ridge and I say won't do any good, 'cause Mr. Ridge is so dumb he can't read or write. I tell him to work on his messed-up computer files. Now they leave me alone."

"Cindasue is correct in her analysis," said her husband, beaming with pride. "You put together a bunch of small incompetent agencies and you get not an arithmetic but a geometric increase in incompetence. But leaders think they can solve everything by mergers. No competent social scientist would agree."

"Them fools not a listenin' to competent anythin'."

It requires only a half tumbler of barley-corn of whatever variety for Cindasue to loosen up and go after her bosses.

"Don't I know that too!" my wife joined the conversation. "First off they take away my green card, then send me back to Ireland because I don't have it. Then doesn't your man clear it up and personally asks me to return and I came back and applied for citizenship papers? And aren't they sitting on them for two years?"

"Your man" in Irish can be any male

32

member of the human race, depending on the context. In this case it meant a president of the United States.

"They got some skunk from down to the holler a poring over them, then he takes and tries to get you thrown out of the country, like poor Ishamel down hyar to the restaurant."

"They wouldn't dare do that to Nuala Anne," Peter Murphy protested as he filled the wineglasses around the table.

"They a tryin' their damnest," his wife warned. "They too dumb to know who she is. Happen they find out, they dig in with their phony evidence . . . Your lawyer woman, that thar Cindy Hurley shunuf she'll break thar backs, but they be a tryin'."

Ms. Hurley is my sister. She is convinced that Nuala Anne is too good for me. Which is true, but she doesn't have to be so obvious about it.

"How do they find out about people like Ishmael?" my wife asked.

"Rattlesnake spies tell 'em . . . Happen spies come up with good stuff, polecats pay 'em. 'Gainst the law but thar's always money for scalps."

We all laughed uneasily. Yet we knew that the country was in the depths of a particularly vicious period of hatred for foreigners, all foreigners. The Patriot Act produced a lot of phony patriots — which it was supposed to do.

"It is what they done to Mr. Ishmael. He too successful here on Clark Street. Competitors done reported him."

"A lot of people picked up in this neighborhood," Peter Murphy said. "I suppose that because of the kind of place it is we'd have more than our share of targets."

"Best damn targets are people with dark skin," his wife agreed. "Polecats and rattlesnakes like to break up families. Send Moma or Dada back home and leave the rest of the family hyar. Best thing is to break up Moslem families. Serves 'em right. Keep 'merica safe from terrorists."

"That's terrible!" my wife protested, her face twisted in pain.

" 'Cept'n they don't think them folks are real humans like we'uns. 'Taint wrong to ruin their lives."

My wife thinks Cindasue is very funny. She had told me that she "just loves" the cute way Cindasue talks. I almost told her that her way of talking was every bit as amusing to those of us who are stuck with Radio Standard English, 'merican style. She couldn't believe that her beloved

America would try to throw her out again.

"Not right we a doing things like that hyar in the Yewnited States of 'merica. Mista Jeffereson, he warned about it."

"I am getting too old for it," Nuala Anne said, "and a peace-loving woman. Yet I really do enjoy fighting the government, don't I, Dermot dear?"

"Woman, you do," I recited my lines on cue.

But in the corner of my head, not the one where the smart-assed Adversary lives, but the haunt of the little wisdom I've acquired, I felt a tremor of fear. One could never tell what the national security state might do next.

Varmints, polecats, skunks, badgers, rattlesnakes.

"Happen they show up early in the morning like them thar holler skunks do, don't be saying a word till your lawyer be thar. 'Member what they were a doin' to that poor Martha Stewart gal."

My wife was quite blasé about the whole matter, even though the American government had taken both her green card and her Irish passport in preparation for her citizenship papers. She had loved the fight over her previous deportation. She would love another. As she had told me once,

"Dermot love, ain't I a shite-kicker?"

I understood the general idea but I wondered how she would define it.

"What's a shite-kicker?"

"Well isn't it like this?" she said, her voice sinking to a conspiratorial whisper. "Don't I come into a room and look around to see if I can find a pile of shite to kick and kinda spread it around the room?"

"A high-powered troublemaker?"

"Don't you have the right of it, Dermot Michael Coyne? And a bitch on wheels too!"

I didn't doubt her for a moment. Last year a couple of eejits were trying to beat me up on the sidewalk in front of the house. My demure Irish wife, looking like Gráinne O'Malley, charged down the stairs, canogi stick in hand, and began to pound on them, canogi being a kind of Irish hockey for women. Also the dogs and the kids joined in. And Cindasue, delicious in halter and shorts, appeared from down the street with a service revolver that was almost as big as she was. I had to pretend that I needed the help.

So she would relish taking on the gobshites (her word) at Homeland Security.

Nuala, like all the rest of us, has many different personalities which fit the various situations in which she finds herself. Unlike the rest of us, they are all colorful personalities and she moves among them with great speed. The ur-Nuala as I call her is the shy, fragile, and modest Irish speaker from Connemara. Then there is the sophisticated woman of the world who has been everywhere and done everything, and the accomplished entertainer and the devoted wife and mother (a bit on the compulsive side) and the wanton wench who loves to seduce me and the mystic who talks about the mountain behind the mountain and the fey detective who knows what's going on in people's souls — or dogs' souls — and the furious shite-kicker and the worrywart who thinks teachers are exaggerating her children's virtues and guilt-ridden old-fashioned Catholic who believes in her heart of hearts that she was personally responsible for her postpartum depression after Micheal and the premature birth of Socra Marie (pronounced, mind you, Sorra) and fishwife gossiping over the backyard fence and mother whose patience had been driven to its utmost limits by her husband and children, a role which is all too familiar these days. And many more besides.

I have slept with all of them. Each has her own erotic appeal.

THAT'S BECAUSE YOU'RE HYPER-SEXED.
I am NOT.

My favorite bedmate is the greenhorn from Connemara.

My wife had not changed much physically since I had first encountered her in O'Neill's pub on College Green in Dublin, the Danish town with the Dark Pool. She was still a graceful Irish goddess, not that I had ever encountered any exemplars of that group of women — slender, lithe, dangerously sensuous, with a voice in which you hear the sound of distant bells over the bog land, long black hair, flashing blue eyes, and a pale, ever-changing face which adjusted to the role she was playing at any given time. Her grimly determined will would not permit pregnancies to affect her bodily measurements and the faint smile and laugh lines on her face made it even more appealing. Marriage and motherhood had added to her beauty, even hazardously so. What does she look like with her clothes off? Well, that's my business and I won't be telling, will I now?

Save for the metaphors in the unpublished poems I've written about her.

Living in the same house, to say nothing of sleeping in the same bed with her, keeps me in a permanent state of semitumescence.

I have no complaints about her in bed either.

People see Nuala Anne and they need a second look, women and men alike — whether she's walking into church on Sunday with her three well-dressed children trailing behind her or swinging a lethal tennis racket in two-piece tennis togs or entering a restaurant as if she owned all the world or strolling purposefully down Michigan Avenue in a business suit. In each of these scenes, no one notices the big, dumb blond guy trailing after her.

So when I returned from walking the dogs I found her in the breakfast nook, bedraggled in Notre Dame shirt and terrycloth robe, hair in disarray, sipping a cup of tea and shuffling through the day's lists. The dogs had dragged me up the stairs because, as much as they like to run, they like even more to come home and find that Nuala is still around. She hugged them both and asked them to go downstairs to the doggie room. They needed water and rest after their run. I sighed mentally. We were in for a serious discussion.

"Did you wake up the children?" she asked.

"Woman, I did."

"Did you feed them their breakfast."

"Woman, I did."

"Did you take them across the street to school?"

"Woman, I did."

"Did you take the dogs for their run?"

"Woman, I did."

"Did you manage to clean up after breakfast?"

"Woman, I did."

"Aren't you the friggin' perfect husband?"

"Woman, I am!"

She sighed loudly.

"I can't even work on me lists! How will I get through the day without me lists!"

Tears poured down her cheeks.

Nuala Anne coped with the demands of her lives by making lists each day of what had to be done — a list for everyone and for every project, cross-indexed for all I knew because they were written in Irish. I'm sure there is a Dermot list because she wouldn't let me look at it.

I had asked her once, "Does it say that I should fuck Dermot tonight?"

"Och, Dermot Michael," she had replied, "I don't have to be reminded of that, do I now!"

"Should I wet the tea?" I asked her that morning in the kitchen as she shuffled again through her scraps of notepaper.

"It will do no harm," she admitted with

40

another sigh as she pushed the papers aside.

That was a more complicated task than you might expect. The very mention of tea bags was solemnly interdicted in our house. Nor could you pour more boiling water over the loose tea already in the pot without removing some of what was there and replacing it. The art was to know just how much to replace. I was learning.

I pushed the button on the electric teapot — which was not too modern because they used such pots back in Carraroe all the time.

"You scalded the pot, did you now?" I ask often when she's making the tea.

"I may have lost me mind, Dermot Michael Coyne, but I haven't lost me soul."

I poured the boiling water over the tea and sat at the table. She buttered an English muffin and covered it with raspberry jam for meself. I left it to her to decide when the tea was ready.

There was no milk on the table because I had talked her out of the Irish custom of, as I said, polluting perfectly good tea.

"You aren't the worst lover in all the world, Dermot Michael."

You must understand that is a very high compliment from an Irishwoman.

"And you have had so many others to compare me with?"

She actually laughed as she poured our tea.

"Did you ever think, Dermot Michael, that if you had it to do over again, you might just sneak out of O'Neill's and not sit at the same table with me?"

That was a fast pitch for which I was not ready. While I tried to cope, she broke off a piece of the English muffin and put it in my mouth, just like she was distributing the Eucharist.

"Well, to tell the truth, woman, I have not."

"Why not?"

A tough question. We were obviously in a mood for a general confession.

"I figured then that you'd be a good ride and there'd never be a dull moment. Both expectations — admittedly of a young man whose blood was drenched with hormones — have been fulfilled."

"I've been nothing but trouble for you."

That wasn't true at all and she knew it wasn't true. Yet just then she was afraid that it might be. I had better tread carefully. So I said nothing.

"I'm a neurotic twit, I get depressed, I almost lost my little girl, I fight with you all the time . . ."

"And you're no good in bed."

"That's not true," she said hotly, "and yourself knowing it."

My wife was fiercely competitive. She had learned to play tennis only in America and was not satisfied till she could beat me half the time. She was already good at golf and, granted her handicap, she also beat me half the time, though she claimed that she won more often than I did. A couple of years ago she had decided that she was not as sexually skillful as other women — she never specified who those other women were. So she began to read books on how to be a better lover.

"You may not read those books, Dermot Michael Coyne," she had ordered me. "Won't they be giving you dirty thoughts?"

"Any poor man who has to live in the same house with you and share the same bedroom with you, woman, will already have all the dirty thoughts he needs."

She had blushed, smiled, and lowered her head.

"Isn't that a sweet thing to say . . . But how do I give you dirty thoughts?"

I read the books without undergoing a noticeable increment in my lust level, though they did provide some insights into woman psychology which I tried to introduce into my poetry. As far as I could tell, however, the books did not improve on my wife's sexual skills, which, as I had told her, were considerable to begin with.

She was furious with me. I should have kept my mouth shut.

She was bantering now, shite kicking, looking for an argument.

"Well, sometimes you take off your bra when you brush your hair before you go to bed."

Her face had turned as red as Cardinal Sean's choir robes.

"And you want me stop such misbehaving?"

"If you do, I'll divorce you."

She didn't misbehave that way every night. Even when she did, I took the brush out of her hand and brushed her hair myself only sometimes. Happen the opportunity, as Cindasue would say, I'll do it again tonight. In the meantime, as I ate my muffin and drank my tea, I calmed her down.

"But all this fey stuff drives you out of your friggin' mind," she said sadly. "You're about fed up with it, aren't you now?"

"It's part of the package, Nuala Anne," I said evenly. "If you are meant to solve mysteries and save people, then I'm meant to be your spear-carrier and research assistant . . . Besides they're fun . . . A live video game for a superannuated adolescent even if the heroine doesn't wear latex . . ."

"There's bad people around, Dermot love," she said grimly. "I knew about them even before me dream. Really evil people. I knew about them even before Cindasue told us about them last night."

"Who are they spying on?" I asked, having put on my invisibility cloak.

"On everybody, especially immigrants. We have to stop them."

IT'S JUST GOING TO MEAN MORE TROUBLE. NOW'S THE TIME TO BREAK HER OF THIS CRAZY HABIT. TELL HER SHE CAN'T BE FEY ANYMORE.

The Adversary had a point. Here I am, a young man with a beautiful wife, three great kids, a steady if not altogether earned income, three homes (one for each kid?) and a wife who on some nights will let me brush her hair. If I let her go on this new venture into feydom, I might lose it all.

Who were the new enemies, spies who were everywhere and spying on everyone? The woman was out of her mind!

So what did I say?

I took charge of our family and said, "Nuala Anne McGrail, go take your shower and wake up. When you're finished, we'll talk about how we will defeat this new crowd of baddies."

"Will you really do that, Dermot?"

She knew damn well that I would.

"Get into the shower, woman!" I ordered, squeezing her thigh. "The game's afoot and we haven't a second to lose."

YOU'RE A FRIGGING AMADON.

"You're sure?"

"Haven't I told you so!"

She hesitated.

"This morning, I think it ought to be a private shower."

Astonishingly I hadn't thought of that possibility.

"Into the shower, woman!"

She put her notes in a neat pile on the table and went upstairs to our room.

I really am a friggin' amadon.

— 3 —

The hot water feels so good . . . I should turn on the cold . . . Och, Nuala Anne, 'tis not like the old days when you and Ma used to go swimming in the ocean! You'd laugh at the cold water! But then you didn't have so much heat to cool as you do now . . . And you weren't hungover . . . A second jar of the creature, Cindasue's stories, me terrible dreams, then Dermot . . . Well, I asked him to take me and he did . . . and I felt wonderful . . . And I wake up with this terrible hangover . . . Loving and the creature never did this to me before . . . It wasn't the loving . . . it was the drink taken. . . . But the loving is still in me . . . It's not right at all, at all for a man to have as much power over a woman as he has over me . . . I've let him know too much about me . . . I'll never get away from him . . . The thing is that I don't want to get away from him . . . He's too good for me . . . I go crazy when I feel him inside of me . . . I want him there all the time . . . I don't deserve a lover and a husband like him . . . So I try to fend him off with me quick tongue and me obsessions . . . My friggin' lists . . . I think I'm nicer to him than I used to be, but I don't know because the poor amadon never complains . . . Even the kids complain when I turn obsessive . . . They laugh at me . . . Dermot doesn't laugh and doesn't complain . . . I should have invited him to come up here with me . . . His hands are so wise when he's bathing me . . . They mess around with me and drive me out of me friggin' mind when I want that and they provide reassurance when that's all I need . . . I was afraid to have him here with me . . . What am I to do about him . . . And now I've got him into another evil mess . . . It is truly evil, worse than any of the others . . . Layer upon layer of evil . . . Spies everywhere . . . The evil is like a big heavy pall weighing me down . . . and it's right here in the neighborhood too . . . We've escaped before . . . But this time it's worse . . . twisted, complex malevolent . . . We'll beat it of course . . . It's going to be difficult . . . And what will it do to us as we destroy it? . . . I better stop dreaming about all my Dermot's wonderful tricks, take a nice cold shower . . . and get back to work, still I wish he were here . . .

— 4 —

I hardly knew where to begin. I knew I could find a manuscript over in the basement of Immaculate Conception Church on North Park Avenue, part of the collection that Ned Fitzpatrick had picked up on his various trips to Ireland. There was always a manuscript over there that somehow fit the vibes that herself was feeling. Sometimes I thought it was the manuscripts that attracted the vibes. My brother George the Priest, always the busy pastor, went through the motions of being glad to see me.

"Your gorgeous witch up to something new?" he asked as he gave me the key to Ned's archives.

"Witch," when George applied it to Nuala Anne, was a positive word. She was after all one of the dark ones. Still, I didn't like it.

"If she's a witch, she's a good witch," I insisted.

"Never denied that, little bro. She's

worked miracles with you . . . The good witch of North Southport Avenue."

That was the family conventional wisdom about me. I was talented, lazy, indifferent, went to two colleges for four years and never graduated. Then Nuala Anne came along and made something out of me. The fact that I had made more money than all of them put together was the result of pure luck. I usually added, "and sound instincts," but they ignored me. They also ignored the books I had published. The truth is, they would say, that without Nuala you'd be hanging around some library reading old books.

Herself lost her temper when she heard their theory. I was not lazy, I was not indifferent, she had not made something out of me at all, at all. I was the one who had salvaged her from a boring life as an accountant and turned her into a concert singer "and a lot of other things besides." I was the perfect husband and father. She was terrible lucky altogether to have found a man like me. The family, who adored Nuala, backed off, but didn't change their minds.

I hoped she was right, but I half thought (as she would have said) that she was wrong. Or half-wrong anyway.

So I went down to the musty old storeroom beneath the side altar where my wife was convinced I should always look for material when she was in one of her dark moods. I told myself once again that we really ought to get an archivist in to arrange everything. Nuala had vetoed the idea.

"I think Ned and Nora would want us to leave the stuff right where it is still," she said. She was convinced that she was related to Nora and in some sort of communication with her — just as she was on the same wavelength as my grandmother ("Ma" as we called her) even though she had never met Ma. So when our first child had been born with bright red hair, we had to call her Mary Anne after Ma and that became Nellie just like Ma and then elided into Nelliecoyne, which Ma had been for most of her life.

Superstition?

How did I know? I was living on the edge of a very strange world, pretty deep into it, and I didn't want to sink in any deeper by trying to explain it.

I searched through the old papers, which Ned had organized into folders. None seemed interesting till I came to a folder which was labeled "1833." The first paragraph, in firm and clear black writing, began:

It was the spies that did in the United Irishmen. The spies were as thick as flies around a dead cow. At some of their meetings half the participants were spies for Dublin Castle, the English headquarters for all of Ireland. Lord Edward, Wolf Tone, and especially Robert Emmet — Bold Robert Emmet — were murdered by traitorous friends. The Castle did not have to establish an organization. Irishmen flocked to it, eager for the Castle's pound in exchange for the blood of Irish patriots. Sometimes the spies even reported on one another. The whole crowd of patriots knew there were informers, but, naïve innocents that they were, were not afraid of them. They killed those whom they caught but remained careless. They would never have thought of spying back on the Castle.

I put the manuscript in my briefcase, left a note in the archives saying that I had removed it on a certain day and planned to return it. All the Irish "risings" till 1916 were romantic, poorly planned follies. Spies sold out the rebels before they ever had a chance, not that there was ever much of a chance anyway. No one ever spied on the Castle. Not till Michael Collins arrived on the scene and infiltrated the center of English power with brave woman stenographers. The Big Fella was always one step ahead of the Brits whom he beat at their own game. The brave young women never earned a penny for their spying and wouldn't have taken it if it were offered to them. The Castle people didn't realize that kind of patriotism could exist among women, especially Irishwomen.

Spies were very much part of English imperialism. They used spies against us when we were getting rid of them. They used them in India in what that poet of imperialism, Rudyard Kipling, called the Great Game. They used them everywhere because pay for a spy requires much less than the death of English soldiers. It was a dirty business dealing with traitors, but not as dirty as sending in English troops. It was not an accident that their counterspies at Bletchley Park helped to win World War II. The Brits knew all there was to know about spies.

"Well," said my wife, impatiently looking up from the book she was reading, when I returned to the house, "I don't suppose you found anything."

"Woman, you're wrong again!"

I read her the first paragraph of the manuscript.

She removed her reading glasses, leaned forward, her blue eyes hard and intense. "Wasn't I after telling you that you'd find something over there?"

"Woman, you were."

That's the way it is in our cases. The spear-carrier never gets credit.

She was freshly scrubbed and wearing neatly pressed black jeans and a matching black sweatshirt, both closely fitting, with a red ribbon holding her hair in place, shoes with high heels, and nylons. For whom had this costume been arranged, I wondered — for herself, for me, for the angels? If it was for me, her neatly displayed curves had their usual effect of causing me to gasp. Do I love Nuala or just lust after her? Both and in an intricate complexity that I try to express in my poems — with little success.

She was surrounded by a pile of books about espionage.

"Would you ever walk across the street and collect the small one," she said, returning to her book. "You know what she's like. If one of us is not there, she'll just cross by herself."

I whistled for the hounds. They came running, doubtless figuring it was about time to collect Socra Marie. If we had delayed five more minutes, they would have complained. Spear-carriers do what they're told.

We arrived in the nick of time. Along with other toddlers she emerged from the door of the school and dashed towards the street, determined as she always was to navigate it herself. A patrol woman of sixth-grade age shouted at her, "Sarah Marie, *you* stop right *now!*"

The child was growing up. A year ago she would have run into the street anyway. Now she'd stop with a sigh of protest and wait for the advent of the doggies.

I scooped her up.

"I always do what Angie says," she informed me piously.

It was like her to know the sixth grader's name. A future precinct captain?

The canine brigade paused to bark at their friends among the toddlers. The Team Coyne then looked in both directions and crossed the street.

"Da looked both ways," the child said, confirming my probity.

"If Angie wasn't there, what would you have done?"

"Wait for Da and doggies," she said piously.

She was fibbing, but she at least knew the right fib.

Her mother, a delectable sculpture in black, waited for her at the top of the stairs. The child squirmed out of my arms and ran up the stairs.

"Ma! I stop for Angie . . ."

Nuala enfolded the tiny bundle of energy in her arms. Unconditional love.

"Didn't I see you, dear? And wasn't I terrible proud of you?"

Unconditional love all the way.

As her mother led us all to the breakfast nook, Socra Marie poured forth a largely incoherent tale of her triumphs during the morning.

"Everyone love me!" she concluded brightly. "Except when I talk too much."

"You wouldn't be your mother's daughter, would you now, unless you had important things to say?" I observed, noting that I was increasingly talking in questions.

Me wife glared at me, then grinned.

She rewarded the dogs with treats and sent them to their room. She allowed no begging mutts at her table, even in the breakfast nook. Despite her obligation to research espionage, she had provided a healthy lunch, bowls of steaming soup and stacks of sandwiches with the crusts cut off, Irish style, a glass of milk for Socra Marie, and two glasses of iced tea for Socra Marie's parents.

The iced tea was a concession to Americanization, one which she never honored when we were "back home."

"Wouldn't it shock me ma and da, something terrible!"

Socra Marie entertained us through lunch with her stories of school. Nuala Anne listened with an indulgent, loving smile, though she had no more idea than I did what our child was saying. The teacher had told us that she was the most popular child in the class because she was so kind to all the others. "She's a little verbal, of course, but no one really minds."

"Verbal, is it?"

My wife is suspicious of any praise from teachers.

"Runs in the family," I had said, earning myself a glare that would wither half the shamrocks in Ireland.

"The other children want to take her home to be their sister, she's so entertaining."

Nuala had not liked that at all.

"Well, don't let her disturb the class."

The teacher was seven or eight years younger than my wife.

"Oh, she never does that!"

Nuala wasn't convinced.

"Little show-off," she had complained to me as we walked home.

The Energizer Bunny ran down suddenly at lunch that day.

"Ma!" She took off her glasses and rubbed sleepy eyes. "Nap!"

Nuala picked her up and headed upstairs to the "girls' room."

Our other kids resisted naps at that age. Socra demanded them. We both worried about it, but the doctor said that the child burned up a lot of energy with her enthusiasm and enjoying the life she almost didn't have.

Nuala returned, shaking her head. I was in our study, working on the document from the rectory.

"The poor little tyke was asleep before I put her to bed . . . I wonder if there's something wrong with her."

"Some kids need naps at her age more than others," I said, echoing the doctor. "She's still a tiny one. Besides, she'll be the Energizer Bunny again in an hour and a half."

"What do doctors know?"

She sat in her reading chair and opened the book on the top of the stack — all of them doubtless sent from Borders on a rush basis.

"More than we do."

"That's not much . . . And Dermot, why are you looking at me lustfully all day long? And yourself unable to wait till nighttime for that kind of shite!"

AHA, YOU'RE IN TROUBLE NOW!

"Well, Nuala Anne McGrail, isn't yourself the only woman that's in the house and my wife at that?"

"And why do you have to talk in questions all the time? That's all right for me, because I'm Irish, but aren't you a friggin' Yank!"

"Haven't I become acculturated?"

She relaxed and smiled, laughed, then collapsed into tears.

"I'm the worst friggin' bitch in all the world and a nine-fingered gobshite too."

I have no idea altogether what a nine-fingered gob of shite is. Neither does she. But it is a marvelous expletive.

I rose from the couch, which is mine by right in our study overlooking Southport Avenue, walked over to her reclining easy chair, and took her hand.

"Well, you're not the worst of them. And

if I should stop wanting you, then you'd better take me to the doctor for an eye test or a hormone test. And if you don't want me to want you, you must not dress in sexy clothes."

I drew her over to the couch and sat her down. She stared at the floor, her book on her lap with a finger still in it.

"We can sit here and do our reading together," I offered.

She nodded.

"You know, Dermot Michael Coyne, that you can fuck me anytime you want."

"I know that, Nuala."

"I love you so much . . . I apologize . . . and I should have asked you to bathe me in the shower this morning . . . I would have loved it."

I put my arms around her shoulder.

YOU'RE GOING TO EXPLOIT HER AGAIN.

I'm not, you eejit. It'll be much better tonight.

"Why didn't you ask me?"

"I was afraid to . . . Och, Dermot Michael, my emotions are still a mess . . ."

She rested her head on my chest.

"The dreams still?"

She sighed.

"And the evil out there!"

We were silent for a few moments.

"All right!" She was all business again. "We both have work to do."

She straightened up and opened her book. But she made no move to leave the couch. Later on in the afternoon, she took my hand and held it.

I knew them all, you see. Bob Emmet, Lord Edward, Wolf Tone. Bold Robert Emmet as they call him now. I was in Bobby's class at Trinity in 1794 and I was there the day they threw him out. I managed to sneak into his trial and listen to his speech from the dock. And ready-made legend it was. I stood there in front of St. Catherine's Church when they hung him, cut off his head, and held it for the silent crowd to see. I saw Wolf Tone dragged out of a coach into Kilmainhum Jail, where the poor idiot cut his throat. I was in the crowd when Lord Edward Fitzgerald was shot in the house where he'd been hiding, betrayed by the spy Magan in whose house he had slept a couple of nights before.

"He won't swing," said a man in the crowd.

"Why not?" someone else asked.

"The bastards will let him die from an infected wound. No public trouble that way."

I was too young to understand that

anyone, even Lord Clare, would do something that evil.

Well, it's 1832, thirty years since then. They're all great Irish patriots. And they're all dead. Bobby would be fifty-five, just my age. He and Sarah would be living in Dublin with a flock of kids around them. Maybe not. All ten of the other Emmets are dead, except Tom, and himself a big political success in New York. Bobby was the fourth Robert in the family, the previous having died as infants. Most of them from tuberculosis. Bold Robert was, even at fifteen when I met him in Trinity College, a sick, wasted little man whose energy and drive did not match his poor body. Sarah died five years after he did, also from the white death, having lost her only child.

God be good to them both . . . I stop writing and weep when I think of Sarah . . . I loved her too . . . Enough of this sentimentality.

What would they think of this "emancipation" which Danny O'Connell has won for us? I personally don't trust Danny. After the 1803 rising Danny went around searching for rebels. He didn't find any because there were not many to begin with and they had returned to the hills. He *doesn't believe in violence, he says. The political way is the only way. Well, he won our rights and that thirty years and more after Lord Edward and Tone and poor Bobby failed. Now Irish Catholics will sit in the parliament in London and won't have to pay tithes to the Protestant Church over here. So that's good, I suppose. God knows that's the way the Catholic bishops want it and themselves in the pocket of Dublin Castle from Archbishop Troy back in 1798 on down. We poor priests of the land out in the bogs don't have a right to say anything.*

The next step, Danny tells us, is home rule. I don't think the English will give us that without a fight. Why should they? They took this island away from us by vio-lence. They beat us every time — Strongbow and Henry and Elizabeth and Cromwell. They believe we're an inferior people that should be killed off like the red Indians in America. They hate us because we persist in our Catholic superstition. If they could kill every one of us, they'd do it and replace us with the lowland Scots that they want to get out of their own island anyway. So they take our land from us and force us to live in poverty and misery and starve us.

Yet poor stupid fools, we fight back. There have been risings ever since Strongbow arrived — fifteen at least since King Billy planted his orange flag. The '98 was only the biggest so far. There will be others, despite their lordships the bishops. We Irish are not only stupid but stubborn. We want our country back. Someday we'll be taking it back.

Still I don't know, maybe Danny O'Connell is right. Maybe we should win our freedom by our political skills. The parliament in Westminster won't know what hit it when forty so of our own come riding into town — fast-talking, clever men with long memories and a gift for making trouble. I'd like to be there and watch it all.

It's true that there are people in England who are on our side. The Act of Union did destroy the Ascendancy and the corrupt Irish parliament in which a couple of score of crooked Protestant politicians ran the country for their own purposes. Some of the English thought that would improve the lot of the Irish. It might have if Lord Cornwallis and Lord Castlereagh, who bribed the Irish parliament to vote itself out of existence, had been able to push through a Catholic emancipation act with the Act of Union. That crazy bastard

George III vetoed their plan and their lordships, to give them due credit, resigned. Castlereagh was a bit on the crazy side, but Cornwallis was a gentleman in the best meaning of that word. Many more of the survivors of the '98 would have died if he had not believed in compassion. He probably would have pardoned Wolf Tone too, if that idiot hadn't cut his throat.

Tone and Lord Edward and Bob were Protestants too. They were also Irish and hated English tyranny more than many of us did.

Most of the priests of the land, no better than their people both the English and our bishops will tell you, have always been on the side of the "lads." I'm not so sure who has the right of it. We Christians shouldn't be killing people. When we kill the English — and their women and sometimes their children — we are no better than they are. The bishops don't so much object to murder as they do to fears of the French Revolution — which shows how little they know of their own people.

There are Whiteboys in my parish down here in Wexford — half bandits, half terrorists. Some of their fathers were in Dublin with Bobby, and my men would return to Dublin at a single word from someone who seemed to be in charge, even if it were a sickly twenty-five-year-old in a silly green uniform. Bobby is a hero to them. "Let no man write my epitaph" — For a Protestant Bobby could outblarney any Irishman I know. The Whiteboys know that I was a friend of his, so they treat me with great respect. I keep my own counsel. I let them know that I don't approve of their violence against the local English but I don't work for Dublin Castle either.

Bobby knew he would become a legend. He designed his own trial and execution to accomplish just that — and to protect poor Sarah, who might have been in the dock too if Chief Secretary Wickham and he had not agreed on compromise. Bobby would admit his guilt and Wickham would keep Sarah out of the trial. So it gave the poor woman five more years of mostly unhappy life before she joined him in heaven. Bob couldn't have known that her tragedy would enhance his legend. He loved her too much even to think that way.

I was in love with her too. I was in the parlor of Casino, the Emmet house down in Milltown, when she and Bob were introduced. Her father, John Philpot Curran, a really nasty bastard if you ask me, and Dr. Emmet were friends. He never did like Bob very much, but he could hardly keep him out of the house. He was too arrogant to notice the fire that leaped back and forth between his daughter and "young Emmet." Maybe I was the only one who noticed it.

I know what Bob saw in her. She was nineteen years old then, in the full and beautiful bloom of youth. It was, as I learned in those days, easy to fall in love with such a glorious woman. It is even now difficult to forget her, so I've ceased to try. I think that God understands. I don't know what she saw in Bob, a pale, weak little fellow. It must have been his mellifluous voice which had hypnotized all of us in the History Club at Trinity and which later would persuade many to accompany him on the folly of the Rising of '03. Or maybe she recognized his inherent nobility which has already become part of our national mythology. It doesn't matter anymore. Her lovely body and his ugly body are long since moldering in their graves.

I was with her when she waved to Bob as he was being dragged to the gallows. I was with her when she visited the grave-yard at St. Michan Church, where perhaps *his body is buried. Her eyes were dry, her body erect, her head held high. Bob wasn't the only one who could lay claim to a noble character. With a few hundred more men, some more muskets, and some help from the French they could have been the first rulers of a free and republican Ireland — much more impressive than George III and his equally mad brothers. Many people back in those days said that Bob Emmet was a crazy young romantic and his rebellion an aftereffect of the '98. In fact, Dublin Castle was taken by surprise. Bob's men fought well against the soldiers and the Yeomen. With some good fortune — more than we Irish ever seem to find — they might have taken control of the city. Then the whole country would have risen. All the disappointed veterans of '98 would have swarmed in from the country. It would have been Paris in 1789 — just as Archbishop Troy had feared . . .*

"It was all my fault, you know," she said to me. "Before we went to France, he wanted me to go to America with him. I was afraid of my father. If I had agreed, we would have left this terrible island behind forever and he'd still be alive."

"You must not blame yourself, Sarah," I

said. "He was an incurable Irish rebel. He would have come back."

"I don't believe that he would."

Even now I don't know what to think about that. Maybe she was right. I thought to myself that, if she didn't choke off such terrible thoughts, she'd soon be in a cemetery herself.

Well, that's all over with. Now we're emancipated — thirty years after Lord Cornwallis promised it to us.

I am ahead of myself. This was supposed to be a memoir for my nieces and nephews of the terrible times in which I grew up. I want to tell them all the truth about Bob Emmet — and Sarah Curran, a truth which is different from the legend. My problem is that, like the rest of Ireland, I find it hard to distinguish between the truth and the legend.

— 6 —

"Well, Dermot," said John Curran, the host of the dinner party, "we've been neglecting you. What is it that you do exactly?"

He was a slender man, in his late fifties according to what I had been told, but looking much younger, with wavy brown hair, edged with touches of gray and parted in the middle. His eyes danced, he smiled often, he exuded Irish charm.

"I'm a retired commodities trader," I said.

"A little young to be retired, aren't you?"

"Oh I've been retired for ten years . . . I made a lot of money once, mostly by mistake, and retired. As Damon Runyan put it, all horseplayers die broke."

"And you invested your money wisely?"

"My wife is an accountant. She does the family investments."

My dark Irish Crystal goddess raised an eyebrow, but uttered not a word.

"I'm told you write some interesting poetry," he said easily. "I'm afraid I haven't heard the names of your books."

"The most recent one was *Anthems for America: Songs for American Feasts*."

"Sounds very patriotic."

Nuala deigned to come down from Cro-Patrick and join the conversation in pure West Galway brogue.

"Wasn't it short-listed both for the Pulitzer and National Book Award? Won't we be back next year?"

The night after we had begun our exploration of spies in Ireland, our eyes bleary from poring over books on the various Irish "Risings" and the manuscript from the Ned Fizpatrick's collection, Nuala Anne and I went to a dinner party. We did not particularly enjoy ourselves because the hosts and the other guests — charming, literate, and erudite — were not our kind of people. It was a literary salon in a big, old mansion on the east bank of the Chicago River, appropriately called River House. Me wife, and meself, oops my wife and I, are not literary salon types, though I had published two novels and four books of poetry and she had set some of my verses to music. We produce literature, of a sort, they talk about it. We were the guests about whose presence they might later brag. In fact, however, through most of the meal they talked to one another while we listened. They showed off for us instead of permitting us to show off for them. It seemed likely that Nuala Anne had brought her small harp in vain.

I didn't want to attend the party. The Currans sounded a little too precious to me with their big old house down by the river among all the yards where the yachts off Lake Michigan are stored during the winter. Nuala insisted. These people lived "just around the corner" and were neighbors and it would be rude to turn them down. I almost said something about her Irish attitude towards aristocrats and thought better of it.

They weren't really aristocrats, but, it seemed to my jaundiced West Side prejudices that they were trying to act like they were — candles in holders on the oak-paneled wall and in an Irish crystal chandelier reflected on the row of Irish crystal goblets in front of each plate and the Irish linen tablecloth. All very high-class Dublin Protestant that you'd never see in Dublin.

Most of the women were beautiful, which would be some compensation, I told myself, for an otherwise wasted evening.

Their conversation was about Catholic writers, some of whom I had even read, others of whom I had heard about, and still others of whose existence I had been unaware. Who the hell was Hans Urs von Baltassar? Also there was much discussion of *papabili,* Cardinals who might become the next Pope. They agreed that it would not be an American. These were Catholics on the inside, not merely regular churchgoers and contributors, but men and women who understood — or thought they did — the inside power structure and the theological heritage. I observed with interest that they did not mention David Tracy of whom my brother the priest had said, "He's the best of them, little bro, best in the world. The Germans and the French don't take him seriously because he's an American."

The group around the table did not seem all that interested in Americans.

They were all tall, handsome, well-groomed, and well-maintained people. The dinner was "semiformal," which in our day means women wear long gowns and the men suits and ties. John was a lawyer of course. His statuesque blond wife, Estelle, was a caterer. She cooked the sumptuous meal herself, and served with the help of two maids. The fish and the meat were covered with sauces that made them unrecognizable. Me wife, suspicious of all "funny food," nonetheless raised an eyebrow in appreciation. The wines were in decanters so, unless you were an expert, you'd have to guess the label. Father Reide a middle-aged Jesuit historian from Loyola (in enemy territory in a neighborhood called DePaul), smiled contentedly after his first sip of the red wine, "wonderful claret, Stelle."

Me wife raised both eyebrows.

Estelle Curran's figure was elegant and comfortable, well-shaped middle-aged sex appeal, full breasts carefully emphasized beneath her gown so that you hardly noticed. Her husband watched her every movement with what might be called clinical appreciation (though not if I were evaluating my own wife). There was still sex in their marriage, maybe a lot of it.

None of my business.

Because I'm a poet of human relationships, I am inclined to watch carefully the tiny signs in such relationships, especially the occasional quick glances, the slight brushing of bodies, the quick touch of hands, the brief smiles which pass between intense lovers. Remote foreplay — or after play. The sexual tension between the senior Currans was tinder that could burst into flames. Not that anyone else around the table, except the romantic poet, was consciously aware of it.

Estelle leaned over me to pour some exotic sauce on some unrecognizable food. Her elegant breast, firmly controlled by a clearly outlined bra was dangerously close to my face, her scent paralyzing.

I gulped and glanced quickly at Nuala. She hadn't noticed.

OGLE YOUR OWN WIFE, FREAK.

Not a bad idea.

Irish Crystal tonight for Nuala Anne meant black and silver — a clinging black gown which fell from neck to feet, with thick silver trim at the neck and sleeveless edges of the gown and silver jewelry, including a silver comb in her piled-up hair. It was all very chaste, if anything that clings to her can be said to be chaste. No one in the room could keep their eyes off her, including, truth be told, her husband. Her silence, except for an occasional thank-you to the servants, was hardly typical. One might suspect (though not this one) that she was silent to enhance her radiant allure. In fact, she was characteristically sizing up the party before she took it over.

"And didn't I write the music for his

anthems and isn't it going to be a platinum record this summer?"

Her blue eyes were dancing with mischief, which made her even more radiant.

"Yes, of course. I thought you were a singer. But, ah, Dermot said you were an accountant."

"Didn't I come over on a green card to work for Arthur Andersen and me husband rescued me from them just in the nick of time, poor dear people?"

"Where did you live in Ireland before you came to America?" Estelle Curran smiled graciously at the charming little peasant goddess.

"Och, so far out in Connemara that the next parish is on Long Island, a place called Carraroe."

Actually it wasn't quite at the end.

"When you're flying back from the Aran Islands you can see Carraroe on the left-hand side of the plane," I corrected her. "It's a little Galway Venice, with a village on roads running between the lakes and the bay."

"And then I went to Trinity College in Dublin," she continued, in effect dismissing my comment as irrelevant to the issue of her autobiography "and I learned accounting and now have charge of all the family finances, including paying the taxes."

That wasn't altogether true either, but me wife was having too much fun putting these folk on that I didn't bother correcting her.

"And I have three children, the oldest makes her First Communion this year. The youngest came a little early and is three."

Nuala Anne always says this about Socra Marie because she is so proud of her.

"How early?" Estelle said with a frown.

"She came at twenty-five weeks."

"You will have developmental problems with her."

"She's tiny and wears glasses," I said, "but exhausts us all with her energy and wit."

"Don't the doctors say that all her measures are well within the curves and that her eyes will get better too?"

"Doctors are not doing anyone a favor when they keep those poor little babies alive."

"She's the light of our lives," Nuala said softly. "A great blessing from God."

"You must sing one of those anthems tonight, dear," John Curran interrupted, gaining control of the conversation again. "And maybe some folk songs."

A flicker of unease slipped across my

wife's wonderful face — a sure sign that her dark side was acting up.

"And maybe some of the rebel songs," Deirdre Donovan, the older of their two blond daughters asked, a woman in her middle thirties, whose husband seemed to be a lawyer.

"I don't sing them songs," Nuala said firmly. "The men who shout them out in the pubs would have run at the first sight of a British bayonet."

We were in deep water now, Nuala's water.

"I take it then, Ms. McGrail," Father Reide mused, "that you favor peaceful means in the solution of Irish problems."

"Didn't the Big Fella have the right of it, Father. You fight till they have to negotiate with you, then you negotiate. And look what they did to him, poor dear fella."

The Big Fella was Michael Collins.

"Do you think that if the Irish Republican Brotherhood had waited in 1916, they would have won home rule without a fight?"

"I don't know, Father. And neither does anyone else. The Brits postponed it once too often, a mistake they often make when dealing with us poor savages. If they had granted Redmond home rule before the war, the Easter Rising wouldn't have happened. Neither would the War of Independence and the Civil War. And there wouldn't be the Troubles up in the North now."

She presented the theory as though she had worked it out after long years of careful reading of Irish history. In fact, she had formed it earlier in the day when she learned about such matters for the first time.

"An interesting theory," Jack Curran, a younger version of his father, and also a lawyer commented. "What about the earlier risings?"

"Well, now," Galway subtly segued into Trinity College, west Brit. "The truth of the matter is that the Irish never did accept the theory that their country rightly belonged to England. They rose every time they got a chance. There was in fact going to be violence until the English and their colonials went home, just as there has been recently and probably will be again. Most of us think it's foolish now. Still, there'll always be an IRA."

"You approve of them?" asked Father Rory Curran, the other son a young man, the oils of ordination still not dry on his hands.

"I do not, not at all. They're a pack of eejits, like the men of 1848, and 1867, and 1916. Losers all of them. With the exception of the Big Fella, they didn't know how to organize or fight. Eloquent rhetoric, grand songs, brave deaths, and not a chance to win anything. That's why I won't sing their songs."

Again this firm opinion had been formed only a few hours earlier.

"And the men of '98?" asked Gerry Donovan, Deirdre's husband.

I realized as I studied his face that there is a tendency for all Irish lawyers to look alike. Every male face around the table had the faintly skeptical, reserved expression of the trained litigator waiting to pounce. I was willing to bet that young Rory was destined for Rome and canon law.

"They were Protestant eejits and brave men too. So I won't criticize them at all, at all."

The woman of the house and the two servingwomen now distributed dessert, some of kind of exotic ice-cream thing. I ate a bite or two, but my wife devoured the whole thing.

The woman of the house and her two daughters were blond. One of the daughters-in-law had red hair and seemed to be a pert South Side Irishwoman, out of her element but defiant. The remaining one was a pretty, petite woman with a perpetual sulk. The conversation bored her and she didn't seem to like the rest of the family. Her name was Annette, it turned out, and she was the wife of Trevor, the oldest of the three sons. He was tall, his hairline receded somewhat, and he wore thick, horn-rimmed glasses which, along with his solemn, legal demeanor, made him look a little like a Celtic Abraham Lincoln.

OK, I counted mentally. The parents are John and Estelle. Trevor is the oldest — about forty — and his wife is Annette. Deirdre is the next, and her husband is Gerry Donovan, who is a lawyer at the Firm. Early thirties. Then there is Jack and his red-haired wife, Martha. He's also at the Firm, late twenties. Father Rory middle twenties and Marie Therese, just out of college and as yet unmarried.

The two daughters were clones of their mother, tall, shapely blondes, Marie Therese the tallest of them — a lot of sexual appeal even for a married man like myself.

"By the way, sir," I intervened in the conversation with me wife, "are you by any chance related to the John Philpot Curran of the '98?"

He responded again with his gentle, urbane lawyer's smile.

"It's not impossible, surely. There are a lot of Currans, however."

"Poor Sarah," Nuala Anne commented, licking her lips to capture the last bit of ice cream. "She deserved better."

"Indeed she did."

The table was quiet for a moment. Most of the guests didn't know about the tragedy of Sarah and Bob and were not about to ask.

The conversation turned to the Church. John Curran announced that he thought Sean Cronin should have resigned as Archbishop at his seventy-fifth birthday instead of staying on.

"I admit that he is in excellent health, but we've had him around for a long time. Chicago needs some new blood."

"Better the devil you know than the devil you don't know," Father Reide murmured.

"That poor little coadjutor Archbishop," Estelle agreed, "he's such a pathetic, innocuous little man."

Me wife stiffened next to me. She and Blackie Ryan were colleagues in the solution of mysteries. Indeed, she owned a sweatshirt which proclaimed her to be a member of his North Wabash Avenue Irregulars.

"Don't underestimate Blackie," Father Rory said. "That carefully cultivated aura of befuddlement only makes him more dangerous."

"Like Chesterton's Father Brown," Gerry Donovan added.

"Well," the host pursued his point, "Cronin has to do something about the homosexual problem. I cannot object to civil unions for them, but I don't think they should be admitted to the priesthood. If the Cardinal doesn't clamp down on them, then the Vatican should. We've had too many sexual abuse problems already."

"Most gays are not sexual predators, Dad," his older daughter insisted. "That's not fair."

"But, Deirdre, how is one to know which ones are and which ones aren't? The only safe strategy is to exclude them altogether."

"How is the Cardinal going to know?" Father Rory asked.

I had the impression that in the family he was always called Father Rory. Our family priest was never called Father George. He would have laughed at it. Except by Nuala, who did it to torment him.

"I'm sure it's obvious enough to those who are skilled in such matters."

"At the seminary it was obvious with

some of them. They'd hang around with one another and you could pick them out easily. Others . . . No way of being sure."

"I feel sorry for them," Estelle Curran said as she was supervising the distribution of tea, coffee, and liquors. Me wife and I had tea, black, and Bailey's — which raised a few eyebrows. But what else could you expect of a young woman from the bogs who thought cognac was poison.

"They don't have any choice in the matter," she continued. "It's just the way they are. They must find celibacy more difficult than other men, just like it is impossible for them to be faithful to their partners."

"I say," her husband insisted, "that they should have their civil unions if they want, even with ceremonies that they can consider marriage. But keep them out of the priesthood. I've had too many cases with such men to have any illusions. I think it should be a diriment impediment. Don't you agree, Father Reide?"

We were involved in sophisticated gay bashing. I decided to stay out of the conversation because the undertones were ugly. Indeed, the dinner table conversation was thick with undertones I didn't understand and didn't like.

85

"I agree that it's a serious problem, John. However, I think we've had gay priests since the beginning even if we didn't have the word. Homosexual priests, bishops, popes, and even saints. It is possible that they bring to the ministry certain important characteristics that straight men do not possess so frequently . . . I have noted — and I may be wrong — that they see the world quite differently from the rest of us . . . That may be disturbing, but it may also be useful."

"Let them be artists and designers and poets and whatever," John Curran said firmly, "but keep them out of the priesthood!"

"I think," Estelle said firmly, "we ought to adjourn to the parlor. Nuala Anne has been good enough to promise us a song or two . . ."

"Or even three," herself said with the vast, joyous smile that always warmed a room and drew all eyes back to her.

She began with my Halloween anthem about trick-or-treaters, a slyly subversive poem about kids exploiting their parents who didn't really mind. Nuala Anne had inserted mischievous little melodies of tiny dancing feet. I saw Socra Marie dancing in her angel garb. Our audience didn't quite get it, but they applauded politely. Then she sang "The Kerry Dance," the way "the Count" sang it — sad, sad music, with the burst of defiance at the end.

Then she settled down for her masterpiece.

"Sure, won't I be keeping you here all night now? Well, I must sing one more song, which is for me anyway a kind of theme song, though it's not about a Galway woman at all, at all, but about a tragic young woman in Dublin's fair city who will be remembered whenever any Irish person sings about her."

So naturally she sang about Mollie Malone, who still pushes her wheelbarrow through streets broad and narrow.

Weren't the tears flowing like the River Liffey when she finished.

"Sure," she went on, "isn't that special to me because I sang it on the night I fell in love with a man? And isn't the ending a sad one too. For him. Didn't he marry me!"

So she sang it again with all her heart. For me, just the way she had done that first foggy night in O'Neill's pub down the street from Trinity College. And didn't my eyes fill up with tears like they always do when she sings the song, very Irish tears for meself and herself and for Mollie and for all the Irish and for all humans who have to die.

The Curran clan — stiff, refined people that they were — cried too.

"Just one more, please, Nuala Anne," Deirdre begged.

"Well, maybe I should sing the Connemara lullaby."

And the winds blew gently down the dark Chicago River, just outside the window and enveloped all of us.

We walked home because as herself insisted, " 'Tis only around the corner to our house and if anyone tries to rob us you can beat the shite out of them, can't you, Dermot love?"

Not out of a couple of guys with knives, but in fact our neighborhood was one of the safest in the city.

"Well," I asked, "what did you think of them?"

"The three blond women are gorgeous, beautiful boobs. They have to be careful with their weight and all of them are."

"Well so are you, Nuala Anne."

"I'm not . . . I don't have to be careful — like Ethne does. Me ma never puts on weight. I do it because I'm obsessive."

"It would be a lucky man who would see

the three of them naked," I commented, just making trouble.

She sighed, her middle-range sigh, and ignored my attempt to make trouble.

"Well, I suppose some lucky women have and wouldn't it be a good lesson for all of them about beauty?"

I thought that I would let that comment go — till I tried to write a sonnet about the three Curran women.

"Sure," Nuala continued, "aren't they a strange crowd altogether and themselves nice people, and so uptight-like?"

"That about says it. They were exploiting you. They can talk to all their uptight lace-curtain friends about what a sweet and intelligent young woman you are."

"I don't mind singing for people, Dermot Michael. You know that. I'm not stuck-up. I didn't have to bring me harp, did I now?"

"No, you're not stuck-up."

I extended my arm around her shoulders. She leaned against me. We turned away from the River, which we native Chicagoans don't appreciate nearly enough, especially now that it doesn't smell anymore.

"You were the most beautiful woman in the room."

"Go long with your blarney. It's just a dress I picked up at a sale."

Nuala Anne does her personal shopping at mark-down sales and in wholesale shops and is inordinately proud of how much money she saves. If you have good taste and a body like hers, you can get away with it.

"I think me hair will need a lot of combing tonight, to get the kinks out, don't you know?

"With or without your bra?"

"Och, Dermot Michael Coyne, you've never been reluctant about that before, have you now?"

My loins tightened, my head grew light. The woman was seducing me.

"Sounds ded friggin' bril," I managed to say.

"Now you're imitating me again! 'Tis not good for the children to hear you talking like a Claddagh fishwife."

"Will we see them again?" I asked, trying to lower the sexual tension a bit.

"Well, I don't think we'll invite the lot of them back to our little cottage, will we, poor dear people? Maybe herself and himself. Invite the Murphys. Different kind of show, if you take me meaning."

"What's wrong there, Nuala Anne?"

"Dermot Michael Coyne! Can't you wait till we get into the house to squeeze me boobs?"

"Woman, I cannot!"

"Ah, well, that's the way of it . . . sure, won't you drive me out of me mind altogether!"

"That's what marriage is for!"

She sighed, as if in absolute despair.

"You'd fuck me all the time if you could!"

"Woman, I would!"

The whole seduction was surely part of her plan to become pregnant, not that she didn't love me and didn't enjoy marital play.

"I don't know what's the matter with them," she returned to the Currans. "There's something wrong, something just a little out of kilter, if you take me meaning. I suppose they've been rich for several generations?"

"Affluent," I said, "not rich. Professional money, like our clan — doctors, lawyers, accountants, you should excuse the expression."

"But your clan does not have to pretend that they're literate and refined and civilized . . ."

"They certainly don't."

"And they don't know everything about the Church either, and his rivirence a priest."

Nuala Anne always treated my brother with a lot more respect than that to which he was entitled.

"The Currans try too hard," I said.

"And themselves a long way from the bogs, unlike some other folks I know."

We laughed. Nuala would admit, at least on occasion, that she could play the Connemara peasant lass role to the hilt.

"Sure, 'tis who I am, isn't it now?" she'd laugh.

I note that she did not say anything that night about how the Currans would be involved in our search for spies. She argues that I had set her on fire and her dark side always tunes out when that happens. Later we would know that the spies were closing in on them.

As we climbed the steps to our front-door entrance, she sighed very loudly.

"The screwing should be solemn high tonight, Dermot love, shouldn't it?

"Long and slow and sweet?"

"With lots of fooling around."

"I understand."

The kind of lovemaking which ought to produce a fourth child.

Ireland has always been a violent country, but most of the people are not violent. That, my nieces and nephews and grandnieces and grandnephews, is something you have to understand. In the old days the kings were always fighting with one another over land and cattle. Anyone who had a hill and ten head of cattle was a king, don't you see. So they and their retainers would go out each spring to fight with one another and the rest of the country paid them no heed. Even the warriors were not good fighters. That's why when Strongbow and the Normans came they took over the country so easily, then became Irish, just like the Danes before them did. When the English came over under Elizabeth and Cromwell and King Billy along with Scotch settlers, it was different. They had no intention of becoming Irish. They decided to convert some of us, the lords and that sort, and kill off the rest of us. God knows, they almost succeeded.

The result was that there was always an element of lawlessness out in the country-side, groups like the Defenders, and the Whiteboys, and the Ribbonmen, which are still with us today, even here in my parish. They're part bandits and part Irish patriots. When a "better class" of people come along and want to drive the English out — there will always be such people on this island until the English leave — the rough men in the countryside are only too happy to join in the mayhem — and maybe kill a few hundred Protestants as part of the game. Maybe they'll lock them in their churches and burn the churches down, just as some fine Catholics did here in Wexford during the '98.

It was different at the turn of the century. The French Revolution had set Europe on fire. Books by French writers spread all over the continent. Lord Edward's mother, the Duchess of Leinster, tried to raise her children according to Rousseau, hired a Scotchman as their tutor, and was un-faithful to her husband with him. The First Duke of Leinster himself (and the twen-tieth Earl of Kildare as he also was) like a lot of our lords in those days had put him-self into debt building a new house for himself in Dublin. That's the way things *were in those days: the whole world was falling apart.*

England was fighting the Revolutionary Army and not doing well against it. So the people who wanted to drive the English out of Ireland thought that was the time to strike, especially if they could get some help from the Frogs, whom to tell you the truth they disliked almost as much as the English. These would-be leaders were men who could read and write and many of them had been to university, which meant they were different from most of the rest of us. They were also Protestants, though their ancestors had been Catholic. Most of them were not very good Protestants. They had become deists, one God at the most if you take my meaning. Poor Bob Emmet was devout, not that it did him much good.

Well, they founded a group called the United Irishmen, which included Presbyterians from the North, and Protestants from Dublin, and Catholics from the countryside. They may have had two hundred thousand members by the '98 but not many of them knew much about fighting, much less organizing an army, things which the English, to give the devils their due, were good at, though the Americans had beaten them pretty badly.

The poverty and misery of the Catholic poor was even worse than it is now in America. You won't be able to imagine the dirt, the filth, the smell, the sickness, the disease, the misery of ordinary people. Around Stephen's Green you see some of the most elaborate homes in the British Isles and hidden behind them, some of the worst hovels. Disease spreads from the poor to the rich. Parents are reluctant to become too attached to a newborn baby because the chances are at least even that the child will die before its second birthday. Intelligent and lively young people die of tuberculosis before they're twenty-five, as did my poor love Sarah. Life is short and ugly. Yet the rich Protestants in Dublin live in splendor and luxury and gross immorality. It could not have been much worse during the black death.

The United Irishmen, and most of their leaders Protestants, were against the oppression of Catholics, which was a novel idea in those days. French revolutionary convictions about equality overcame their religious prejudices. The Irish parliament, which met in a big ugly building on College Green, was completely crooked and corrupt and controlled by maybe fifty families at the most. Dublin Castle, with the viceroy (the Lord Lieutenant) and the First Secretary, was the center of English rule and often fought the Parliament. However, they were not eager to permit Catholics into it because that would cause real trouble.

The United Irish reckoned that if they could time a rising at the same time the French would land troops in the west, they could take over the country. They might have been right. When the French finally got a small force ashore in County Mayo a year after the Rising, they beat the English in a battle at Castlebar before Lord Cornwallis got a large enough army out there to rout them. The Mayo people, however, did not trust the French and did not rise. What would have happened if they had come a year earlier, we'll never know. The truth is that the French never quite got into the game. Their ships always had a hard time finding Ireland after they sailed from Brest. So the theory that the French would come to the aid of Irish freedom just as they did twenty years before come to the aid of American freedom didn't work out.

We even had our George Washington in Lord Edward.

Before I tell you about him I must tell you more about the spies. Dublin Castle had spies everywhere, a few of them were loyalists to the crown, a few others were threatened with prison if they didn't co-operate, and most of them eager for money. Magan demanded and received four thousand pounds for betraying Lord Edward.

There were few things that the United Irishman planned or did that the Castle didn't know about. The English weren't completely prepared for the Rising and didn't have the troops they thought they needed to fight it, but they knew it was coming. You could hardly have a meeting of ten United Irishman without two of them being traitors. Even the lawyers who sup-posedly represented United Irishmen were spies. McNally, Bob Emmet's lawyer during his trial (because that bastard John Philpot Curran refused to represent him), reported directly to the Castle.

Why would men betray their friends and neighbors and colleagues, you might wonder. Like I said earlier in this long letter, money was the main reason. Even if a man didn't need the money, the chance of making more was irresistible. Whatever chance the '98 had was swept into the sewers of the Liffey when Magan betrayed Lord Edward.

He was supposed to be the George Washington of Ireland. He was a tall, handsome, gracious man — all the Geraldines were that if nothing else. He had served in a regiment in the American colonies during the war and had returned to Canada in command of a regiment. He had traveled across the Canadian wilderness and explored down the Mississippi River to New Orleans (sleeping with an Indian woman on the way). Like all his kind he was an immoral man. He stole the wife of the playwright Richard Sheridan and had a daughter with her — both of whom later died. He frequented the gambling dens and the whorehouses of Paris and was notorious for his immorality both in London and Dublin. He fell in love finally with Pamela, the illegitimate daughter of the Duke of Orleans (who called himself Philip Egalité during the Revolution but lost his head just the same), married her, and brought her back to Ireland just before the Rising. His family hated her of course and did their best to separate her from her two children after he died.

If you were a leader of the United Irishmen in those days, you had to go to

France to seek help from the damn Frogs, whether it be the leaders of the Revolution, or the Directorate which took over and brought some order, or Bonaparte. They all made promises. Invading England through Ireland sounded like good strategy. Yet they were skeptical of the claims of men like Lord Edward and Wolf Tone. Would the Irish people really rise when French troops landed? Looking back on it, they had reason to be dubious. We never did like the Frogs. The one time the French ships were able to find a shore on which to land enough troops to win a battle, most of the local Irish did not join in.

Yet through all those years the plan invariably was that the United Irishmen would rise at the same time the French landed. The wish being the father of the thought, the landings were always expected momentarily. Both the '98 and the '03 began when they did because our brave leaders expected Frogs on the beach the next morning. I'm still astonished that intelligent men could so completely deceive themselves. At the end of the day both of the Risings happened because the leaders thought at the last minute a rising would convince the French that the Irish were serious about revolution.

In fact, most of us were not. Those of us who were had little notion of how to do a revolution. However, as the winter of '97 turned into the spring of '98 the country-side was restless, both here in Wexford and up in Kildare. Even some of the Presbyterian merchants in Belfast were ready to go.

I still remember the excitement of the time, the rumors and the counterrumors you would here on every street corner, the Yeomanry (brutal Protestant militia) swaggering through Dublin with the curses of Dubliners following after them, reports of French sails off Waterford and Kinsale, anxious and intense discussion in the pubs, important Dublin men reporting to their friends what the Castle was doing, whispers in the night for fear the spies might be listening — which they were more often than we thought.

I'm angry as I think about it, angry at Lord Edward — whom I adored in those days — and his colleagues for being fools, angry at the spies who betrayed them, angry at the English who had no right to be in our country, and angry at myself for yielding to the enthusiasm and the folly.

I was on the fringes of the Rising. I

carried messages back and forth. Yes, I knew Lord Edward and worshiped him, as did everyone who knew him. His father, the late First Duke of Leinster was an irresponsible spendthrift and a cuckold. His brother, the current duke, was a bungling incompetent, barely able to read and write. But in Lord Edward, the bloodlines of the Geraldines ran true.

He walked through the streets of Dublin in those days, his head high, a smile on his face, like he was already the Irish George Washington. You could see him on the steps of the Four Courts where they did the legal business of the country, or in front of the House of Lords in casual conversation with his colleagues. His smile, his wit, his charm disarmed everyone, perhaps even the Castle spies who followed him wherever he went.

The countryside was restless. Almost every day we heard reports of random violence out in the counties, particularly down in Wexford. Catholics were already killing Protestants and Protestants striking back with more murders. Young romantic that I was I waited eagerly for the explosion.

I met Bobby one morning in March as he trudged across the Green. I had no idea whether he was involved with the United Irishmen. We chatted briefly. He gave away nothing.

"Will there be a rising, Bob?"

"Who can say?"

"I'm told that Lord Edward has appointed adjutant generals in all the counties."

He sighed.

"That is as may be."

"And that battle plans are all prepared."

"So it is said."

"On the day of the Rising, the mail won't leave Dublin. That will be a signal to the rest of the country."

He merely sighed and asked me to give his respects to my family.

We were both little more than children. I was caught up in the exuberance of youth, Bob steeped in the caution, I thought then, of old age.

In the event, he was deeply involved in the Rising. But he left no footprints. Neither the Castle, nor his own family, nor most of the United Irishmen knew that "young Emmet" was a key conspirator. After it was over, he was the logical one to emerge as the leader of the next effort, though he was barely twenty years old.

Impulsive and generous, Lord Edward had made friends with a young Catholic named Thomas Reynolds and invited him into the conspiracy. Reynolds at first was eager to join, then had second thoughts about what might happen to him if he were captured. He changed sides and provided the Castle with the detailed plans for the Rising.

In May the Castle issued orders for Lord Edward's arrest. Everyone in Dublin knew that a rising was coming and that Lord Edward would lead it. Wild rumors spread that there were two hundred thousand men in arms all over Ireland who would attack at his word. After the Castle issued an order for his arrest and despite the work of scores of informers, they could not find him. Almost like a ghost, Lord Edward strolled the streets of Dublin and met with his fellow plotters whenever he wished. The legend grew rapidly.

Despite his audacity and his apparent optimism, he was privately, as I had reason to know, growing more dubious about the project. He had no confidence in the French. His "generals" were not trained military men. He did not trust most of his troops. He was uncertain how large the Rising would be. Only in Wexford and perhaps in Kildare could he be confident of reliable fighters and even in those counties there was no unity of command. Only some local priests like Father John Murphy in Wexford had any leadership instincts.

"A revolution led by priests," he said with a sigh in my presence. "I supposed it is always that way in Ireland. What need does this island have for Norman lords like my family."

— 8 —

"Poor dear men," Nuala Anne said, closing the manuscript. "I know what's going to happen, but I still hope and pray that it doesn't."

"It's two hundred years late to pray for them."

"God doesn't pay any attention to time . . . The priesteen escaped to write about it, didn't he?"

I was not altogether sure that God didn't pay attention to time, even if he lives in eternity. However, my wife, typical West of Ireland mystic that she was, believed that boundaries of time, like all other boundaries were permeable. She may well have imagined herself to be on Stephen's Green that morning that our author had encountered the mysterious Bob Emmet.

However, I was not going there. I did not want to find out.

It was early afternoon. Socra Marie was in nap mode. Danuta, our Polish house-keeper, was resting her eyes. Ethne was in the exercise room, working herself into the physical condition that Nuala insisted was necessary before marriage. "And don't ever let yourself get out of shape after you're married," me wife had insisted.

The dogs were pacing around restlessly, their own snoozes interrupted by the crackle of lightning and boom of thunder. Perhaps a perfect time to read about Dublin's fair city in 1798, a city that wasn't fair at all.

"Do you still feel that there are spies around us?" I asked her.

"Pardon, Dermot love?"

She startled, as though I had wakened her from a daydream.

"We're hunting modern spies, aren't we?"

" 'Tis true."

"And who are they?"

"Well" — she reordered her stack of books — "let's consider it logically."

I didn't know that logic applied in the world of the fey.

"First there are them nine-fingered gobshites who are denouncing immigrants to Homeland Security."

"Why would they be interested in us?"

"I'm still an immigrant, Dermot."

"You have a green card."

"Do I now? Weren't they after taking it when they seized my citizenship application? Couldn't they come in here this afternoon and remove me out to O'Hare and send me back to Ireland?"

"They'd never do that to you, Nuala Anne. You're not a Muslim."

"You can't tell what them fockers might do and your man not president anymore."

It had required presidential action to retrieve her green card the last time. I resolved to call my sister, Cindy Hurley, about forcing the citizenship papers out of the bureaucrats at Homeland Security.

"Then," she went on, "there's your man across the street who sent the police to lift our doggies."

At the word "doggie" both the hounds moved to her feet and curled up for protection from a thunderbolt that seemed to hit the rectory across the street.

"We coped with that easily enough."

"But, Dermot love, there are people out there who don't like us."

Clad in black jeans and a black leather jacket against the fierce April winds, she had walked the dogs, now on a leash, over to school with the children the morning after our dinner at River House. She was very careful to keep them on the parkway

108

and off the parish property. The kids had swarmed over to make their obeisance. Mutts hugged, kissed, shook hands, and rolled over despite the mud. As I watch, a police car pulled up.

That miserable bastard!

I had dashed down the stairs and across the street, wearing only my red-and-gold Marquette gym suit.

By the time I had arrived on the scene, Fiona was shaking hands with the officers and Maeve rolling over on her back.

"She's a retired member of the Dublin Garda," Nuala explained. "She loves cops."

"How does she know we're cops?" the bemused officer asked. . . . "Good girl, good girl!"

"Maybe all cops smell alike," herself said innocently.

A lovely woman can say something like that to a cop and get a laugh. The second cop bent over and scratched Maeve's belly. She rolled over and offered to hug him.

"Maeve, you'll get the nice man's uniform dirty."

"That's all right, girl," the cop said, "you're a great dog. Someday I'll bring my kids over to meet you."

"I don't think we're breaking any laws, officer," my totally innocent Galway wife, continued. "Aren't the dogs on leashes and don't they have all the right tags and aren't we on the parkway which is public property?"

"And don't I have the shite shovel?" I asked, holding up the poop scoop.

"I don't see anything wrong," said the first cop.

Nuala Anne reached in her pocket and produced two treats for the cops to give to the hounds. They both politely begged for their treats, removed them delicately from the officers' fingers, and destroyed them altogether.

The gathered kids cheered. So did the parents who had appeared on the sidewalk. The cops departed in an atmosphere of good feeling as the beasts barked in protest at their leaving without a second treat.

"What was that all about?" a mother about my wife's age asked.

"Oh nothing much . . . Didn't Ms. Carson complain to the pastor and didn't he call the police and tell them we were creating a public nuisance on his school yard and ourselves on the parkway."

And didn't the mothers and the few fathers turn and glare at complainers who were watching from the steps of the church. Then the bell rang and our enemies took advantage of the sudden silence to beat a retreat. Our children fell into the ranks and marched off into the school.

"Would you ever take the doggies home, Dermot Michael. I want to have a word with your man."

She had looked quite satisfied with herself when she returned to our study.

"And you said?"

"Didn't I tell him that he was a loser and that he'd lose every time he tried to hassle us? And didn't he complain about our not being real parishioners and ourselves going to Old St. Patrick's on Sunday? And didn't I tell him that maybe since we weren't real parishioners we shouldn't send in the thousand-dollar check every month?"

"Is that what we give him?"

" 'Tis . . . besides our extra contribution to the school endowment."

"Was he properly frightened?"

"Nothing like money to threaten a priest . . . And himself knowing that Father Coyne is your brother!"

"We did indeed, Dermot Michael," she said on that afternoon when it seemed, as the lightning crashed all around us, like the whole parish had incurred divine wrath. "But where was your man down the street?"

"He moved back to his old neighborhood where he belongs. Mike Casey said his wife made him go to AA."

"He's not likely to forget us, is he now? People just don't like us. I'm not sure about those Curran people either. What do you think they've been after saying to their friends?"

"Will they say anything?"

"Why else would they invite us to supper?"

"Well, what do you think they've been saying?"

"The poor sweet little thing is just a peasant girl from the bogs with a nice voice and her husband is a big handsome ape without a brain cell in his head. I don't know what will happen to them if any big problems happen in their lives."

I burst out laughing.

" 'Tis not funny, Dermot Michael Coyne. They're that kind of people . . . What did Father George say when you asked him about that uptight priesteen of theirs?"

I repeated George's words, which Nuala had already heard.

"George said that he was just a little too smooth by half. Smart, ambitious, conservative, wanted to study canon law and become a bishop."

"And he also said?"

"That both the Cardinal and Blackie never send people to study canon law who want to do so."

"They don't like us very much either, Dermot. We have people like that all around us."

"Are they the ones you dreamed about?"

"I don't know. There's bad things happening and meself not knowing what they are and who's doing them."

"And yourself wanting to be pregnant again."

She drew me over to her couch and wept in my arms.

YOU KNEW SHE WAS A WEIRDO WHEN YOU MARRIED HER.

She's not a weirdo. She's just a little different.

Wasn't that brilliant altogether! Isn't me poor dear husband the most brilliant lover in all the world! I keep saying that to You. But I must give thanks every time. And himself not sure that I really want him or I'm just trying to get meself pregnant. Well, can't I want both? Me husband is not just a sperm machine . . . Well, I'm sure you know that. I would want him pushing into me tonight regardless of the kid . . . Every night . . . I hope You don't mind me desire for another child . . . It's all up to You . . . I'm grateful for the three wonderful ones I have. I'm not complaining. It would be nice to have four but I'll not question your decisions . . . Still . . . Och doesn't he play me body like I play a harp . . . Sure, don't I know how to delight him too . . . you're the Dermot beyond Dermot . . . the Love to which all loves lead. I've known that since I was a small one . . . When I don't treat him right I don't treat You right . . . Forgive me ingratitude . . . Also protect me from the evil that's around us . . . Whether it be Homeland Security or people who want to hurt my doggies . . . What's that noise . . . Whose ringing the doorbell this time of night . . .

— 10 —

"Federal Bureau of Investigation!"

I held the door half-open despite the efforts of these two sleazy characters in trench coats to shove their way into the house.

"Special Agents Dowd and Dunn."

They both flashed warrant cards. In the dark and the rain the cards looked authentic. I didn't trust them. Never trust the Feds, my sister Cindy always said, especially when they come in the middle of the night like the Gestapo used to do.

"What do you want?"

"We want to talk to Ms. Marie Coyne."

"There's no Marie Coyne in this house."

"You've just committed perjury, sir."

"You have lied to federal agents.

"We arrest you on suspicion of perjury."

"The only Marie in the house is my three-year-old daughter Socra Marie . . . I'm not about to wake her up for two goons."

They had pushed their way into the

house and were greeted by two menacing growls.

"Sir, please restrain your dogs!"

"Their presence constitutes resisting arrest."

"As long as you stay right where you are, you're safe. Take one more step and we will resist home invasion."

"We demand to talk to your wife."

"We have reason to believe that she is a threat to the national security of this country."

After our romp earlier I had fallen into deep sleep. I wasn't sure that these two creeps were not a rather tasteless nightmare.

"We have a warrant for her arrest."

He flashed a document at me. Fiona growled loudly. Her affection for cops did not extend to the Feds.

I picked up the phone and punched a rapid-dial number.

"Tom Hurley," said my long-suffering brother-in-law.

"Tom, the Feds are in our house with a warrant for my wife's arrest, though they have the wrong name."

Cindy took the phone.

"Feds!"

"Special Agents, they say."

"What are their names?"

"Gog and Magog."

"Why do they want to arrest Nuala?"

"She's a threat to national security . . . They think her name is Marie Coyne. That's what the warrant says."

"Homeland Security creeps. Is there a woman agent with them?"

"I don't see one."

"Let me talk to them."

"Our attorney, Ms. Cynthia Hurley . . . Stay, girls."

The pooches withdrew a couple of inches.

I turned on the speakerphone.

"We have a warrant for the arrest of Ms. Marie Coyne who we believe is a resident in this house. Your client has already perjured himself by denying her presence."

"First, Special Agent, I hereby notify you that I am turning on a tape recorder. Secondly, do you have a woman Special Agent with you?"

"We do not," said Gog. Or maybe it was Magog.

"Then even if you had a proper warrant, which you do not, we would not permit you to take Ms. McGrail into custody. You can't be such an asshole as to be ignorant of your own regulations."

118

"We have reason to believe that she is a threat to national security, whatever her name is."

"Special Agent, you will have a desk job in Tupelo, Mississippi, by the time we're finished with you . . . Mr. Coyne's wife has a proper legal name and as long as it is not on your warrant, we will not honor it. Nor will we permit her surrender into your custody unless there is a woman agent present."

"We will not leave this house unless she is in custody."

"Yes, you will, Special Agent. Since your warrant is patently flawed, Mr. Coyne has every right to order you from the house and take whatever means is appropriate to remove you. In the interest of expediting this matter, we will surrender his wife at the Dirksen Federal Building tomorrow at ten o'clock. We insist that both the Special Agent in Charge and the United States Attorney for the Northern District of Illinois be present for the interview. I'd advise you to leave that home immediately. I will go into the United States Court for the Northern District of Illinois tomorrow to seek relief from your idiocy. You are already in serious trouble."

My sister is a sweet, pretty, strawberry

blond mother of three lovely kids. She thinks I'm a slugabed and a layabout (as the whole family does) and she adores my good wife. In her lawyer mode, however, she is hell on wheels.

Egged on perhaps by Cindy's tone of voice, the dogs growled loudly.

"We will wait outside and make sure she is delivered to the Dirksen Building."

"Wait wherever you want. Only get out of the house."

They left. As soon as the door closed, the two hounds went wild. They rushed the door, howled, barked, then howled again.

"Good dogs," Nuala Anne said as she appeared in an elaborate white robe, her hair combed, and her minimum makeup in place. "Now settle down. The bad men are all gone."

"I want a couple of Maeve's puppies the next time you breed her," Cindy murmured. "Is herself there?"

"I am."

"Don't worry about those gobshites, Nuala Anne. We'll take care of them. They're frigging eejits."

My wife laughed uncertainly.

"Sounds like fun."

"Dermot," Cindy said to me, "have your

good friend Mike Casey provide a limo and a couple of bodyguards. I'll meet you and Nuala in the lobby of the Dirksen Building at five minutes to ten. We'll sink them without a trace."

My wife extended her arms around me. I noticed that's she'd used mouthwash and scent. You confront Gog and Magog only with the proper persona.

"Och, Dermot Michael, isn't it the same thing all over again!"

"A little different this time, Nuala Anne. We hold all the cards."

"Well, if they send me back, they'll have to pay the plane fare and that will save me a lot of money . . . sure, didn't I want to be here for Nelliecoyne's First Communion?"

"I guarantee that you will be."

Yet anxiety stirred within me. Homeland Security and the Patriot Act had edged us pretty far along the road to a police state, especially if you were an immigrant. We might hold all the cards, but the United States was not the country that it used to be.

Herself went right back to sleep. I tossed and turned and worried.

The limo from Reliable Security appeared promptly at nine-fifteen, after the kids were safe in school and Danuta and

Ethne in charge. My wife was wearing her black trousers, her black sweatshirt trimmed in crimson, and her black leather jacket. She was carrying a very large black purse, also trimmed in crimson. The outfit was complemented by nylons and very high heels. It was, I thought, one of her shite-kicking ensembles.

Mike himself walked over to the FBI car and had a word with Special Agent Gog. Then he and his two assistants — Sergeant Carmen Lopez and Officer John "Buck" Jones, old friends from previous battles — walked up the steps to the second floor of her house (where the entrance was). The pooches went crazy at the sight of them. Nuala calmed them down as we descended to the Lincoln Town Car.

"You are calm, cool, and self-possessed, Ms. McGrail," Mike said, as he held the door open for her.

"Didn't me sister-in-law say that we'd beat the friggin' gobshites and meself ruining her vocabulary."

"The Bureau car is following us, sir," Buck Jones reported. "Should I lose them?"

"Why not?"

They were nowhere in sight when we pulled up to the Everett McKinley Dirksen

Federal Building. The media, however, were already there.

"Is it true you're being arrested, Nuala Anne?"

" 'Tis true."

"What's the charge?"

"They say I'm a threat to the national security of the United States?"

"Is that true?"

" 'Tis not."

"Do they want to deport you?"

" 'Tis true."

"Will they?"

"They won't."

Cindy had set this up. My wife would be on the noon news and probably the evening news, maybe even nationally. She behaved with poise and charm and a bit of mischief in her eyes. Her dolt of a husband, blond, blue-eyed trailed uncertainly behind, looking like he wanted to find a special agent whose face needed bashing.

Cindy met us as soon as we came in the door. Mike's people were sent to park the car and wait for a call on the cell phone. He and Cindy led us through the security machines. One young Mexican woman asked her for an autograph. Nuala Anne produced a disk from her purse and signed it for her.

We had to wait in the Homeland Security office for a half hour before Agents Gog and Magog, looking much the worse for wear, stumbled in.

"Get lost?" Mike Casey asked.

We were led to a very small interrogation room. On one side of the government-issue metal desk Gog, Magog, and a U.S. Attorney identified as Tim Novak, barely out of law school, arranged themselves and their sheaves of paper. They played the role of businesslike, professional defenders of the United States of America. On our side, cramped in limited space, the suspect and her legal team and her husband seemed outnumbered.

"Might I ask you in what capacity you are here, Mr. Casey?" Tim Novak inquired pompously.

"I'm a backup to Ms. Hurley," he said mildly. "I have some experience in matters of proper police procedure."

Indeed he had written the book on it, which none of these losers knew.

I felt a lot better.

"It is ten-forty-three," Novak continued his role as a TV prosecutor. "Present in the room are Special Agents Dunn and Dowd, United States Attorney Novak, Marie Coyne, the suspect, her husband ah . . ."

"Dermot Michael Coyne," my wife said helpfully.

"Dermot Coyne and her attorneys Cynthia Hurley and Michael Casey."

"Michael Patrick Vincent Casey."

"Now we can get down to business."

"No, we cannot," Cindy interrupted. "I specified that I want the United States Attorney and the Special Agent in Charge present for this conversation. We will not continue until they are present."

Nuala Anne removed from her purse the latest book of poems by Seamus Heaney.

"You have no right to impose that condition, Ms. Hurley."

"Look, sonny boy," Cindy replied, her voice dripping with contempt, "you tell both of them that I want them here and they'll come a-running. They're afraid of me and with good reason. You should be too."

A quarter hour later, the two gentlemen arrived, tall, silver-haired Irishmen in dark blue suits. They both looked quite upset.

"What the hell is this about, Cindy?" the Agent in Charge asked.

"You'll see soon enough . . . Very well Agent Dunn, you may begin the questions."

"Your name Ms. Coyne, I believe, is Marie Coyne."

" 'Tis not."

"Your Irish passport says you are" — he tried to read it — "Marie Phinoulah Annagh McGrail Coyne, is that not correct?"

" 'Tis me Irish name. And the first word is pronounced Mary, the mother of Jesus like."

"Mary" with a west of Ireland accent sounds mystical, a hint of music over the bogs.

"So that is your real name, Mary Coyne."

" 'Tis not. I've never been called that in all me life."

"We'll stipulate," Cindy broke in, "that my client's legal name is Nuala Anne McGrail. If you had that name on your warrant, it might be legal. We are here this morning to expedite a situation created by your poor legal work."

" 'Tis true," Nuala said brightly. " 'Tis me real name in America."

"Damnation," muttered the Agent in Charge.

"And your occupation, Ms. McGrail."

"Housewife," she said even more brightly.

"You earn a lot of money for a housewife." Agent Gog looked at her tax return.

"I note that you may have illegally taken her tax return," Cindy observed.

"I do a little singing on the side."

"And where do you sing?"

"Here and there."

"Pubs."

"Well, I used to when I was young. Now I pretty much stay out of pubs."

"Is it not true that you sing at IRA pubs in both Ireland and the United States?"

" 'Tis not. They're a bunch of eejits."

"We have evidence that you do."

"We'll have to see that evidence before Ms. McGrail goes beyond her denial."

"Where do you sing," Tim Novak demanded, "that you make all this money?"

"Well, I sing for me children . . ."

"I'm sure they don't pay you."

"Don't I make some records now and again and sing on the telly at Christmastime and at your mall on the Fourth of July?"

"And what mall is that?"

"Och, isn't it the one down in Washington by the Capitol Building?"

"Shit," muttered the United States Attorney for the Northern District of Illinois.

I knew then that we'd won. Cindy would let them play out the game to gain material for the motion she would shortly file in Federal District Court.

"Isn't it true, Mrs. Coyne, that you have two children?"

" 'Tis not!"

"We have birth certificates . . ."

"We'll stipulate" — Cindy sighed — "that she has three children. You seem to have missed one of the birth certificates."

Unfazed, Gog continued.

"What nationality are these children?"

"Aren't they Irish now?"

"Yet, madam," he said triumphantly, "the records show that they were born in the United States. How can you expect to be granted citizenship when you deny the citizenship of your children?"

"I never said they weren't Yanks," Nuala replied, genuinely confused. "Can't they be Yanks and Irish at the same time like all the other Irish-Americans?"

"Don't argue with him, Nuala," Cindy said. "Let the record show his incompetence."

The United States Attorney winced.

"I see," Agent Magog returned to battle, "you have made substantial donations to various Irish funds. How many of them are affiliated with either the IRA or the Sinn Fein?"

"None of them."

"There's one called Trocare? What is Trocare, Ms. McGrail?"

"Isn't it the official social action fund of the Catholic Church in Ireland?"

"I'll direct my client to answer no further questions about her financial contributions unless and until you offer proof that any of the recipient organizations are affiliated with violent groups."

Agent Gog took over.

"You were deported once, were you not, Ms. McGrail?"

"I was."

"And the reason?"

"They said I didn't have me green card and I didn't because they'd taken it away. Like youse did when I filed my citizenship papers."

"How long has been the delay on your papers, Ms. McGrail?" Cindy asked.

"More than two years. They keep saying it's a routine delay."

"Are you suggesting that the Department of Immigration and Citizenship is lying, Ms. McGrail?" the U.S. Attorney asked.

"Not at all, at all, your honor. I'm just saying they're eejits."

"How did you finally get back into America? Did someone retrieve your green card?"

"Didn't I get a new one?"

"Might I ask from whom?"

"From your man."

"And who is my man?"

"Wasn't he the chief executive of this republic, once removed?"

Dead silence in the room.

"I'm going to end this conversation right now," Cindy said, standing up. "Enough is enough . . . I don't know what to be more angry about — the gratuitous harassment of my client or disgrace to the United States of America caused by such sloppy legal work."

"Sir," Magog insisted, "we still have lots of evidence against the detainee."

"Let me see it," snapped the Agent in Charge. He scooped up the papers from the table and scanned through them. He made a face and passed them to the United States Attorney. The latter performed the same ritual.

"Cindy," he said slowly, "this investigation is over . . . Ms. McGrail, I apologize for your inconvenience."

"I want those papers, Joe," my sister said.

"You can't have them!"

"Then I'll subpoena them. I warn you not to destroy any of them. Mr. Casey, you are my witness to this warning."

"What are you intending to do?" the U.S. Attorney asked irritably. "I've apologized. Isn't that enough?"

"Not nearly enough. I'm entering the court of Judge Ramona Garcia at noon to seek injunctions barring the federal government from further harassment of Ms. McGrail and ordering the Secretary of Homeland Security to issue her citizenship papers by the end of next week or show cause why he should not be held in contempt of court."

"Wouldn't that be brilliant! Meself a real Yank!"

"Cindy, I promise both . . . Why go public?"

"To show in public how close my country has come to Fascism and how stupid and inept that Fascism is . . . Ted, if you're going to send storm troopers out in the middle of the night, at least make sure they're competent! . . . Remember, Joe, I want those documents you have in your hand."

"You're not thinking of a damage suit against us? You won't win that!"

A beatific smile transformed me sister's face.

"I may not win, but in the court of public opinion you'll lose! Come on, guys, let's get out of here!"

She led her troops out of the interrogation room like we were a conquering army. Maybe we were.

"Wasn't that fun now!" my good wife said as she grabbed my arm.

"You didn't get much chance to kick shite. Me sister did it all for you."

" 'Tis true, but didn't I enjoy it altogether!"

"Will you really sue them?" I asked.

"Probably not. But we'll file suit just to describe in full detail what they tried to do to this new Yank of ours and her family."

We went up a couple of floors in an elevator and found a lawyer's room where a paralegal and a stenographer from Cindy's firm were already waiting for us. They set to work drafting motions for Judge Garcia. I went in search of tea for everyone. When I returned, the legal folks were working rapidly. My sister could dictate a motion off the top of her head. Mike Casey had left. Nuala had the phone number of his agents in the car. She closed the Seamus Heaney book and gave me the sheet of paper with numbers.

"Didn't he say to call them as soon as we go into the courtroom? He thought there might be a bit of attention to the case and we'd need our security guards? Security everywhere, isn't it, Dermot love?"

Would it be that way for the rest of our lives? Who had done this to us? Why?

"There are a lot of crazies in the world, Nuala Anne."

" 'Tis true" — she sighed — "all around us . . . What will happen to those poor men?"

"Which poor men?"

"The men who came to our house last night?"

"I hope they come back again. I'll let the dogs take care of them."

"That's not a nice thing to say, Dermot Michael . . . Will they lose their jobs? What will happen to their families like?"

My shite-kicker has a soft heart.

"They'll be reassigned to some harmless desk jobs . . . They didn't care about breaking up our family."

"Our family?"

"If we didn't have Cindy, they would have dragged you before one of their immigration judges and you would be dragged in chains this afternoon and shipped off on Aer Lingus. The rest of us would have had to follow afterwards as soon as we could."

"What about Nelliecoyne's First Communion?" she said in genuine dismay.

"Homeland Security couldn't care less about that."

"Gobshites," she said with a loud sigh.

"Haven't I been telling you that there's a lot of evil around us?"

"Woman, you have."

I wondered if this were the end of it. I was afraid to ask.

At precisely twelve o'clock, we walked down the corridor to Judge Garcia's courtroom, Cindy leading the phalanx.

"Call Ethne," Nuala ordered me. "See how the small one is."

I pushed the code on my cell phone.

"We're fine, Mr. Coyne. Little Socra Marie loved her mother on television."

The small one babbled away.

"Ma gorgeous on telly. She beat up on bad guys. More!"

I passed the phone to my wife as we waited at the door to the courtroom wing for another security search. Her face lit up and tears poured down her cheeks as she listened to babble.

She did manage to slip in, "I love you, Socra Marie" before Ethne regained control of the phone.

"I could have lost her," she leaned against me and wept. "They might have taken her away from me."

"Not for long. Nuala Anne. We're Irish-Americans, a race of lawyers. We would have beat them one way or another. If you were a Moslem or a Mexican-American or even a Polish immigrant, it might have been another matter."

"Gobshites," she said with considerably more vigor. "Dermot, who could have told them awful things about me?"

"That's what Cindy wants to find out."

"The little brat wants me to kill all the bad guys . . . We better be careful about those Westerns she loves on television."

"Real 'Mercan television."

"I hope they don't lose their jobs, still."

The media were waiting for us at the door of Judge Garcia's courtroom. Her bailiffs were struggling to maintain order.

"Will they deport you, Nuala Anne?"

"What makes them think you're a terrorist?"

"Why are you in so much trouble?"

"Who's behind this plot against you?"

"Are you going to sue the Department of Homeland Security?"

"Would this happen to you in Ireland?"

My wife smiled at them, which temporarily stopped the flow of questions — and the flow of blood to my heart.

" 'Tis good to see you all, again, but I don't think I can sing a song just now . . . Back home and across the Irish Sea too, they can lift you and your lawyers can't stop them. So I'm glad I'm here in Yankland. And didn't your man say the case was closed. So, thanks be to God, I'll be going home to me children this afternoon."

"Which man?"

"Himself."

"The United States Attorney," Cindy interjected. "Now we must go into Judge Garcia's courtroom."

"I feel terrible sorry altogether for the poor people, Mexicans and Muslims and Asians and suchlike who them fellas separate from their spouses and children. I'll pray for them and support them that fights for their rights."

Cindy rolled her eyes and guided me wife into the courtroom. The brick throwing and the shite kicking had started again.

The media piled into the courtroom after us. Every seat was taken. Nuala beamed at everyone, kissed Cindasue, who was there in her Coast Guard blue, embraced a proudly grinning Tom Hurley, and kissed the ring of the little Archbishop, who was seated right behind us, practically invisible as he always was.

Judge Garcia, a thoroughly gorgeous Mexican-American woman in her middle thirties, frowned in displeasure at the disturbance in her courtroom and pounded her gavel.

"I will have order in this courtroom or I will clear it immediately."

I caught my wife sending a "good for you smile" to the judge, who moved her lips in response.

"You have requested two injunctions, Counselor," she said to Cindy.

"Yes, Your Honor."

My sister described at some length and in rich detail the indignities heaped on her client and the client's family.

The judge nodded.

"I have heard such stories often in this courtroom . . . Is there a United States Attorney in the courtroom?"

"Stop staring at the judge, Dermot Michael Coyne," me wife whispered in my ear.

Young Tim Novak erupted to his feet.

"Your Honor, the United States will not oppose the granting of these injunctions, but we believe that the injunctions are unnecessary. The United States Attorney for the Northern District of Illinois has already dropped the charges against Ms. Coyne and apologized to her. This emergency hearing is simply an attempt by counsel to turn the courtroom into a media circus."

Bad move. Judge Garcia's jaw tightened and her eyes flashed dangerously.

"Look, sonny, the only reason I will not ask my bailiff to lock you up for contempt of court is your patent inexperience. However, when you return to your boss's office, tell him that I never want to see you in my courtroom again."

Tim Novak, poor jerk, melted back into his chair.

"She is beautiful," Nuala whispered. "Pretty boobs."

"You'll be held in contempt if she hears you."

"She won't at all, at all. Doesn't she like me?"

"Well, Counselor," the judge said to Cindy, "I will grant your injunctions and note for the record that the incidents you describe are not only appalling and incredible, they have become commonplace in our country. Please God they will cease soon."

"Yes, Your Honor. Thank you, Your Honor."

"And Ms. McGrail . . ."

"Yes, your worship . . ."

Me wife popped up like she was a kindergarten student being called by her teacher.

"I hope that this is the last time you have to suffer such indignities from the government of the United States. If they violate these orders, I'll put the lot of them behind bars."

"Thank you, your worship, fair play to you!"

"Now I wonder if you would give me your autograph so I can show my children that you were in my court today."

"Certainly, your worship."

Me wife bounded up to the bench, pulled a disk out of her purse, and signed it with an immense flourish. Then she and Ramona Garcia showed each other pictures of their respective children.

"She never fails to surprise me," Cindy observed. "I hope you realize how lucky you are."

"She thinks she's the lucky one," I responded.

The media were waiting in the corridor when we came out.

Cindasue sidled up to me at the entrance to the court, huge but attractive in her Coast Guard blues.

"Them thar vermin you a stompin' on be the ones who been a harassing folks in our part of the holler."

"Homeland will leave them alone."

"Happen the spies complain, they send out new varmints."

The supply of varmints was apparently unlimited.

"Nuala, why do you want to become an American after what the United States has done to you?"

She waited for quiet.

"The Special Branches in both Ireland and England might have done the same thing. America is a great free nation that's in a bad patch just now. Didn't your Mr. Jefferson write that everyone has inalienable rights? Wouldn't that include immigrants and aliens and suchlike — Arabs and Chinese, and Mexicans, and Cubans and Haitians, and even the odd Irish person that comes along? Isn't it wrong altogether to try to break up families in the name of patriotism?"

National news tonight. All networks.

"I'm proud of you, wife."

"Me too, sister-in-law."

And didn't the tear ducts open and spill on the corridor of the Federal Building named after Everett McKinley Dirksen, aka "The Big Ooze."

Me wife sagged against the cushions in the Town Car as we rode back to the DePaul neighborhood.

"I'm tired, Dermot Michael. It was great craic, but I'm worn-out."

"And your sleep was interrupted last night."

" 'Tis true . . . and didn't you wear me out before I fell asleep."

"You wore me out."

We giggled and leaned against one another.

"Well, it will be a quiet night," I said.

"Is that a promise?"

"I'm making no commitments."

Quiet it was not when we entered our house. The kids screamed and shouted and cheered when they saw their mother on the three TV sets we had assembled in the playroom. Ethne and Damian applauded fervently. The dogs barked, recognizing not the image but the voice. My siblings called and repeated their frequently stated praise of my bride and the warning that I didn't know how lucky I was. The friends and neighbors who knew our phone number also called to celebrate her victory. I was what I usually am, the big lug in the background. I turned on her Web page and deleted hundreds of hate mail letters before she got to them. There would be more. Goonlike people assembled in front of our house at supper time, sullen folks of both genders, in jeans, old sweatshirts, and sports jackets. The police and the Reliables kept them moving. The rain, which had stopped in the morning, returned and drove them off eventually. Thanks be to God, my exhausted wife˙ never noticed them.

Would they hassle the kids in the morning? Would we need the dogs to be serious escorts?

Nuala Anne and I huddled protectively in our bed that night, too weary to consider anything else.

"Are you still awake, Dermot love?"

"Woman, I am."

"Didn't I think the evil would disappear after this morning. It's still around and it's thicker than ever. The spies are still watching us."

11

Didn't I do a brilliant job altogether? Only this poor dear husband of mine knew that I was scared and he didn't realize how scared. I was afraid You were angry at me because I was such a poor wife and You were going to send me back to Ireland and poor Dermot and the kids wouldn't come after me? I'm the worst gobshite of all! I fooled them still. They thought it didn't faze her at all, at all. Well, it did faze me. I knew Dermot would take care of me, no matter what. Now I'm totally exhausted-like. It will take a week before I recover. I'll be an angry little bitch with me poor children. Fine example I'm giving to Nelliecoyne before her First Communion. I don't know what to do about Dermot. Doesn't he distract me something terrible! A look, an accidental touch, and I melt. It isn't healthy for a woman to react that way to her husband, is it now. There's probably something wrong with me. Or maybe there isn't. Maybe that's the way You want a husband and wife to feel about one another. I don't know. I'm a nervous wreck. I must get some sleep. I have so much work to catch up with tomorrow. Well, I love You anyway. Thank You for sending Dermot to represent Yourself.

12

*Francis Higgins and Francis Magan be-
trayed Lord Edward. The former was a
well-known Castle spy, a man who played
the game for amusement, a bibulous, gos-
sipy fellow who brought other spies, more
sinister and dangerous than he, to the service of the Castle. None of us in the United
Irishmen — and I was only on the fringes
in those days not a formal member —
would have dreamed of entrusting Lord
Edward to Higgins's protection. Magan
was another matter. He was one of us. I
didn't like him much, he was a sly reclusive
man, but I never thought he was a traitor.
Neither did anyone else.*

*Lord Edward had already tried on his
special uniform as Commander of the
Revolutionary Army, something like the
red coat the Brits wear but green with
fancy trim. He had many doubts about the
Rising but typically wanted to appear
beautiful when it happened.*

He never had a chance to wear the uni-

form. In the middle of May he was hiding out in the Yellow Lion, Moore's tavern on Thomas Street. Moore heard a rumor that the Castle was about to search the tavern, so he left town, having told his daughter to find another place to hide Lord Edward — down the street in the house of a certain Mr. Murphy. The young woman, however, was fearful that the police would search Murphy's house too because he was known to be a close friend. So she decided to take Lord Edward to the house of another friend, Francis Magan on Usher's Island. The young woman's intelligence was admirable. However, little did she realize that she was delivering him into the hands of his worst enemy.

Magan could hardly believe his good fortune. However, he did not want Lord Edward to be captured in his own house. He alerted the Castle. Major Sirr, the head of the Dublin police, threw a ring of police around the island.

Sirr was one of the worst of the enemies of Ireland. He was almost killed in a skirmish on Usher's Island, but, worse luck, he survived. Lord Edward escaped from the island and was brought back to Moore's on Thomas Street. Magan found out and promptly informed Sirr, who swept down Thomas Street to search every house. I had visited His Lordship to bring him a letter from his wife, whose hiding place over on Usher island was close to where His Lordship had been hiding. He was up in the attic, tired and, it seemed to me then, unwell. Still, he grinned at me and thanked me for the letter. I declined his tip as I always did. Then, when I went into the street, I saw Sirr and his Yeomen striding down the street and breaking into every home with noise and brutality. I slipped back into the Yellow Lion and warned them that Sirr was coming. I escaped from the tavern just as the Yeomen arrived. I understood that Moore was going to hide Lord Edward in this storeroom on the roof.

Lord Edward was reading a book Gil Blass by Le Sage. Lieutenant Swan, one of Sirr's henchmen, broke into the room and cried out for help. Lord Edward, determined to die rather than surrender, grabbed the black-handled dagger he always carried and slashed Swan on the forehead. Then Captain Ryan charged into the room and seized His Lordship. They struggled desperately. Ryan, brave in an evil cause, would not let Lord Edward go, though he stabbed Ryan repeatedly.

Sirr entered the room, drew his two pistols, and calmly shot Lord Edward. Wounded, but still shouting defiance Lord Edward was dragged off to Newgate Prison, where he died a painful and horrible death. Sirr and his Yeomen destroyed all the houses on Thomas Street where they thought Lord Edward might have hidden. Magan went back to Usher's Island and a promise of a lifelong pension.

The Rising was still set for May 23. Samuel Nielsen, Lord Edward's second-in-command, met with his colonels and gave them their orders. The mail was to be stopped from leaving Dublin in the morning. This would be a signal that the Rising was to commence. But Nielsen was arrested in front of the prison as he contemplated an attack to free Lord Edward. There were no leaders left. The Dublin United Irishmen went back to their homes to hide their weapons. In the countryside the news that Dublin had not risen and that Lord Edward was dead spread quickly. Most of the United Irish vanished into the mists. In Wexford, however, twenty thousand men stormed into Wexford Town, under the leadership of Father John Murphy, and proclaimed a Republic. Hundreds, maybe thousands of

Protestants were slaughtered. The Yeomanry and the English army battled the rebels at Vinegar Hill and destroyed them. The Wexford men continued to fight in a cause that was lost before it was begun. Lord Edward died of his wound in Newgate on June 4, murdered by the Camden, the Lord Lieutenant who refused adequate medical help until it was too late. Thirty thousand would die before the Rising collapsed.

Lord Camden was replaced in part because the accusations of Lord Leinster (Edward's brother) that he had deliberately let Lord Edward die. The new Lord Lieutenant was Lord Charles Cornwallis, conqueror of India and conquered by America, a strange, upright, and compassionate man, a paragon of Christian virtue in a social class permeated by corruption and immorality. The Rising was mostly over, but Cornwallis put an end to hanging. There's many a Dubliner who's alive today, successful in his work and respected in the city, who would be in the cemetery with Lord Edward if it were not for the sense and moderation of Charles Cornwallis.

I dined with him one night at the viceregal lodge. Well, to be truthful, I was present at a dinner with many other people. What I was doing there is irrelevant to this story. I was the youngest one there. Lord Cornwallis did not know who I was and indeed most of the others at the table did not either. He was gracious to me as he was to everyone. Our conversation turned to the American war, a revolution that he was not able to put down.

"Is it true, sir, that General Washington was a colonial bumpkin and an incompetent commanding officer?"

"Quite the contrary, he was a perfect gentleman in all respects, much more so than some of my English colleagues at the time. I invited him to dinner after I had surrendered at Yorktown. We had a delightful conversation. I told him quite candidly that as a Whig I thought the war against America was a mistake. I added that we had not lost the war at Yorktown, where, as I have often said Sir Henry Clinton never sent the reinforcements I needed. We lost it in New Jersey. My very words in my toast to the victor were, if I remember correctly, 'when the illustrious part Your Excellency has borne in this long and arduous contest becomes a matter of history, fame will gather your brightest battles rather from the banks of the Delaware than from those of the Chesapeake.' "

"New Jersey, sir!"

"Indeed yes. I had routed him in Long Island and at White Plains with few casualties on our side. The ragtag Continental Army retreated across the Hudson River to New Jersey. It appeared that the war was over. Yet he resisted with irregular forces and beat me very badly at Trenton and Princeton. We suffered heavy losses. The army that had triumphed in New York scarcely existed anymore. I knew then that the war was lost. It dragged on for five more years only because of stubbornness in certain quarters in London."

He meant because of the stubbornness of King George III who was, as the saying went in Dublin, half-mad, half the time.

"It was much different here, was it not, sir?"

The Lord Lieutenant shifted uneasily in his chair and permitted himself a small sip of claret.

"Was it, sir? I agree with Lord Castlereagh, that there was never in any country so formidable an effort on the part of the people. Far more formidable than in America or in France."

"If Lord Edward had not died."

"Lord Edward served in one of my regiments in America. He was a fine officer. I would not have tolerated his death."

No one dared to ask whether he would have pardoned Edward as he had pardoned so many others.

If England had sent other men like him to govern Ireland, the history of the two nations might be different.

As I walked back towards the Liffey from Phoenix Park, where the Viceroy lives, I wondered about the Rising. Cornwallis probably knew more about it than anyone else. He thought that the United Irishmen might actually have won, an opinion few in Dublin shared.

Well, they didn't win. Near victories do not count.

Months later I encountered someone else who seemed to agree with Lord Cornwallis — Bob Emmet, walking along the beach south of Dublin, lost in thought. At first I didn't recognize him. I could not say why he looked different. He always was a master of disguises when he wanted to be.

"We might have won," he said, as soon as he saw me, "if it were not for the failure in Dublin. If we had seized the Castle, there would have been a general rising."

"I doubt it."

"Kildare and Wexford would have joined and we would have squeezed the Yeomen and the army between his. We had them frightened for a day or two. If only they had not taken Lord Edward."

"I'm not sure we would have won even then. We were terribly disorganized. Lord Edward and Sam Nielsen were unbearably reckless."

"So, my friend, was the English army. Perhaps the leaders next time will not make those mistakes," he said mysteriously.

After we set off in opposite directions, I pondered what he had said.

I wondered if Bob fancied himself the leader of a better-organized and more successful rising. He was only twenty-two. Was he already planning another and better rising?

I dismissed the thought, but it remained with me.

Ironically, he would make the same mistakes that Lord Edward made with the same disastrous results, though many fewer casualties.

— 13 —

"What a terrible story," my wife cried out. "What ever happened to his wife and children?"

"His family gained control of the children. His daughter became Lady Pamela Campbell and contributed to the first biography of her father. His wife fled to Hamburg, a hideout for refugees from both England and France in those days. She remarried — the American ambassador. She did not have a happy life."

"Thank God we live now instead of then."

"I don't need to tell you that governments are cruel these days too."

" 'Tis true. So are people."

I had been able to clean up her e-mail before she saw it. The S mail got through. A lot of it. The main points of it were that if she didn't like it here in America, she should go back to Ireland and that like all other immigrants she was exploiting America and should return the money she had taken from her fans. Americans, all of them immigrants, even if they came across the Bering Straits long ago, have always hated immigrants, especially if a given immigrant is rich and successful. Nuala's fan mail had always been good. Now she was hearing from the eejits. And the nine-fingered shite hawks too. May Rosen, our media adviser, said that it would last just one news cycle and that the people who loved her music would keep right on loving her. That sounded like something God would have said to Joan of Arcadia.

We had encountered a couple of haters when we went over to the parish for our First Communion classes.

Herself objected to the classes. I'm not making me First Communion. Why do I need to go to school? The answer from the school was that either we came to the classes or Nelliecoyne would be denied the sacrament.

"Can they do that?" I asked George the Priest.

"They cannot, but a lot of them do it just the same and you lay folk don't figure it's worth the fight."

"How do we fight?"

"Call the chancery and demand that they vindicate Nelliecoyne's right to the sacrament. Or better yet call your very good friend the coadjutor Archbishop."

Nuala vetoed that. We'd embarrass our daughter.

I doubted that. Our little redhead was incapable of embarrassment.

So we strolled into the ancient school hall and promptly encountered a tiny woman with fierce eyes and tight lips.

"You have a lot of nerve," she spit out at us. "If you get rich in America, you should respect America or go home to where you came from."

Nuala stopped in her tracks, took a deep breath, and replied quite calmly, "I do respect America. That's why I hold it to its highest ideals."

The little woman's husband was a large man in a leisure suit, overweight commodities broker perhaps.

"You make me sick, both of you," he growled. "You are a disgrace to the Catholic Church. I'd like to beat the shit out of you."

"Catholics don't settle differences of political opinion by fighting," I said lightly.

"You want to come outside and settle this like a man?"

"Go find a bar and another drunk," I suggested.

"I'm not drunk," he shouted.

Everyone in the hall turned to look at us.

I wished that he would take a poke at me. Then I'd have an excuse.

"Come along, Dermot," my wife warned. I did.

The lecturer was a thin elderly nun who stirred in my metaphor-deprived imagination images of a praying mantis.

She passed out an attendance sheet and warned us that if our names did not appear on all three of the evenings, our children would be denied the privilege of the Eucharist.

Nuala opened her collection of Seamus's poetry and tuned the nun out. The daimon inside me, not to be confused with the Adversary who would also doubtless get into the fight, made me stand up and say, "S'ter, may I ask a question."

And myself urging patience to my wife.

"You may not till after my lecture."

"I'm going to ask it anyhow. What authority do you have to deny a child the sacrament of the Eucharist? As I read canon law, the Catholic laity have the right to the sacraments and no one can deny them that right."

"I am the DRE, Director of Religious Education, in this parish."

"Again, as I read canon law, the DRE is not given such a right . . . I have inquired and I am told that the Chancery Office will vindicate my daughter's right to the sacrament. I'm willing to come to these classes. Maybe I'll learn something. But I won't sign this paper."

"I'll begin my lecture now."

I noted with some satisfaction that most of the people in the group did not sign the paper. The pastor had a rising on his hands and would back down, because of fear of a declining collection if for no other reason.

"Now who's kicking the shite," said a voice next to me.

The lecture was allegedly about the Eucharist as a sacrament of community. In fact it was an anti-American diatribe. Americans were unworthy of the Eucharist because of their consumerism, secularism, materialism, selfishness, pollution, destruction of the environment, global warming, and so on and so on. I am not an admirer of American foreign policy but there's a bit of rebel in me. I don't like being hectored with clichés, especially by a nun.

Me wife's hand rested firmly on me and not as a gesture of erotic invitation either.

"Keep your friggin' shanty Irish mouth shut, Dermot Michael Coyne."

So I did. Naturally.

After sister had wound down, there were no questions. She departed in the highest of dudgeons. She had borne witness.

The pastor waited at the door to greet us as we left, doubtless having pulled himself away from the television.

"How do you get away with this sort of shit," I said amiably, "forty years after the Vatican Council?"

"Sister is elderly and she works very hard."

"You know damn well you can't deny any of these children the sacrament unless for extremely serious reasons. A refusal to sit through this nonsense is not a serious reason."

Nuala tugged at my sleeve.

"Why do you two have to spoil everything?"

"Funny thing, Father, I thought we were the Church too."

Me wife and I walked out into the deluge that was still falling on Southport Avenue.

"I'm ashamed of you, Dermot Michael Coyne."

"You're angry because you didn't get a chance to say the same things."

159

"Weren't you brilliant altogether . . . and yourself shooting them ducks in the shooting gallery — an elderly nun and a clueless priest."

Good enough for me. Anyway, we didn't return for the second lecture and neither did most of the rest of the parents.

BIG-DEAL VICTORY

SMALL-BORE VICTORY

"What do the kids say about Sister Anattracta?" I asked Nelliecoyne in her mother's presence.

She did not look up from her work.

"I can't tell you the word they use, Da, and herself standing here listening to me."

"Where do second-grade girls learn that word, Mary Anne Coyne?"

"From their ma."

FAIR PLAY TO YOU, DERMOT COYNE.

Safe in our study, me wife said, "We're not getting anywhere, Dermot love."

"Oh?"

"We're having a brilliant lesson in Irish history and learning about the traitors and spies, but we haven't done anything about the spies all around us."

"We got rid of Tweedledum and Tweedledee. We frightened off the man down the street. We put Ms. Carson in her place. We've frightened the pastor."

"Small fry." She waved her hand, partly in pride at her use of colloquial American.

"Well, who's the big fry?"

"Them as sent them terrible lies about me to the FBI."

I was worried about them too.

"Happen it the same low-down, hollersulking polecat bad'uns who a-denouncing everyone else."

She giggled at my imitation of her friend Cindasue.

"Are they the evil you sense are near?" I asked, edging into the dark domains where her fey self lurked.

She shrugged her shoulders, causing a current of desire to run through my nervous system. Damn woman was ruining my powers of logical deduction.

"There's terrible evil all around us, Dermot. Isn't something horrible going to happen?"

"To us?"

"Maybe. I don't think so."

"Can we stop it?"

"I don't know . . . Isn't there's going to be a big explosion somewhere?"

"Does Nelliecoyne know about it?"

Our older daughter was fey. The other two kids apparently not. The canines?

Only sometimes. Thunderstorms were explosions for them.

"She knows it's going to happen. She says I shouldn't worry about it. It won't interfere with First Communion."

"That's a relief . . . Terrorists?"

"It's not like the evil before September 11."

"What should we be doing?"

"Reading our Irish history. Still, nothing good is going to happen."

Something good, however, did happen. The following afternoon, Judge Romana Garcia and Commander Cindasue McCloud, USCG, appeared on our porch, the latter, perhaps two weeks away from childbirth breathing heavily after climbing the steps. They announced that they had Ms. McGrail's citizenship documentation and had come to make her a "shunuff Yank."

Ethne brought the older kids home from school. She had collected Katiesue on the way. Our small one dashed downstairs in her nightie, glasses in hand.

"Gwasses, Ma!"

Damian came from the back of the house with the two beasts, who were excited by the crowd but were quiet and polite when introduced to the judge. Danuta appeared from the kitchen.

There would be a hog-killin' do at the Murphys' on Friday to celebrate our new Yank. This was the private ceremony.

The judge told us how much American citizenship meant to people for whom it was a new gift and how silly we were to forget what a treasure it was. Her parents are immigrants and they celebrate citizenship every year on the anniversary of their oath of allegiance.

Nuala replied that now she was a real Yank as well as real Irish, with the help of her husband and especially her children, she'd do her best to live up to the traditions of both republics.

The small ones were duly impressed.

"Why did you come all the way out here to make Mother a Yank?" Nelliecoyne asked.

"Because she's such a special woman, Nellie."

"Shunuff!"

Using our family Bible, my wife swore her allegiance to the United States of America, so help her God. We all cheered, Socra Marie louder than the rest of us. My wife cried. Naturally.

We drank a cup of tea in celebration. Nuala sang "Shenandoah," her favorite American folk song. We promised we'd see each other at the Murphys' on Friday night.

"We a-singing shunuff 'merican songs, about the Yewnited States 'merica."

"Shunuff," Socra Marie agreed.

"You knew they were coming," my wife still a-cryin'.

"Woman, I did. They said you were entitled to something personal and private. Now I think you and I ought have a drop of the creature to celebrate."

We withdrew to our study and toasted the Yewnited States in our best Jameson's hundred-year reserve. I thought about possessing me very own Yank, but decided it would be better later on in her bedroom.

"How will Cindasue prepare for her party and herself pregnant and working all day?"

"I imagine that the Ryan clan and the Coyne clan will sweep into the place."

"Won't I walk down and help?"

"Woman, you will not. It's a party for you."

"I'll have to make something."

"No way."

"Won't I make me soda bread!"

I accepted that compromise. Everyone, except perhaps Ramona, would bring their own soda bread. My wife's would be the best. Wasn't it a West Galway special recipe?

As it turned out, Nuala Anne made five batches of soda bread, a yield which outnumbered everyone else's — and disappeared before the partygoers turned to other people's soda bread.

I was eating some of it as she prepared the fifth batch that morning.

"Dermot Michael Coyne, will you ever stop eating me soda bread! I'll have to make another batch. Go over to the Murphys' house and eat your mom's. It's almost as good as mine."

I hugged her in a nonerotic way and said, "Doesn't me wife make the best soda bread in all the world!"

She sighed loudly.

"I wish we weren't having this friggin' party."

"Why not? It's a great thing you've done and yourself now being a Yank and a Mick!"

" 'Tis true." She sighed again. "But there's evil in the air."

"We beat all the bad'uns. That's part of the celebration."

"No, we've haven't, Dermot love." She slipped the final huge loaf of bread into the oven. "They're out there. 'Tis a very heavy day?"

" 'Tis not. 'Tis a glorious April day, specially made for a big party on Southport Avenue."

"It's closing in, Dermot," she insisted. "Something terrible is going to happen."

Then she shook it off and went back to her music room to practice her singing. She was going to sing 'Mercan music, mostly spiritual and gospel, an advance tryout for her record, *Nuala Anne Sings Gospel!*

The exchange heightened my unease. I had always figured that if Nuala Anne couldn't stop something bad from happening, then I couldn't either. I had to wait till it happened and pick up the pieces. Since there was nothing I could do, there was no point in my worrying.

Just the same I had called Mike Casey and asked him to ring the party and the street with a lot of his people. I didn't want any of the immigrant haters messing things up.

I've always believed that the Coynes go all out for parties. I learned that they are pikers compared to the Ryan-Murphy clan. The event was more of a mass meeting than a party, a noisy Celtic patronal feast than a welcome to a new American.

"Me always a-saying Papists are crazy," Cindasue murmured as the two clans took over her house. She looked very tired and very pregnant.

"When that little no-count boy chile a coming?" I asked my wife — whose predictions on matters relating to the birth of children — time, weight, gender are frighteningly accurate.

She glanced at her diminutive friend.

"Thursday afternoon."

It was not a matter for discussion.

The party exhausted me, not that I did much work. However, the sight of so many people contributing to the food and the drink and fun wore me out.

"Go sit down and rest, Dermot Michael," Nuala said to me. "You've exhausted yourself just watching."

I thought that was an unnecessary dig, especially since I had cooked up the idea of the party.

Our dogs were enjoying themselves enormously. Rarely did they have so many children with whom to play.

Finally, the little Archbishop arrived to say Mass for us. We all gathered in the yard, under an amazingly warm April sky. My brother George helped him to get his robes on properly, for Blackie always a challenge.

"This event," he said, "reminds me of

the story of the Irishmen who got off the boat at Ellis Island, walked along the dock, and watched another boat pull in. The newcomers swarmed down the gangplank, babbling in a foreign language.

" 'This is a fine country, Mick,' he said, 'but there's one thing wrong.'

" 'What's that, Paddy?'

" 'Too many foreigners!'

"The Irish, you see, are never foreigners."

For a homily he told a story that fit in with the events of recent days.

"Once upon a time a new family moved into an elegant suburban parish, one which was very progressive. It had all kinds of committees, and ministries, and there were meetings all the time, and teenagers went to Appalachia in the spring to help build homes, and adults ran soup kitchens for the homeless, and there were clothing drives and blood donations, and the people in the parish figured that they were pretty good at what they did. But the new family was a challenge. They had dark skins but they were not African-Americans or Hispanics. They talked a funny, guttural-sounding language, and seemed to have a lot of money. There were a father and a mother and three kids of grammar-school age and two grandparents, and they had a lot of visitors in their big home. They improved the landscape of the house and painted the window frames and put up a backboard on the garage. They had three cars — a Lexus, a Caddy, and a Lincoln Aviator and the women in the family, including the girl who was probably in eighth grade never appeared outside the house, except in the latest fashion. The word spread around the neighborhood that they were drug dealers. Then another neighborhood rumor began that they were Arabs, probably Saudi oil millionaires. Then yet another rumor reported that they were, would you believe IRAQI! Well, someone in the parish called the FBI and the Bureau said they knew all about them and were watching them closely. Then some of the kids said that the Lincoln Aviator was packed with things that looked like they might be bombs. The neighborhood began a nightly "watch" in which cars drove by the house, just to make sure there were no dangerous meetings. All they observed were big but quiet parties of very well-dressed men and women. Well, when school began, didn't the three kids show up for the first day of Catholic school, wearing the approved uniforms. So a committee of the parishioners went to see the pastor to protest letting these "non-Catholics" into the Catholic school. They're Catholics, the pastor said. They're Iraqi, the chairman of the committee insisted. They're Chaldees replied the pastor. What's a Chaldee? Iraqi Christians. They were Christians when we Irish were still painting our faces blue. They have a parish downtown, but the family moved out here so they could send their kids to a Catholic school. The older girl is quite a basketball player. They made a big donation to the parish. They own a string of camera stores. The committee went home, thinking that the pastor had been joking with them. They looked up Chaldee on the Net. Sure enough they were Catholics. They wondered why all Catholics couldn't look alike!"

Laughter and applause from the congregation.

Nuala's official singing was scheduled for suppertime. Nonetheless, she led us in singing the music from Liam Lawton's Mass for Celtic Saints.

Our kids were running themselves ragged. The two younger ones had had naps earlier in the day. Nelliecoyne wandered around looking worried, as though she were worrying for her mother.

Less and less did I like this two generations of dark ones.

Socra Marie and her inseparable buddy Katiesue were already running on empty, but there would be no slowing down until they both collapsed.

"Happen they a-fallin' down, I put them thar two li'l ragamuffins in Katiesue's bed."

"How you doing, Cindasue?"

"A-getting ready to get shet of this li'l polecat."

After Mass the picnic began, hamburgers, hot dogs, sausages, steak sandwiches; iced tea, Coca-Cola, beer (nothing stronger at my wife's insistence), forty different kinds of ice cream.

And of course soda bread!

Then herself sat on a chair in the middle of the yard, the little kids in front of her, and the doggies curled up on either side, and began to strum the harp as the sunset clouds bathed Southport Avenue red and gold.

She was wearing blue jeans, a red, white, and blue sweatshirt that proclaimed, "God Bless America," and white baseball cap with "USA" on it in red and blue.

She began with "I'm a Yankee Doodle Dandy," then continued with a medley of songs by George M. Cohan.

"I'm going to sing a couple of American folk songs I like a lot, then I'm going to do some gospel music in honor of my Irish friend and neighbor Cindasue, who made her house available for this celebration. Cindasue as you know is a hard-shell Baptist from down to Stinkin' Crick, but also somehow or other one of them gosh darn Papists. Happen I git out 'nother one of them thar records of mine, it may just be gospel music."

I knew, though no one else did, that Cindasue had taught my wife how to sing gospel music, right proper-like.

All the mutter in conversation stopped. The reverence in Nuala's manner and music imposed reverence on the rest of us. It was not quite what we would have heard in a hard-shell Baptist chapel. Rather it was a one-person, solemn choir of Irish-American Catholics singing with deep respect a music which deserved all the respect we could give.

SHE'S A FRIGGIN' GENIUS.

You've just figured that out?

NO, YOU HAVE.

A superb actress, me wife revealed no hint of the impending doom she felt. Now only the inherently optimistic music transfixed her body and soul.

"Last one," she said. "I try to conclude this one with my theme song about a young woman who should have had the chance to emigrate to America like I did, a woman who died young but will live forever in the minds and hearts and voices of the Irish wherever they may be in the world. And as you all know by now this is the first song I did for a good-looking but obnoxious Irish-American boy in O'Neill's pub just down the street from me college."

So we heard once again, the sad and triumphant song of Mollie Malone.

The kids all joined in, Socra Marie before any of the others.

Then as the sun slipped out into suburban Chicago and the sounds of the harp died away and the shades of night slipped in from over the Lake, there was a moment of respectful silence.

Then there was a terrible explosion just behind us, like the whole neighborhood was blowing up.

The ground rocked beneath our feet. The lights flickered and went out. Then they flickered back on. Nuala Anne and Nelliecoyne were hugging one another. All around us women were screaming, children were crying.

"A house exploded," Nelliecoyne cried out.

"Down by the river," Nuala Anne agreed.

"The Curran house?" I gasped.

"Of course."

An orange glow seeped into the sky west of us. Fire! Would it be another Chicago Fire?

— 14 —

I had never met Theobald Wolf Tone, never even set eyes on him till he was dragged into Newgate Prison in the autumn of '98. Yet I felt I knew him. I had read all his writings. He was the intellectual power behind the United Irishmen. He made the arguments about Ireland's right to be free. Although he was a Protestant — and a vague, deistic one at that — and skeptical about Catholicism, he insisted on full rights for Catholics in prose that no one can ever refute. He was also one of the primary organizers of the United Irishmen. Lord Edward was the political and military leader, Wolf Tone was the organizer and the intellectual leader. In the final years he would also become the principal foreign agent, the man who finally persuaded the Directorate to launch a major invasion of Ireland.

You must remember that this was during the time when France still was a revolutionary government but after the

Reign of Terror. The Directorate was a committee that presided over the government and the army and had waged successful war against England and its allies. Bonaparte was only a successful general still lurking in the background.

Tone had lobbied in France for years to promote the cause of Ireland, especially with Talleyrand, an ex-bishop who skillfully served any master who came along. Finally, in 1798 the French were ready to invade Ireland, several months after the Rising, when it was too late to join forces with the United Irishmen. The French came too late, there were not enough of them, they were shadowed every inch of the way by the English fleet, managed to lose themselves in the Irish weather, and landed at the wrong place. The following year, General Humbert managed to put a small force ashore in County Mayo and win a battle at Castlebar before Lord Cornwallis overwhelmed them. However, this second effort was also doomed from the beginning by the same incompetence and mistakes. In neither case did the Irish peasantry rise to help, the peasantry already having risen once that year.

Wolf Tone's ship was trapped in Bantry

Bay and defeated in battle by the English fleet. Tone, a commissioned officer in the French army — he wore his full uniform when he came ashore — was recognized and arrested. He expected or at least hoped he would be treated as a prisoner of war and exchanged for an English officer held by the French. Then he would be able to live with his wife and family again in Paris. Both Tone and his wife came from large families but were the only surviving children, all the others having died from tuberculosis. As a priest without a family of his own, I wonder how parents endure such tragedy. Losing a babe must be bad enough, but a child or a young adult whom you've grown to love as a person . . . that must be unbearable. Yet parents survive and go on. I observe that each of the three great revolutionaries of the turn of the century — Lord Edward, Tone, and Bobby — came from families where the White Death had taken a terrible toll.

Tone was arrested, dragged off to Dublin, tried in a military court, and convicted of treason. He wore his full French uniform in the court, knowing that it would not help him. I managed by utilizing some of my usual resources to get into the trial.

The English officers were courteous and respectful as Tone himself was. I couldn't help but think that both the accused and the judges acted like English gentlemen. I jotted down his remarks at the end of the trial.

Mr. President and Gentlemen of the Court-Martial. It is not my intention to give the Court any trouble; I admit the charge against me in the fullest extent; what I have done, I have done, and I am prepared to stand the consequences.

The great object of my life has been the independence of my country; for that I have sacrificed everything that is most dear to man; placed in an honorable poverty, I have more than once rejected offers considerable to a man in my circumstances, where the condition expected was in opposition to my principles; for them I have braved difficulty and danger: I have submitted to exile and to bondage; I have exposed myself to the rage of the ocean and the fire of the enemy; after an honorable combat that should have interested the feelings of a generous foe, I have been marched through the country in irons to the disgrace alone of whoever gave the order; I have devoted even my wife and my children; after that last effort it is little to say that I am ready to lay down my life.

Whatever I have said, written, or thought on the subject of Ireland I now reiterate: looking upon the connection with England to have been her bane, I have endeavored by every means in power to break that connection; I have labored in consequence to create a people in Ireland by raising three millions of countrymen to the rank of citizens.

Having considered the resources of this country and satisfied she was too weak to assert her liberty by her own proper meal, sought assistance where I thought assistance was to be found, France, where without patron or rector, without art or intrigue I have had the honor to be a citizen and advanced to a superior rank in the armies of the Republic; I have in consequence faithfully discharged my duty as a soldier; I have had the confidence of the French government, approbation of my generals, and the esteem of my comrades.

Such are my principles and such has been my conduct; if in a sequence of the measures in which I have been engaged mischievous times have been brought upon this country, I heartily lament but let it be remembered that it is now nearly four years since I have quitted Ireland and consequently I have been personally concerned in none of them; if I am rightly informed, very great atrocities have been committed on both sides, but that does not at all diminish my regret; for a fair and open war I was prepared. If that has degenerated into a system of assassination, mass murder, and plunder I do again most sincerely lament it, and those who know me personally will give me I am sure credit for that assertion.

I will not detain you longer; in this world success is everything, I have attempted to follow the same line in which Washington succeeded and Kosciusko failed; I have attempted to establish the independence of my country; I have failed in the attempt, my life is in consequence forfeited, and I submit; the court will do its duty and I shall endeavor to do mine.

It was a dignified and respectful legal argument, presented by a skillful lawyer who wanted more to explain his life than to save it. Bobby's final statement four years later would be quite different.

The court then did its duty and sentenced him to death for high treason by hanging and beheading. Lord Cornwallis crossed out the beheading, which to my mind didn't make any difference. However, it was confidentially expected he would further commute the sentence.

Then Joseph Philpot Curran intervened at the King's Court Bench, on a day when a terrible thunderstorm rocked the city, with a plea for habeas corpus. Civil law, he argued, still applied in Ireland. Executions on the basis of military tribunal decisions were illegal. Lord Kilwarden, Tone's neighbor and mentor in Kildare, instantly ordered a writ. Only when the writ was brought to Newgate did the prison officers reveal that Theobald Wolf Tone had slit his throat with a razor or a penknife and was hovering between life and death. Major Sandys, the provost marshal, reported that the prisoner had not seemed himself in the last days but gave some indications of incipient madness before he attempted to kill himself. He was lingering between life and death and could not be moved.

"Good old Wolf," a man in a Dublin pub said to me. "The Red Coats wanted to cut his throat and he beat them to it."

Such is the humor of Dublin's fair city. However, if he had waited for a few more days, he might have had a new trial and a somewhat more lenient verdict.

Or maybe he was deliberately murdered. A lot of people will tell you that some of his old enemies in the Dublin Corporation bribed the gaolers to make Wolf Tone's death slow and painful just as Lord Edward's had been. He was buried quietly in the rain in his native Bodestown. Pilgrims go there every year on his birthday. One of the final letters he wrote from Newgate was to Robert Emmet in Paris.

His wife, Matilda, and his only surviving son, William, remained in Paris. The boy lived to fight in Napoleon's army. After Wellington (Dublin-born but denying that he was Irish) finally disposed of "Boney" at Waterloo, the two migrated to America, where Matilda remarried (happily) and now defends and protects her husband's memory.

(Wellington, hard old Tory that he was,

was six years younger than Wolf Tone, probably knew him or knew of him from his time as Irish Secretary, bitterly opposed Catholic emancipation until he became prime minister and made a deal with Danny O'Connell. Irish history has more than its share of ironies.)

That Tone wrote a letter to Bobby, then only twenty-two years old, suggests that he knew Bobby was his successor.

"You two stay here," George the Priest ordered the Cardinal and the little Archbishop. "There's no point in risking the whole future of the Archdiocese of Chicago when there are younger clergy around."

"I'm going over there," Cardinal Sean insisted. "I'm still the boss."

"No, you're not," my wife informed him. "It's my party and I'm the boss. Stay here until we find out what happened."

"Hit be the big home down thar by the crick, uh, River. Fireboats and craft of the Yewnited States Coast Guard a-comin' up the River. I better see if they a-needing my help."

"No, you're not going to the fire either, Commander McCloud," my wife ordered, "not with Johnpete on schedule. You're on maternity leave. You're staying here."

"Everyone better do what Nuala Anne says," Peter Murphy agreed. "She's the only one with her head screwed on right."

Dr. Mary Kate Murphy, the little Archbishop's sister and Katiesue's gramma, put her arm around my wife.

"Nuala Anne is definitely in charge."

There was no doubt about that. In the chaos and confusion after the explosion, the howling of the hounds, the screaming of sirens, the rumble of fire trucks and ambulances, the growing orange blot a couple of blocks away, Nuala started giving orders. Ethne was to take the kids home, including Nelliecoyne, who definitely did not want to go. Damian was to corral the howling hounds and take them to his apartment for the night. The mutts didn't want to go either. They knew that a terrible thing had happened and felt that they should be involved in doing something about it, though they weren't sure what. But they obeyed me wife's orders.

"What should I do, Nuala Anne?" I asked only ironically.

"Stay here and help me, of course. What else?"

She directed guests on the best way to escape the neighborhood — North on Halsted to Belmont, then over to the Kennedy Expressway — instructed Peter Murphy to sit Cindasue down and Dr. Murphy to put Katiesue to bed. She put me in charge of the cleanup crew — what else do blond apes do? Then she sat down on a chair in the middle of the yard and played soothing music on her harp. Those of us who were still around settled down and relaxed.

MAYBE THEY DO PLAY THOSE THINGS IN HEAVEN.

Mike Casey returned from the fire scene.

"It's a real mess," he said. "A car bomb most likely. Ruptured the gas line. The house is an inferno, so is the lumberyard next door and the yacht storage yard on the other side. Some homes across the river are on fire too. The fire people are doing a good job. One of the fireboats came up the River, though it ran aground. It's soaking everything, as good as a rainstorm. The media are out on the river too and on the other side. Some of them are taking terrible chances. I don't know how they get the fireboat off the river bottom."

"Victims?" I asked.

I noticed that my wife had stopped her harp music.

"No bodies yet. No one knows whether any of the Currans were in the house or whether there were any people in the lumberyard or the yacht storage. If there were any people in the house, there'd be nothing left of them."

I glanced at Nuala. She merely raised her shoulders slightly. She didn't know either.

We went home about midnight, meself carrying the friggin' harp and herself with an arm around me.

"Wasn't it a grand party altogether?" she said.

"Except for the end."

"Well, they'll always remember the night the neighborhood blew up to celebrate Nuala Anne's party, won't they now? And won't they see, sure, wasn't it a friggin' brilliant way to end a party?"

"With all those people killed?"

"All what people?"

"No one killed?"

"No, Dermot Michael, not a single one."

"So the evil is still out there?"

" 'Tis, but it lost this one. Even poor little Nelliecoyne knows that."

"Why? How?"

"Och, if I knew that, wouldn't I tell you?"

As soon as we were inside the house we looked in the children's rooms. All four, counting Ethne, were sound asleep, the latter with Nelliecoyne curled up in her arms.

We went up to our study (which is also

my office, herself having a study of her own to which I am permitted only by invitation for purposes of lovemaking).

All the TV channels were still playing the story of the explosion in "West Lincoln Park." Typical of such hasty improvisations, they moved back and forth from live shots, interviews with bystanders, and shots taken previously. The big old fireboat sitting in the river and regurgitating its water became the centerpiece of reporting. Weekend anchorpersons, seemed surprised that Chicago had such things as fireboats and blissfully unaware of the real Chicago Fire. However, they did understand that they had a great story and a great picture.

A photogenic African-American deputy fire commissioner, his yellow slicker covered with water, was answering stupid questions from a young reporter (male) who must have thought he was Peter Jennings.

"Is it true, Commissioner, that the fireboat has run aground?"

"I'd rather say it is temporarily stuck in the mud."

"Has the Fire Department any contingency plans available for refloating it?"

"Bring some tugs up the river maybe."

"Wont it interfere with traffic on this side of the river?"

He blinked at that one.

"Most commercial traffic is on the South Branch of the River. On this branch almost all the traffic is boats going down to the Lake for the summer."

"I see. Which branch is this?"

"The North Branch," he said, no longer bothering to hide his astonishment.

"And when will the fireboat run out of water?"

"Only when the river runs dry. The boat pumps water from the river into the fire."

"I see." Alas, he didn't see at all.

"Is the fire under control?"

"We've struck the fires on the other side of the river, thanks be to God . . ."

"What does it mean to strike a fire?"

"It means that, while we are still pouring water and fire retardant on it, the fire is no longer a danger. The fires on this side, especially in the lumberyard, are not yet under control. It has stopped spreading, we hope."

The camera panned the blazing lumberyard, the ruins of the Curran house, still glowing like a hellish skeleton, and the shipyard beyond.

Nuala gasped, "Isn't it beautiful, Dermot Michael?"

"I'd be more likely to say terrible . . .

Think of all the beautiful things the Currans have lost and the gorgeous boats that will never run before the winds in Lake Michigan again."

"Och, aren't they all insured?"

"Do you have any estimates of the number of deaths, Commissioner?"

A shot of the ranks of ambulances waiting, almost eagerly for burned bodies.

He sighed softly.

"So far we haven't recovered any bodies. We will have to wait till the fire ends in the house to begin searching."

"They won't find any at all, at all," herself said, flouncing out of the room.

"And you have yet to determine a cause of the fire?"

"Not yet. That may take a while."

"So you don't suspect arson?"

"Any determination of that will have to be made by our arson investigators."

"Thank you, Commissioner."

"Aren't you full of horseshite?" my wife, in briefs and bra, said as she turned off the anchorperson. Her hair hung loosely on her white shoulders, making her look, if not really lascivious, at least gloriously attractive.

"Oh," I said, entranced as I always am by such an apparition.

"Wouldn't it brilliant altogether if we make love?"

"It's an offer that under the circumstances I can hardly refuse."

I'M GETTING OUT OF HERE.

She sat on my lap and kissed me tenderly as she unbuttoned my shirt.

"Shouldn't we be celebrating that we're still alive and still free Americans?"

"I can't argue with that," I gasped.

"And won't I be riding you tonight, just for a change."

I discovered that all my clothes were gone. It would be an interlude of delicious, delectable torment. Then my ability to reflect disappeared. Altogether.

We woke up at eight. No alarm in the study.

"You are a fiendishly wicked woman," I murmured.

"Dermot, where are the children?"

"Downstairs with Ethne."

"We've got to get them ready for school."

"It's Sunday."

We were on the couch, covered with throws.

" 'Tis not."

" 'Tis."

"Then we gotta get them ready for Mass."

"We went to Mass yesterday."

"We did not!"

"We did so . . ."

"Dermot, I don't have any clothes on!"

"You're a terrible woman altogether."

"Neither do you!"

" 'Tis true!"

"Dermot Michael Coyne! Put on your own clothes and go get mine. We have to hurry downstairs."

"Yes, ma'm."

"And bring me shoes."

"Yes, ma'am."

I grabbed a clean sweatshirt, clean jeans, clean underwear, and a pair of loafers. She was sleeping again when I returned to the study.

She woke up when I stumbled into the room, not altogether conscious myself. In a frantic burst of modesty, she dressed and rushed for the stairs.

"What will Ethne be thinking?"

"That we slept in after the excitement of yesterday."

I grabbed the lingerie she had left on my desk, shoved it into a drawer, and followed her down the stairs.

"She'll know we were screwing."

"Married people do that!"

The breakfast nook was chaos. Unlike

my wife, our nanny had given up on the thankless task of organizing the breakfast table. However, even I was a bit surprised when we bumbled into the nook, to see our younger daughter standing on a chair and screaming at the TV.

"Katiesue ma on TV! Shunuff!"

The mayor, huddling under a rain poncho was speaking to the camera, behind him, covered by a huge poncho but with her Coast Guard cap in evidence was Commander C. L. McCloud.

"We're very proud," the mayor was saying, "of the way that Chicago and the federal government responded to this terrible fire. The Police Department, the Fire Department, and the United States Coast Guard responded rapidly and efficiently and brought the blaze under control before much greater harm was done to the adjacent shipyards and neighborhoods. We're grateful for the help of this rain" — his impish grin appeared briefly as he looked up at the dismal gray clouds — "in extinguishing the flames. We are also grateful that there haven't been any human casualties."

The camera panned the river, the fireboat, and two police boats as well as a small Coast Guard craft. The latter three had portable pumps on their decks. All four were somewhat languidly pouring water on the smoldering ruins.

"I now want to turn the microphone over to my good friend and neighbor Commander C. L. McCloud of the United States Coast Guard."

The "C. L." stands for Cindasue Lou, about as classic an Appalachian name as one can wish. She was the mayor's neighbor because the Ryan-Murphy clan had a compound of a sort at Grand Beach.

My wife brought me a chair to sit on, a cup of tea, and touched my arm lightly. Now she remembered last night and our love.

I sighed. How clever of God.

"Be quiet, Socra Marie dear. We all want to hear Ms. Murphy."

Someone lowered the mike for her. Peter Murphy stood right behind her.

She started, as she always did in these public episodes of her life, in flawless bureaucratic English.

"At 2100 hours last night, the Chicago Fire Department called the Port of Chicago to ask if it was possible to bring one of its fireboats up to the Webster Street Bridge. The duty officer informed the Fire Department that there were no records of a fireboat ever proceeding that far up the river but that there was some reason to believe that draft of the boat might not scrape against the bottom of the river at that point — which was mushy and unpredictable. In any case the Yewnited States Coast Guard in the circumstances would send one of its cutters along as an escort. In the event, the fireboat is temporarily stuck in the mud but the Coast Guard will offer all possible help to the city of Chicago in this matter. The Coast Guard cutter, as you can see, has been joined by Chicago Police boats. All have mounted temporary pumps in case more water is needed."

"Commander, how will you remove the fireboat from the mud?"

"Maybe the rainstorm will add temporarily to the river level."

"Can you not draw in more water from Lake Michigan?"

"Unfortunately in its present configuration the North Branch and the Main Branch of the River empty into the South Branch, then into the waters of the Chicago Metropolitan Water Reclamation District. Lake Michigan won't help us, I'm afraid."

"But you can't permit the river to be blocked while the yachting season begins."

"Worse comes to worst, we uns bring up a couple tugs and pull hit out."

Now, as the Coast Guard always planned, C. L. McCloud was about to return to her native language.

"Given the problems with the boat running aground, was it wise to bring it up this far in the River?"

"Happen hit not a-coming up hyar, mebbe the whole neighborhood a-going up in smoke."

"Why do you say the other craft are boats and the Coast Guard boat a cutter?"

"We the Yewnited States Coast Guard, the oldest armed service. A-starting out in 1793 as the Yewnited States Revenue Cutter Service. We right proud of that. All our vessels, happen even with an outboard motor, are cutters."

Commander McCloud's solemn eyes sparkled with laughter.

"One more question, Commander — Are you pregnant?"

"I dono. This hyar little varmint inside me shunuff think so."

"And you're still on active duty?"

"Johnypete, he ain't coming till Thursday afternoon. We uns always prepared. *Semper Paratus.*"

We all cheered enthusiastically. Socra

Marie held out her arms to me to be lifted off the chair.

"What happened to the baby?" the Mick asked.

"The raincoat covers him," I explained.

"Oh," he said, filing the information away for future use.

Damian appeared, to take the dogs for a run in the rain, which being Irish, they enjoyed even more than a run when it was not raining. Ethne led the brats to the playroom for rainy-day amusements, mostly on TV — though only after a quick exchange of affectionate glances with Damian.

"If you don't mind, Nuala," he said, "I'll come back and do some more sketches."

"Please do," she said, glowing over the very slow-moving romance she was supervising.

The phone rang.

"Father Ryan, Dermot . . . I have three matters of interest to you. I hear on very good authority that your brother behaved with great courage and wisdom at the fire site, not that such intelligence will surprise you. Secondly, it would seem that the pastor of the local parish did not appear until this morning and seemed quite upset about the traffic problems the fire was causing for his parish. Thirdly, the Currans,

197

including the admirable Father Rory, are skiing in the Italian alps, after having paid a visit to Rome in an endeavor to enroll him in Milord Cronin's alma mater, the College of Noble Ecclesiastics."

"Indeed."

"My term . . . Despite his love of said loving mother, Milord Cronin is not a little upset at this presumption."

I relayed the information to Nuala Anne, who responded by pouring me some more tea and giving me a slice of soda bread with raspberry jam.

"I saved some of it for you, Dermot love," she said with her shy, peasant girl smile.

"Thoughtful of you, my dear . . . Any special reason?"

"Because I love you so much."

"Funny, I was about to say the same thing."

We finished our breakfast in contented silence.

"Let's go over and look at the mess. . . . We can stop and congratulate Commander McCloud on another public relations triumph."

Peter Murphy greeted us at the door. Like all the Ryans, save the little Archbishop, he was a tall black Irish type.

IRA gunman, my wife suggested.

The women in his house were both sleeping, hangovers doubtless. Peter Murphy told us that there was no chance they could keep Cindasue away from the camera and the mike. She was "right proud" of her performance. And she had Nuala Anne's guarantee that the li'l varmint wouldn't come till Thursday afternoon.

"What if you were wrong?" I asked my wife as we turned west on Webster and walked towards the river.

"Happen I'm wrong, I'll apologize. But I'm never wrong, not when I know. I knew that the tiny one was a girl and that she would be tiny. I didn't know how tiny."

What good is it to be one of the dark ones if the messages are often incomplete. But then, as herself says, she does not take it seriously when something important is at stake, like a stock market investment.

THE BIRTH OF A BABY ISN'T SOMETHING IMPORTANT?

Beats me.

Clyborn Avenue is one of the slanted streets in Chicago that violate its stern cross-street grids, like Ogden and Milwaukee Avenues and Mr. Dooley's fabled Archery Road. Unlike the other slanted streets Clyborn had been a minor street until the urban professionals invaded the neighborhood, lined with small stores, aging homes, and low-end factories. Now it has become an upper-middle shopping mall for said urban professionals (who include the McGrail-Coyne ménage). On the corner of Clyborn and Webster, however, there survives an old neighborhood tavern which prospers because of the patronage of the professionals who feel like they're in a real neighborhood when they drink in a bar with members of other social classes, from west of the River. Nuala calls it our "local" because insofar as we go into any bar, it's that one.

When one crosses Clyborn and approaches the River, the ambience changes. The down-at-the-heal houses on either side of Webster have yet to be rehabbed. Then one arrives at a thin strip of small machine shops and tool stores, and finally the shipyards along the River, where Lake Michigan sailing craft are stored out of the water during the long winter months.

Just short of the river is Dominick Street, at the end of which we beheld the ruins of a shipyard, then the ruins of the Curran house, and beyond that, a smoldering lumberyard. That segment of the bank of the Chicago River looked like it had been taken out by a flight of jet fighter bombers or perhaps had been the scene of a house-to-house battle like the one in Faluja in Iraq.

The fireboats out on the river were still distributing gentle streams of water all along the bank, like irrigation systems in prairie states. Police cars, fire trucks, and a couple of ambulances were lined up in a disorderly row, safely out of the range of the falling water. A Fire Department helicopter hovered in lazy circles overhead. Upriver a Coast Guard chopper, with its trademark red bar, stood guard to warn summer sailors that this first Sunday in April was not, after all, a good time to try to begin the summer season. Though the rain had stopped, temporarily if one were to believe the morning forecasts, cops and firemen and various suit types stood around in slickers and jackets, huddled against the legendary Chicago winds. A lone TV truck rested next to an empty ambulance. The whole area was ringed by the usual police investigation tapes and two young persons in uniform to warn off unauthorized personnel. Like us. It was a comment on the weather — twenty degrees colder than the day before — that we were the only such breaking the Sunday morning peace.

We walked back to Webster and stood on the bridge, where we had a full view of the wreckage on our right and the two police boats and the Coast Guard cutter on the left, the latter distinguishable only by its red stripe. Their temporary pumps were not operating, but the crews kept a careful eye on the darkened ruins on the west bank.

Nothing remained of the Curran house but a few brick pillars and unidentifiable pieces of rubble. Even the water and heating pipes had melted.

"Dear God, those poor people! All the things they prized so much don't exist anymore."

Nuala Anne never takes God's name in vain. When she uses it, she's praying.

"Yesterday you said it was all covered by insurance."

"Memories can't be insured, Dermot Michael."

We ambled back across the bridge.

"Do you have any vibes, Nuala?"

"I know it's all wrong, Dermot, all wrong."

"None of this happened?"

"Not for the reasons everyone thinks."

"What are the reasons?"

"Won't we have to find out?"

Well, that was clear enough as a mission statement.

"Only authorized personnel can cross these tapes, ma'am," the cop told me wife.

"Is Commander John Culhane here?" she said.

"The Chief of Detectives of Area Six," I added.

"Yes." The cop was getting suspicious. We probably were media.

"We're not media," I assured him.

"Would you ever tell him that Dermot and Nuala Anne are out here if he has a minute or two."

"Same name as the singer?" asked the woman cop.

"Yes."

"People ever tell you that you look like her too?"

"Once in a while. She's a lot prettier."

"I wouldn't say that . . . I'll get Commander Culhane for you."

John Culhane, a big, trim man, with sandy hair and piercing brown eyes strode up to the tape with a vast grin on his Irish face.

"I figured you two would show up. Something like this in your neighborhood. You're kinda late . . . Congratulations on being a citizen, Nuala. I hear you had a grand time with those bastards."

"Well, we managed to hold them off, if you take me meaning."

"I can well imagine you did . . . Do you want to take a look around?"

We agreed that it would be interesting, Nuala Anne thanked the cops with her most gracious smile, and we walked under the yellow tapes into a sea of mud.

"I think they must have emptied half the river last night," John said. "Do you know these folks?"

"Didn't we have dinner with them last week?"

"Ah! And what did you think?"

"Interesting people, very cultivated, a little shallow maybe but well-meaning, and not our kind of people."

We walked by the hulks of burned-out yachts, a mess that looked like Florida after a hurricane.

"From what I hear about them that's not a bad summary. They've been a major player in Chicago politics and law for over a hundred years, discreet, behind the scenes, capable, quietly affluent . . . The Germans built this place in the 1850s, all by itself on the side of the River, very pastoral . . . Built it to last, which it did until someone blew it up . . ."

"Certainly arson?"

"Not much doubt . . . See that crater? That was the garage. Someone parked a car in there loaded with high explosives. The house went up at once, the lumberyard and the yacht storage were enveloped. By the time the fire engines arrived there was a solid sheet of flame. If they hadn't brought the fireboat up right away, it could have spread all the way to Clyborn and across the River for a couple of blocks anyway. The plan was not merely to destroy the Curran house; but to create a neighborhood conflagration."

"Another Chicago Fire!"

"Not that bad, but bad enough. Most of the homes around here are wood . . . The other buildings too . . . We could have lost a lot of people . . . Panic . . ."

"Will you find who did it?" Nuala asked.

Our house was wood. Her children had been threatened.

"Our arson guys are the best. They'll put the pieces together and analyze all the rubble and identify the explosives and the kind of car. But this is a superprofessional job. Not just some jerk throwing a milk container of gasoline through a window. So my job will be to find out who would want to do this to the Currans. It won't be easy."

"Terrorists?"

"My guess — and that's all I have now — is that it's too big for just ordinary arson and too small for the terrorists."

"Pretty spectacular way of collecting insurance, huh?"

"I would think so, but we'll have to look into that too. Kind of interesting that they're over in Cortina. Doesn't prove anything either way."

"It wouldn't fit their image as multi-generation respectable professionals," I said.

"Irish professionals," Nuala added, skeptically. "Gombeen men maybe."

"But not mad?"

She sighed.

"No, I don't think so."

"Beautiful house, was it?"

"Most elegant I've ever seen besides the Georgian places in Dublin."

She displayed no inclination to walk any farther into the swamp the fireboat had created.

"Shame . . . Not much of a location anymore . . . You folks going to be working on it?"

"Och, Commander Culhane, would we even think at all, at all of trying to compete with the Chicago Police Department?"

"Yes you would and we both know you

would. I learned a long time ago that it was better to cooperate with you two . . . Do we still have a deal?"

"We do!" She raised her hand for a high five.

Spear-carriers do not participate in such rituals.

I guided her through the least swampy parts of the boatyard and back to Webster Avenue.

She was silent till we crossed Clyborn.

"Someone wanted to send a message, Dermot Michael, didn't they?"

"And they risked burning our little house down."

"It isn't very little."

"I don't like that they did that."

"Then they're in trouble, aren't they?"

" 'Tis true . . . and, Dermot love, it has something to do with them Currans, even if they didn't do it themselves."

"I'll call Mike the Cop as soon as we get back to the house."

The whole family, except the tiny one who was sleeping, were gathered together in the playroom watching *Bambi*. Ethne and Damian were sitting on chairs near one another but disclosing no hints of intimacy. Ethne had a notebook in front of her, half-studying for an exam. The pooches were snoozing quietly.

"Anyone for brunch? We have Sunday brunch at this house!"

The kids shouted gleefully.

"I'll help." Ethne rose from her chair.

"Ah, no, 'tis the job of the woman of the house. And haven't I found a couple of loaves of me soda bread that somehow didn't find their way over to the Murphy house!"

The kids cheered again.

"You make the best soda bread in the world," Nelliecoyne said firmly.

"Galways Soda Bread."

"West Galway."

"Connemara."

"Carraroe."

"I'll help," I volunteered.

" 'Tis good of you, man of the house. Don't forget your phone call."

I went up to the study and punched in Mike Casey's private number.

"I figured herself would want to know more about them," he said. "I've got a complete line on them . . . Got a pencil handy?"

"Sure."

I didn't of course. Fortunately for me when I worked with Nuala I had an excellent memory.

"To begin at the top, John Curran, managing partner of Curran and Sons law firm. One of the 'sons' was his grandfather. Born 1946 a boomer, Loyola Academy 1962, Loyola University 1967, Loyola Law School 1970. Went into the family law firm immediately. Grandfather lived in the house on the River. His family born and raised in St. Jerome's on the North Side."

"There are no North Side Irish," I repeated a mantra from my West Side family.

"I quite agree. The grandfather, Bart, was quite the boyo. Sanitary district, among other things. Would do jail time these days. The father, Tomas or Long Tom, was a straight arrow professionally, though a little dubious personally. Survivor of the Bataan Death March in World War II. People called him Long Tom because of his moods. John is as clean as they come. With the old man out of the way they turned the firm into a boutique operation — wills, trusts, taxes, discreet divorces for the money Irish up on the North Shore. The firm has made a lot of money because it has a deserved reputation for competence and discretion. The grandfather, Bartholomew, known as Black Bart, left the house to John, apparently because the father hated the place. When John married

Estelle Keane in 1970, they moved in. She had a lot of money and they became involved in the restoration of the house, which has kept them busy for the last three decades or so. The firm has some clout which it uses with its usual discretion. Close to the Daleys, but not friendly, if you know what I mean."

"Indeed."

"Democrat in local politics, probably tends to vote Republican nationally, but doesn't admit it to anyone in the ward. Moderate on most issues. If he's pro life, he's quiet about it. Supports civil unions for gays. Has a gay man working for the firm, which offends his wife and one of his daughters-in-law. Practicing Catholic pro-Jesuit as you might imagine. Does not, however, get along too well with your good friend Sean Cronin over the subsidizing of inner-city schools — Catholic schools should be for Catholics."

"Ah."

"Presumably doesn't like our mutual friend down at the Cathedral either."

"Serious mistake."

"He learned early on that if they avoid long coffee breaks and longer lunch hours, lawyers don't have all that much work to do, that their junior partners, sons, paralegals, and legal secretaries could do just as well for them or better. So the family owns a home in Dorr County, condos in Ocean Reef and Vail, and an apartment in Rome."

"Rome!"

"They bought the apartment when their son, Father Rory — always called that by the way — began his studies at the North American College in Rome. They'd spend time over there every year to keep an eye on him and promote his career, just like old man Cronin did with the present Cardinal."

"Interesting."

"They don't need money, Dermot. They're not filthy rich and don't want to be. Maybe they blew up the house on the river for insurance money, but there's no obvious reason why they would need it. The Feds hassle them about taxes now and again, but never find anything. One has the impression that, for the Currans, corruption would be too much work."

An interesting characterization.

Nelliecoyne appeared with a plate heaped with soda bread, bacon, an omelet, and a scone.

"Ma says that we'll all go back on our diets tomorrow. I'll bring the tea."

"Estelle Keenan Curran, born in 1951 married John in 1970 after two years with Madames of the Sacred Heart at Barat. Great beauty from a new rich construction family. First child, Trevor, born fifteen months later. Stay-at-home mom, but managed to collect her degree, and now runs a successful catering firm. Good cook apparently. More straitlaced than her husband. Goes to Mass every day at the Loyola chapel. Takes Jesuit advice very seriously. Still quite attractive. Reads a lot, as they all do, but hardly an intellectual. Doesn't like gay people."

And bossy, I thought to myself, remembering her dialogue with Nuala in which she disapproved of the existence of Socra Marie.

Aloud I said, "Trevor!"

"It is said he has aristocratic pretensions. Trevor is a lawyer with the family firm. Estates. He is said to be boring but very good at his work. His wife, Annette, is an Opus Dei enthusiast and supports Estelle's objection to the young gay man in the firm. Their kids go to the Opus Academy up north. Trevor agrees with his father that the man is a good lawyer. On the other hand the dad is furious at the Cardinal for not forcing all gay men out of the priesthood."

"And out of the Jesuits?"

"That question does not seem to arise . . . Jack, born in 1978, is anything but quiet and dull, a throwback maybe to the old days. He says they should hire a lesbian woman for the firm too but only if she's Haitian. He likes to make trouble. Bright as they come. Specializes in tax problems. Would be a great litigator. Likes the drink taken, but not compulsively. Kept in line by his new red-haired wife, Martha, South Side Irish type. Loves to argue with her mother-in-law and sister-in-law about abortion and gay rights. Lawyer too works for the public defender. No kids yet."

"Troublemaker?"

"She rocks the boat but I gather she can take care of herself."

"I know the kind."

"Indeed you do."

The subject of that remark entered the study, teapot in one hand, cup in the other, poured me tea, and kissed my forehead to indicate that I was not in trouble.

"Gerry Donovan, the husband of Deirdre (born in 1974) is a quick, sharp lawyer who would also make a great litigator, but would sooner work in a low-pressure firm where he can read history. He's a lot like the head of the firm, moderate, middle-of-the-road in all things. His wife is a quiet, stay-at-home mom like her mother, reportedly very deep."

"Worst kind."

"Mary Therese, born in 1977, is not married yet, though she's engaged to an investment banker at William Blair, where she serves as their mathematical genius. She's the only one among the children who is not a lawyer."

"Father Rory is a canon lawyer?"

"He stayed over in Rome after he was ordained to study canon law. I gather he wants to have doctorates in both canon and civil law."

"Is he kind of a free agent or does he work for Sean Cronin?"

"Well he's a priest of the Archdiocese so I guess he works for Cardinal Sean, but he acts pretty much like a free agent. Since the Cardinal did the same thing when he was a young priest, he can hardly complain. My sources tell me that the Cardinal has other things to do besides worry about young Father Curran."

"Why is he not a Jesuit?"

"No one seemed to know. The family was disappointed that he didn't choose to be a Jesuit so decided to make him a bishop instead. There are ways, they say, if you know Rome, to get around Sean Cronin."

"What did Blackie say about him?"

"That he's a man of great intelligence and skill and might even be able to save his soul if he becomes a bishop."

"Sounds like Blackie."

"I asked him what he would do if Father Rory were assigned to the Cathedral. He said he would ask him if he were willing to assume responsibility for the young people's club. I gather that this generation of clergy doesn't like that work."

"Blackie is a very dangerous man."

We both pondered that truth for a moment.

"That's all I've got so far. I'll keep my ear to the ground. However, there's no reason to think any of them either needs a lot of insurance money or is in trouble with the law."

Just as I said good-bye to Mike, me wife appeared in the room with a dish of chocolate ice cream with chocolate sauce for me.

"The rugrats destroyed the brunch altogether; that tiny one has a fearsome appetite. I wonder if I should ask the doctor about it?"

"You'd worry if she wasn't eating."

" 'Tis true. I like to worry. It's what

wives and mothers exist to do."

"Among other things."

"Among other things," she said, her face turning crimson. "Eat your chocolate ice cream, Dermot Michael. We go back on our diets tomorrow."

I didn't know I was on one.

It was raining again outside. I needed a walk or a swim or exercise.

DON'T YOU NEED SEX TOO?

I'm not a maniac.

NEWS TO ME.

"What did Mike know about the Currans?"

"Quite a lot."

I reported in full. She nodded through my recitation and frowned often.

" 'Tis the mother. She's the one to blame. Uptight bitch. She's messed up the whole family and she ordered the explosion because she wants the money to make her son a Cardinal."

"Is that the end of the investigation?"

"I don't like her because of what she said about Socra Marie . . . and herself having five children in nine years."

"A real Catholic family," I said. "She still looks like she'd keep the bed warm at night."

"Typical male chauvinist remark . . . Still

I don't suppose that someone as anal retentive as she is could tolerate the loss of that mansion."

"Nice tits."

"I won't let you aggravate me, Dermot Michael Coyne!"

"Shall we call John Culhane and tell him to arrest her?"

"Be serious . . . I half suspect that she's a lovely woman and I'm just being a witch."

"Not possible!"

She laughed.

" 'Tis and you know it . . . Maybe it's none of them at all, at all. Maybe it's someone who hates them, someone who didn't know that they were flying over to Italy, and our United States not being good enough for them to ski in. That person might try again. Find out, Dermot Michael, whether it was a trip they had planned for a long time."

"Yes, ma'am."

"And eat your ice cream."

— 16 —

Bob was fifteen when I first met him at Trinity College in 1793. He looked like he was closer to ten, a shy little fella with a quick grin and a propensity to blush. No one would have imagined that in ten years he would be leading a rising, the last gasp of the Protestant Irish nationalism of the eighteenth century. However, when he spoke for the first time at the meeting of the Irish Historical Society he was a different man, bold, brave, a master of argument, and a powerful speaker. I thought to myself then that he would go a long way. He did, all the way to a scaffold in front of St. Catherine's Church on Thomas Street.

It will be difficult to write a biography of him, though men will have to try. He did not live long enough to leave behind a record of a life about which a book could be written. Moreover, most of the time after his resignation from Trinity a few months before we would have graduated, he was in hiding. An ingenious and clever little fellow he left few traces behind him. The spies knew nothing to report to Dublin Castle. The Castle itself knew only that Tone had sent him a letter as he was dying. They thought it strange that he would have wasted his time on an innocuous letter to a twenty-year-old who, as far as anyone knew, had not been actively involved in the '98. Indeed they could have made a better case against myself who, as far as they knew, had been at best a messenger boy.

Bob was a master of disguise. He used many different aliases, wrote letters in invisible ink, forged different signatures, even changed his handwriting a couple of times. This may sound like romantic play-acting, but the Castle had no idea that he had slipped away to France and was trying to persuade Bonaparte to attempt one final invasion of Ireland. They were utterly astonished when the Rising occurred.

His infrequent letters to me were always signed "John Peel" and were written in invisible ink on the reverse side of a harmless letter in real ink.

We had experimented with such trickery when we were at Trinity. I don't know where he learned about invisible ink and I won't tell you how to create it. You merely immersed the letter in water, the real ink would wash away, and the invisible would appear, then fade away after five minutes.

The message in his first letter when I uncovered it read, "I'm here in a country across the sea trying to find material for our research. It is difficult but I meet frequently with Herr Hand and even his employer, who seems very interested in our work."

I was astonished by the message. What was my little friend doing in France? For whom was he acting? Was he leading yet another rising? I laughed at the very thought. Bob Emmet a revolutionary general, what could be more absurd! If I understood the message correctly, he was claiming frequent meetings with the Prince Talleyrand and an encounter with Bonaparte, who was now the de facto King of France under the title of "First Consul."

I heard much later, after he died, that others had received such letters, which pertained more directly to his plans and plots in France. I may have been the only friend who received messages. But there may have been others who are still wary of admitting it. However, such materials would be useless to a would-be biographer because the ink will have long since faded.

I suppose I took some risks in copying them immediately. Yet even if the Castle spies had found the letter I have quoted, they would not know what to make of it. By that time I was in Carlow College studying to be a priest. The Bishop of Wexford sent me to Carlow rather than Maynooth because he thought I would be at some risk from the Castle Catholics up there. I had told him, truthfully enough, that I wanted no more of Protestant risings. He may have believed me. It was the truth, however. I believed that the leaders of the '98, even my admired Lord Edward, were incompetents and that their reliance on the French was a serious mistake. I was also sickened by the murder of Protestants by Catholics in Wexford. We were no better than our oppressors when we did that sort of thing.

The only time a rising would make sense would be when you had enough resources and organization to be certain of victory. I'm not sure that will ever be the case.

I received two more letters from "John Peel," who had somehow learned that I was in Carlow.

"I hate this country. It is degrading to have to work with these people. They are degenerates, the women especially immoral. They wear garments that are designed to seduce men. They are often as drunk as the men. They play at cards and offer themselves up as payment when they lose a hand. They also cheat shamelessly when gaming. Few men or women are faithful to their spouses, even at the very highest levels. All the virtue of earlier years has been swept away. They are no better than the English aristocrats. Ireland has nothing to learn from them. We must understand that, when dealing with them, they may be worse than the present alternative."

Very few of my Protestant classmates at Trinity were that censorious. Yet there was always a bit of the Roundhead in Bob. He would have made, I often thought, a good member of Cromwell's New Model Army.

I could not reject his advice, however. The French had let us down repeatedly, whether by design or ineptitude, I was not sure. Ireland was happier as part of the English Empire than it would be as part of any imaginable French Empire. The French, in fact, were a filthy people.

I have modified my thinking since then. The English are also a filthy people and so, given the wealth and the time, will we Irish be. However, we will be filthy with flare.

The third and last letter was even more mysterious.

"I have been home briefly and saw you in the streets of Carlow Town. You look in great form. I always knew you would be a priest. I will pray to the God we both worship that you will persevere in your calling. Great days are ahead of us."

At that point I was not so sure that I would persevere in my calling. I had met Sarah Curran during a holiday from Carlow and was in serious danger of losing my heart to her, though she seemed, as she always did, interested in me only as a loyal and trustworthy friend.

I now realize that my seemingly harmless young friend, had gathered around him a new band of leaders and was organizing another rebellion in Ireland. Moreover, he had developed elaborate and detailed plans which were far superior to anything that the leaders of the '98 had devised. He had laid out schemes for storing arms and making weapons inside the city and even of a rocket that was to be fired into Dublin Castle. He had also made it a firm rule that no rising would occur until a French force of sufficient size was already on the ground.

The men of '98 had not given up. Some of them, mostly workers, were ready to try again. Bob was extremely persuasive. His schemes made sense. This rising would be better organized. Chains of command would be clear. Communication would be efficient. Weapons would be stored in places where they could be obtained easily on the day of the Rising. The new Irish army of the new Irish republic would have learned from past mistakes.

In fact, all the plans and all the lines of command were drawn up by a young man in his middle twenties with no experience except his extensive reading of history and military texts. At night in the excitement and uncertainties of combat, his plans fell apart. Yet his ability to keep the Rising secret, caught the Castle by surprise. His men fought well in the streets. If all those who had promised to come in from the countryside had arrived, he might have captured Dublin Castle, raised the green flag, then . . .

Then I don't know what would have happened. As it was, the Rising was a *miserable failure. Reports from France indicated that the French would land in October. Like all such reports these were false. Bonaparte, once more at war with the alliance, had no intention of wasting troops in Ireland, whatever the alliance's agents in France believed. Nor would he risk his fleet on the foggy, rocky west coast of Ireland. Rather he sent the fleet to the Mediterranean and its eventual meeting at Trafalgar with Lord Nelson. I have the impression that Bob resisted pressure from his lieutenants to move up the date for the Rising in a cockamamie notion that an early rising would force Bonaparte's hand. I don't think he wanted a fight on that hot July evening in 1802. He was smart enough to know that he didn't have enough troops or weapons yet and that the French were not coming. His brother Thomas had already left France with his family for America, where he would have a distinguished career. I've thought that he was a coward and a deserter. Yet I also wish that Bob and Sarah had gone with him.*

I did not realize that he was back in Ireland until I encountered him the previous summer at Sarah's. I was paying my re-

spects to the Curran family during my summer holidays from Carlow College. Bob was also paying his respects to Sarah in the drawing room of their home. I knew I was risking my calling by visiting Sarah. The very sight of her made me forget about the priesthood altogether.

She was a far more beautiful young woman than the pictures reveal. In the full flush of her youthful beauty, Sarah made everyone who met her smile, if only in response to her own dazzling smile. Brown curly hair, lovely skin, dancing eyes, quiet laugh, she dominated a room. In those days she seemed vigorously alive, with only faint hints — at least to one who loved her — of the delicate health which would eventually consume her.

"Mr. John Peel, I presume, sir," Bob said with a bow when I entered the drawing room.

I returned the bow.

"Pardon me, sir, but I thought that was your name."

"You two seem to know one another." Sarah laughed.

"We were at Trinity together," Bob explained, "and good friends. I was expelled because I was a Protestant and he was permitted to remain because he was a Catholic."

We all laughed.

Bob was a man transformed, courtly, witty, sensitive. It was astonishing how the smile of a beautiful woman had transformed him. I was envious of him because Sarah had never smiled at me that way. I also realized that he had captured her heart and that I would return to Carlow the next day with one open door I thought I had in my life permanently closed. I would be a good sport and say to myself that if I had to lose her to another man, there could be no one better than Bob Emmet.

I have little memory of what we said at tea that afternoon, under the unsmiling eye of that scum of the earth, John Philpot Curran. The words were not important in any case. All three of us were young, healthy (it seemed), and exuberant in our life and hope. The images of their two faces, so very much in love, I will never forget. It was, I believe, an interlude pregnant with grace. I don't know why I feel that way. My two friends were doomed. I would live with melancholy memories. Yet grace filled the room. I believe, most of the time anyway, that I will see them again and that they will welcome me. Bob and I *finally left their house and walked in companionable silence along the canal in the strong sunlight of an early-summer evening. The warmth and light made Dublin look beautiful, despite the awful stench.*

"We will try again," he said suddenly. "The French will come again, and we will be ready."

"The French will never come, Bob . . . You yourself have said that they are a nation of liars . . . who will lead us?"

"I will. And I will not make the mistakes that Lord Edward made."

I didn't believe him, not a word of it.

"We will capture the Castle and the city, the country will rise, the French will land, and Ireland will be a free and independent country in the family of nations."

I of all people should have been immune to his rhetoric, but that afternoon, the canal gold and rose in the setting sun, I believed at least temporarily.

"And you will become the President of Ireland, just as George Washington became President of America."

He waved his hand in dismissal.

"Not at all. The Irish people will choose their own president. I will retire from public life. I don't think I'm suited for it. It is enough that history record I led the Rising."

I did not doubt that he was speaking what he believed. Lord Edward might have become the king of Ireland and thought it only proper. His family was as close to royalty as we had. He looked like a king. Bob looked like a shy little boy.

I saw him several times during the year as 1802 turned into 1803. His headquarters was in a small house at Harold Cross on the south edges of the city. I had received a letter at Carlow, in invisible ink naturally. He had invited me to stop by Harold Cross and visit during our Christmas Holiday. I visited him on Boxing Day.

"I thought it was the wren knocking at my door," he said with a laugh.

There was a large stack of foolscap on the deal table in front of him. He laid his pen aside and rose to shake my hand.

"Writing a revolutionary proclamation?"

"Just so. We must have a public record of the reasons for deeds which will necessarily be bloody."

Try as I might, I couldn't see Bob Emmet shedding anyone's blood.

"Will you win?" I asked.

"Oh, I think we will. We have a very good chance. The present rulers are quite incompetent. Their spy system has fallen apart. They don't expect another rising for a half century. We will surprise them and sweep them before us. There are pledges from the neighboring counties of enough men to capture Dublin the first night. Then the other counties will rise."

"And the French? Are they coming?"

"I have every reason to think they are. My brother Thomas has spoken with Bonaparte himself. Arthur O'Connor is interfering as he always does, but he too expects a massive French force will land in late summer, perhaps in Waterford, which will bring them very close to Dublin."

"Will Tom accompany them, or Naper Tandy or Wolf Tone in a French uniform?"

"I doubt it, though if he does, he won't be drunk like Naper Tandy was . . . Tom is planning to transport himself and his family to America to begin life again. He has decided that his days as a revolutionary are over . . ."

Bob hesitated.

"I can't say that I blame him."

He started to say something, paused, then described how there would be no lack of weapons for the Rising. There were several armories working in the city, right under the nose of the Castle. They were making pikes and munitions and fuel for rockets. Blunderbusses would arrive shortly, weapons convenient for carrying under one's coat. They would fight the Yeomanry and the English army as equals.

I was skeptical. I had heard that the new Lord Lieutenant and First Secretary were easygoing gentlemen who believed that Ireland was thoroughly pacified. They devoted much of their time to enjoying the life of English royalty. The commander of the army, General Fox was thought to be something of a clown. There was no one on the island like Lord Cornwallis, who may have ruled with a gentle hand but ruled nonetheless.

Yet, for all the truth of the laziness of the Crown, the army was still professional and the Yeomen still ruthless. Bob might take them by surprise. Yet often unprepared, the English were usually brutally efficient in destroying the military pretensions of Irish amateurs.

He poured me a small glass of poteen — "against the cold of your ride back to Carlow." Then he got to the point of our conversation.

"You have been close to Miss Curran, have you not?"

"We are acquainted, Bob, but I would not say closely."

"A very lovely woman," he murmured.

"I have every intention of becoming a priest," I replied cautiously. "However, she is certainly a striking beauty."

"Would it surprise you if I say that it is my intention to make her my wife after this wretched business is over?"

He was asking if I would object.

I wouldn't, but I would.

I was destined for the priesthood. I had no rights on Sarah, no claim on her, no grounds to object. Yet I had known her first. I was courting her, however remotely and uncertainly, before Bob had ever met her.

"It would not surprise me. On the contrary, such a plan merely indicates your usual good taste, in women as in everything else."

I meant every word. Yet my heart beat faster.

"If I should die in the Rising" — his face flushed as it did so often — "I hope you would see your way clear to taking care of her. John Philpot Curran, as you know, is a fine lawyer, but a rather defective human being, thinks only of himself and his public persona."

That request I had not expected. I stammered in response.

"I will of course discharge such a task as best I can. I fear that I lack the resources and, given my commitment, the uh, freedom to do so completely."

"I would not expect that," he said awkwardly. "I ask only that you care for her within your own limitations . . . I do love her very much . . . But I love Ireland too."

"Maybe you should forget the Rising and invite Mistress Curran to join you and your brother Thomas in America."

He smiled ruefully.

"Believe me, I would very much like to do just that. However, like you I have prior commitments."

"You think you will die, Bob?"

"I would be a fool if I did not admit that possibility . . . If I do, and I promise you this, I will die in such a way that it will not be a meaningless death. I will leave a sentiment that Ireland will never forget . . . Thank you for stopping by. I hope to see you at Easter."

On the cold and rough coach ride back to Carlow Town, I considered the conversation, though I tried not to. Bob was a romantic fool. He and Sarah should elope immediately and escape both Ireland and John Philpot Curran. His chance of surviving this cockamamie rising he had fan-

tasized into existence were thin. If he were not a fool, he would not have permitted himself to fall in love. Ireland was a wet and rocky and unfeeling island. Sarah was a lovely young woman. There ought not even be a choice between them. Now he was drifting like the Liffey to the sea towards almost certain death. He was offering Sarah to me, if I wanted her.

Of course I wanted her.

But I also wanted to be a priest, of that I had no doubt. I realized that Sarah might not approve of his offer to me if she knew about it. Yet if she did want me, how could I reject her?

I was doing very well in my studies at Carlow and the faculty were pleased with me. No one knew about my activities in the Rising of 1798. Nor did they even suspect my relationship with Bob Emmet. There was some discussion of sending me to Rome to finish my theology training. I resisted because I wanted to be Irish in my training. I wasn't anxious to be a bishop. I told my own bishop and he just laughed.

"You're a bit of a republican, aren't you?"

"With all due respect, milord, the butchery here in Wexford a few years ago suggests that Risings don't work."

He nodded wisely.

There had been a fierce street battle in Carlow Town during the '98. That was the same year the college opened. Most of the seminarians were militant republicans, great admirers of Father John Murphy, who led the Wexford forces at Vinegar Hill — and was hung for his troubles. Like all the local clergy I know even now, they were on the side of their people and hence against the English. I steered a middle course. Only when the Irish were very well organized, had effective commanders, and could count on help from the outside, should they even attempt a rising. Some of my classmates assured me that everyone knew the French would land before the summer. I said that I would believe the Frogs would keep their promises when they really did.

However, during the Easter Holidays, when I rode the abominable Carlow Coach back to Dublin, I observed signs of preparations in the countryside in Carlow and Wicklow and on the edge of the Dublin mountains. Small groups of rough-looking men walking along the roadside with serious frowns and no apparent destination — Whiteboys, perhaps, but much more public about it than they should be. I would not have suspected anything un-

less I knew what was afoot.

A Castle spy, and there had to be such in County Wicklow at least, might not have smelled trouble. So far, Bobby's Rising was a secret — as it would be until the day of the Rising. As usual the fighters would come down from the mountains, always reserving the right to return if they didn't like the smell of things.

The spies could still do a lot of harm, however.

I paid my respects to the Currans in their house on Westmoreland Street. Sarah seemed happy to see me, though she was clearly very anxious. We talked about ordination and my possible trip to Rome. Once again, I had no sense that she was attracted to me.

She remarked that Mary Anne Emmet Holmes was ill with tuberculosis and was not expected to live much longer. A fierce young woman, she had sneaked into Kilmainham Gaol and into her husbands cell when he was a prisoner there after the Rising of '98. She wouldn't leave and the English were afraid to throw her out. Her courage and energy, however, were not protection against the White Death. The elder Emmets were already dead. Only Thomas, Addis, and Robert were still alive, and Thomas had already migrated to America, the only survivors of twelve children. The thought crossed my mind that Sarah had lost all but one of her siblings to the same plague, including a twin sister. Their mother had left the family when she was eleven, unable to live any longer with John Philpot's cruelty. Yet perhaps Sarah would be the Tom Emmet of her family. Despite her worry about Bob, she exuded health and vitality.

"Good decision on Tom's part," John Philpot Curran announced, puffing on a big cigar, whose stench filled the whole drawing room, and sipping from his jar of whiskey. "America is the place to be if you want a peaceful society without bloody battles every couple of years."

"They had their own revolution, which ended only twenty years ago," I said.

"But they have their own country."

"Because they took it, sir."

"Do you think Ireland can take it, young man?"

I hated his pomposity. A marvelous lawyer and in his own way something of a patriot. But he would never take risks for Ireland. Even his brilliant attempt to save Lord Edward was little more than self-aggrandizement.

"Only if someone like Rochambeau comes with a force the size he took to America."

"You think it would be better if the French ruled Ireland instead of the English?"

"No," I said. "I wouldn't want Frogs swarming over the countryside. They're an immoral people."

Curran laughed, then belched. Sarah smiled because she knew whom I was quoting.

She shook hands warmly with me at the door and enveloped me in her smile. Though I knew it was really a smile for Bob, it remains with me even to this day.

17

"Teach says I'm verbal," Socra Marie informed Estelle Curran, on whose lap she was sitting. "She means I talk a lot. I say that me da says I got it from me ma."

The Currans, looking like they had just been released from jail, were in our parlor, apparently engaged in a relaxed conversation with the good Nuala Anne (in jeans and a Trinity College sweatshirt). The two white hounds had arrayed themselves on the floor in their friendly/protective mode. Tea and soda bread were available on an end table. For a moment I thought I was in a cottage in the West of Ireland. All that the scene lacked was the acrid smell of peat fire.

The Currans, devastated but resilient, were somehow more attractive than they had been at the dinner. Nuala seemed to have changed her mind about them too.

"Aren't John and Estelle after asking us for our advice?" Nuala said, a warning note in her voice that said, just sit down and be quiet Dermot Michael.

I did both.

The mutts thumped their tails on the floor in a low-key greeting to the titular alpha male of the house.

Our daughter rubbed her eyes.

"Nap, Ma!" she demanded.

"This one goes down real quick, like," she said, scooping up Socra Marie. "I'll be right back . . . Dermot, you look like you're perishing for the want of a sip of tea. Why don't you pour yourself a splasheen?"

We had followed the plight of the Currans in the various media for the last several days. John Culhane had provided more background information. There wasn't much doubt in the minds of the journalists that they had ordered the torching of their own house on the river.

Emerging from the Customs Hall at O'Hare — surely one of the antechambers of hell — they encountered a mob of angry, screaming journalists who had to get clips for the five o'clock news. The vultures had swept aside the Curran family, despite Jack's efforts to protect his parents, and closed in for the kill.

"What was the insurance on your mansion?"

"What will you do with the money?"

"How do you respond to the charges of arson?"

"Was it a terrorist attack?"

"Why did you leave town so suddenly? Was it so you wouldn't be in the house when it blew up?"

John Curran put on his lawyer-outside-the-courtroom face.

"We've just returned from Italy. We don't know what happened to our home, which we dearly loved, and whose destruction breaks our hearts. We can hardly comment until we learn more of the facts."

That wasn't enough for the five o'clock news. The vultures followed them as Jack and Gerry Donovan led them to a waiting limo.

"Why did you want your house destroyed?"

"Do you know that the FBI suspects you hired the arsonists?"

Two suits waited at the door of the limo, waving their warrant cards. I noted with some relief that they were not our old friends Gog and Magog. They were hoping, no doubt, to pry loose some remark that could be interpreted as obstruction of justice. The vultures pushed them aside.

The Bureau was already involved in the case on Monday morning, John Culhane had reported to us, eager to take the case away from the Chicago Police Department on the grounds that there was a possibility of terrorism. The CPD refused to yield jurisdiction. He confirmed that the Currans' departure was a sudden decision, which left open two possibilities: they had the great good fortune to escape murder or they knew what was about to happen and were guilty of arson. The United States being what it is today, they were assumed to be guilty until they proved themselves innocent. Both the United States Attorney for the Northern District of Illinois and the State's Attorney for the County of Cook held press conferences at which they promised thorough investigations. The Currans, in the company of their son, son-in-law, and a phalanx of lawyers — including my redoubtable sister-in-law, who looked like she was having the time of her life, faced two days of questions from the cops and the Feds.

The government never says that there are no grounds for criminal charges. It doesn't arrest you, it doesn't convene a grand jury. It lets you swing in the wind. Spokespersons for both jurisdictions informed the media that "no decision has been made about convening a grand jury."

The ineffable Ms. Hurley fired back in a statement.

"Both the federal government and County of Cook know that they have no evidence at all of criminal behavior. The Feds intruded because they wanted publicity, and the locals had to fight back. We hope that now the games are over the Chicago Police Department will get on with the serious business of finding who destroyed that beautiful old home and endangered the entire neighborhood."

"Do you anticipate grand juries?"

"No more than I anticipate a World Series between the Cubs and the Sox."

While we were waiting the return of the woman of the house and I was sipping my splasheen of tea and destroying altogether a plate of herself's soda bread, John Curran asked me, "Cindy Hurley is your sister, isn't she?"

"I'm usually identified as her brother, indeed her little brother."

"She really is a terror," Estelle said admiringly.

"Actually, she's a very sweet young matron who just doesn't happen to like cops or prosecutors."

The Maeve inched forward and extended her head so that it was available for petting. I obliged. She rumbled contentedly, a wolfhound's equivalent of a purr.

"I assume that they don't have any evidence against you?"

"Only that our home blew up when we weren't in it." John Curran sighed. "Apparently in the world of the prosecutors, that's grounds for suspicion. I'm happy I stayed out of that world and even happier that your sister did not."

"As we were telling Nuala Anne, Commander Culhane told us that his investigation might take a long time. So he hinted that we should contact you people . . ."

"That was a wise hint."

"Is she psychic or something?" Estelle asked.

"In Ireland they call it fey and she is that. More to the point, she is very, very smart. Moreover, as long as I've known her, she has never failed to solve a mystery . . . I'm the spear-carrier."

The woman of the house thundered down the stairs, the Good Witch of the west riding in on the wind.

"Och, Dermot Michael Coyne, haven't you destroyed the soda bread altogether?"

Without waiting for me to say that there

244

was almost as much more where that came from, she sank into her presider's chair and turned to our guests.

"That one never objects to going to bed, then bounces out like she's the recharged Energizer Bunny."

"We had a son like her, my last pregnancy, one we hadn't planned. Of course we loved the poor little kid. The doctors at Children's said he would not survive, but we wanted them to try. He didn't make it . . ."

Her eyes filled with tears.

"They say" — there were tears in her husband's eyes too — "that they've improved the chances lately. But our guy wouldn't have made it even today."

"The real challenge," I said ponderously, "is finding ways to bring such pregnancies to full term."

"So now he's a little angel" — Nuala too was weeping now — "taking care of you and protecting you and maybe himself whispering that you should come visit us."

We were silent as we digested that bit of Connemara piety.

"Commander Culhane said you were better than any private detective he knows."

"And we don't take any pay," I added.

"And aren't we from the neighborhood," me wife added. "And ourselves endangered by the fire!"

"I don't know what more I can tell you," John Curran said. "Our kind of legal practice doesn't make one the kind of enemies who would do something like this."

"You can never tell what some crazy people might think," Estelle added. "You can make enemies without realizing it."

"That's certainly true."

"And our children might have made enemies, though I hope not. We often had family dinners on Saturday night at the old place."

"They're pretty good kids, but they live their own lives," John agreed.

She was the smarter of the two and her husband knew it and apparently did not mind.

What good does it do to mind?

"How much is the land worth without the house?" I asked.

"A lot of money, I'm sure," John Curran said with a shrug of his shoulder, "as is the land on either side. Riverfront property is suddenly very valuable in Chicago. I'm sure developers will want to gobble it up as soon as they can."

"You're not planning to rebuild?"

Estelle raised her hands in a gesture of despair.

"We could never rebuild the memories . . . And it would take a long time and a lot of money . . . We have been thinking for some years that we ought to move our empty nest to a smaller condo or co-op downtown. Now the decision has been made for us."

John Curran became for a few moments the brisk, competent lawyer that he was most of the time.

"We'll sell the land to a developer who will promise to put up first-rate homes, pay off the rest of the mortgage we owe to my father, buy another place and furnish it, and then when we get the insurance money use most of it to fund a chair or two at Loyola."

"That way," Estelle added, "we'll feel that something good has come from it all. We'll mourn, but it's not like losing a child. It was only bricks and mortar . . . And memories."

She dabbed at her eyes.

Nuala and I were silent. This was no way the same couple at whose house we had eaten a little while ago. No, they were the same couple when they weren't, as my grandma would have said, "putting on airs." They deserved our help.

"How will this work out?" John Curran asked. "We really need a solution soon to clear our reputations and fend off the insurance investigators, who will take forever."

" 'Tis easy," Nuala Anne said, complacently I thought. "Won't poor Dermot make the rounds and talk to everyone in the family to see if they have any ideas who might want to blow up the house and kill you two and as many others as might be there? And won't I sit here and think?"

And exercise and practice her singing and take care of the kids and make soda bread. And worry, which is the obligation of all mothers, one which increases with the number of people to worry about.

And determine whether she's pregnant yet.

"So if you will talk to your family and tell them that I'm on your side, I'll phone and make appointments with them for Dermot."

They agreed, though they seemed a little disappointed that we planned nothing more elaborate, no séances or anything like that. There was always a touch of the unusual in Nuala's solutions, but most of the explanation came from shrewd insights and powerful intelligence.

"We'll sort it out," Nuala promised. "We always do."

"That's what Commander Culhane said."

The two mighty mutts stood up to accompany us all to the doorway.

"Good dogs." Estelle patted them both. "Take care of everyone in this house."

"And Jesus and Mary and Patrick go with you," Nuala bade them the usual West of Ireland farewell.

"What do you think, Dermot Michael?" she asked, after bringing me another plate of soda bread and a glass of iced tea which she knew I preferred after lunch.

"Well, I think they're a lot nicer than I did after dinner the other night . . . And a little afraid."

"A lot afraid or why would they trust the likes of us?"

"Why indeed?"

"I'm thinking that this is a deep one."

"Something in the family?"

"Maybe something very dark!"

"Are they in danger?"

"More than they know. Whoever blew up their house might try again."

"They were the targets then?"

"Och, aren't the eejits at the Bureau

stupid? Does a smart lawyer like Mr. Curran expect to get away with arson just because he's gone out of the country? Wouldn't it be a brilliant idea altogether to have Mr. Casey's friends keep an eye on them?"

"Woman, it would indeed."

"I asked my spiritual director, Father Charles, how I should deal with this conversation," Annette Curran said primly. "He told me that I might be present but I should not participate unless he were here. Trevor thought that it would be inappropriate. So I will say nothing."

So two days later as the full moon rose over the Lake I was at the home of Mr. and Mrs. Trevor Curran in suburban Winnetka. A large but not pretentious Georgian home on a street with similar homes and large frontyards and backyards and careful landscaping, this home cried out that those who lived there were affluent but not quite rich. Though I knew that they had four children, there were no signs of the presence of kids, none of the mess of abandoned toys that kids usually leave when they're called for supper.

Inside, the house was equally faultless. Trevor, a man in his middle thirties, wore a dark blue suit coat and tie and horn-rimmed spectacles that, combined with his high forehead, suggested a scholarly and conservative lawyer, cautious in all his dealings. Annette, in a modest beige dress, brown hair, and a rigid face, suggested a novice nun temporarily wearing lay garb. My data said that he was thirty-four, but he looked several years older. She was thirty, and despite her four children, looked much younger.

"Father Charles is from Faith, Hope?" I asked.

Reputedly the richest parish in the Archdiocese, SS Faith, Hope, and Charity (named after three virgin martyrs not three virtues) was often called "Faith, Hope, and Cadillac." My observation as I picked my way carefully through its elegant streets that "Lexus" might be a better name even if it were not alliterative with "Charity."

"Father Charles is my spiritual director," she said in the tone of one who thought having a spiritual director was a high honor.

"My wife," Trevor said in a deep, somewhat weary bass voice, "is a member of Opus Dei. Our school-age children attend their school. I have not joined yet, though I am sympathetic to their beliefs."

Creeps, I thought.

"That picture is your great-grandfather," I asked, nodding towards a painting on the wall.

"Yes indeed, not the founder of the firm. Alas we have no paintings of him, but Black Bart, as he is often called, is the man who in effect reconstructed the firm . . . Looks a little like Mephisto, does he not?"

"I'm not the one who said it."

He chuckled, a gentle, wise old man laugh.

"He flourished in the Roaring Twenties, a different era. He brought many important clients to the firm, and, to be honest, a considerable amount of money. My grandfather, Long Tom Curran, and my father saw that the times were changing and we have achieved some respectability, though even my grandfather, now retired and living in Ocean Reef, had a bit of the 'boyo' in him. A charming man, nonetheless, very charming."

"A terrible sinner," Annette said through tight lips.

"Perhaps, dear, perhaps. But the Bataan Death March did strange things to him . . . However, that is neither here nor there, is it Mr. Coyne? My father, who is also charming but hardly a 'boyo,' has asked me to talk to you about the obliteration of our childhood home."

"We might have been inside when the old dump exploded," Annette said with a sign of the cross.

Trevor ignored her.

"I assume that the police are looking into the activities of the developers who have wanted to buy the house for half a decade at least. They made my father offers that another man could not refuse. However, he and my mother loved the place, as well they might have. Besides, he pointed out that offers increased dramatically every year, thus implying that it was, even purely from the point of view of appreciating value, a property that might well be retained profitably for several more years."

"I see . . . what kind of development, Mr. Curran?"

"Luxury homes, Mr. Coyne, and I use 'luxury' in its usual connotation, not the sense that developers normally utter the word."

"Indeed!"

I was sounding like Archbishop Blackie. I'd better watch it.

"You are aware of a small community named Ravenswood Manor farther up the River, Mr. Coyne."

"A little bit of River Forest in the city . . . The governor lives there, I believe . . ."

"The developers think that they could build much more luxurious homes north from Webster Avenue to Ravenswood Manor, a little bit of Kenilworth in the city. Such a development would transform, if I may use the word, the hinterland of the Chicago River in which in a few years one might be able even to swim. The city government as you may imagine is greatly interested in the project."

"I can imagine."

"The money to be made on the sale of our house and land would enable my father also to retire to Florida. While he likes working very much, Mr. Coyne, he also likes not working. My mother, however, loves Chicago."

"She should dress her age," Annette snapped.

"Nonetheless, she is my mother," Trevor rebuked her gently. "For me and my siblings a very good mother."

"And," I added in the interest of truth and respect, "a very beautiful woman."

Trevor Curran beamed.

"I am pleased you agree, Mr. Coyne. I can in full honesty return the compliment about your wife."

Annette's face was transformed by a moment of pure hatred — for both beautiful women, perhaps for all beautiful women. I gave Trevor full credit. He knew how to deal with his wife. But why had he married her in the first place?

People change.

"So this disaster might please the developers?"

"Oh, indeed yes. Moreover the destruction of adjoining yards will give them a wide space of frontage. They can advertise three or four elegant and spacious homes in what they might well call Riverview."

"Assuming that no buyers will remember the honky-tonk amusement park of the same name."

"Precisely" — he beamed — "not that you or I really remember it either . . . But you grasp my point surely. We have no reason to destroy the old house, but now the development can begin. At the end of the day, my father will not really retire to Florida. He loves the city too. I have made it clear that I will never accept a managerial role and my little brother Jack requires more, ah, seasoning."

Annette opened her mouth to say something, but thought better of it.

"So you doubtless get my drift, Mr. Coyne. One or other of the potential developers contact an outside, ah, firm that specializes in dramatic arson. Like the legendary hit men, they come to Chicago, do their job, and vanish. The police are not likely to find them."

In the distance I heard a sound like television. Annette Curran jumped from her chair and dashed, with the fury of the just woman, out of the room.

"The children and their mother disagree about the use of the television," he said. "I try to preserve a benign neutrality."

We shook hands and I departed.

Riding back to Chicago I pondered that little scene of family life in Winnetka. There might be just a touch of sadism in Trevor Curran. He seemed to enjoy tormenting his wife, bound by her Opus rules, to honor and obey him in all things. One might find some sort of amusement in such behavior as well as pleasure if one played the cards well.

He was a bore and a bore deep in love with the sound of his own voice, half the battle if you're playing the role of a very wise tax lawyer.

As I rode back to Chicago, I discovered slowly all the loopholes in what he had said. His sonorous legal scholar voice had bemused me. He was in fact talking nonsense. If I wanted to make a lot of money for myself and my family, I might just pay someone to torch my house and force the developers, egged on the city administration, to engage in a bidding war for the land that was finally available, even if this wasn't the best time to try to build truly luxury homes in the city — and in the meantime collect insurance money on the house. Moreover, in Chicago of the present big-time developers, even those connected to the Outfit — especially those connected to the Outfit — would not be likely to put out a contract on a historic landmark.

The Currans were what the Irish call a "cute" family, each generation knowing how far to push the envelope without ending up in jail. But Trevor Curran's explanation pushed the envelope too far.

When I returned to Southport Avenue the house was quiet. The sleepy dogs came to the door when I opened it, sniffed in approval, and went back to their stations. The kids were all abed. Nuala was in the exercise room maintaining her figure. I had been explicitly forbidden to enter the room when she was working out on the grounds that I would ogle her in her shorts and running bra and that would distract her from the task at hand.

The charge was true on both counts.

So I called Mike Casey. His wife, Annie Reilly, answered the phone.

"Hi, Dermot, why don't we see you and that beautiful wench of yours over here in our swimming pool anymore?"

"Busy," I said. "Three kids."

They lived in the Hancock Center, where herself and I kept my old studio apartment as our "athletic club," which appreciated in value every year — and also as a secret love nest when we wanted one.

"Mike," I said, "tell me more about Grandfather Curran."

"John's grandfather?"

"Right."

"Let me see what I got here in my notes — Bart Curran born in 1896, died in 1960. Three sons died in the war. The oldest, Thomas or Long Tom — John Curran's father — was a victim of the Bataan Death March. He was a lieutenant in the First Cavalry Regiment. He had volunteered for the army in 1938, when he was eighteen years old, to get away from his father, Black Bart as everyone called him. Battlefield promotion. Somehow escaped and worked his way down the islands to Australia. After his escape he became a major in the Thirty-third Division — Illinois National Guard — when MacArthur returned to the Philippines at Leyte Gulf. Real war hero. He never talked about it and usually showed no effects."

"You can't bottle those things up."

"Well Long Tom Curran did . . . He went to college, then law school. Married his grammar school sweetheart — Liz Manion when he was still in law school. Joined the family firm and shoved old Black Bart into the background, took over the firm and cleaned it up. Tough, honorable man. Mostly. Usually."

"So?"

"I'm of his generation, Dermot, a little younger. He was a good guy — until he went into his black moods. He was usually even-tempered, but rarely and unpredictably moody. He would go into towering rages, drink himself out of it, then apologize. We all wrote it off as some kind of war memories. Liz knew how to deal with him, poor woman. She insisted that he was never violent to her. But he got into fights for which his friends had to cover up. John was born as you know in 1946. There weren't any more pregnancies. No one asked why."

"He's still alive down in Florida, isn't he?"

"Oh, yeah. Never comes up to Chicago.

Washed his hands of the whole business. Liz died in 1960, not even forty. Cancer. Wonderful woman. I imagine she stood between John and his father. You will never hear a bad word from one about the other. Maybe not much affection between either. Old Black Bart died the same year. The loss of the wife whom he loved and the father he never much liked put him into a long-term black mood. He kept the firm alive for John who joined as a clerk while he was in Loyola and then as a partner when he graduated from law school in 1970. Long Tom let the firm drift, taking care of the business he had built up but not seeking much else. He still made a lot of money, all of it honest. I wonder what it was like in that old house when Long Tom and John lived in it alone."

"Probably didn't talk much at all outside the office."

"Real Irish way of coping with grief. Liz was a great lady . . . Anyway when John married Stelle in 1970, Long Tom moved out of the house, then two years later went off to Florida — three decades ago — where he practiced a little law when the mood suited him. He was only fifty-two when he gave up on Chicago and the firm. He's been in Florida for thirty years."

"His troubles, which his friends covered up, got worse after his wife died?"

"They did . . . Also a few love affairs, always discreet, always ending quietly. They say he was a womanizer for a while when he moved to Florida. Probably not anymore, though age doesn't end the game."

"I hope not," I agreed.

My wife insisted that Mike and Annie were still lovers. That was fine with me.

"Sad life, Dermot. I can't imagine that he's involved at all in the destruction of the old house. It was Liz's after all."

I thanked Mike and hung up to wait for the noise of the exercise machine to cease.

I fantasized a bit about having a wife whom I could not only compel to have sex but also compel to enjoy it — obviously Trevor's game, for which Opus was a major support.

I dismissed the fantasy before the voice of my Adversary pointed out that such a relationship was not in the cards for me and I wouldn't have liked it anyway.

Finally, my wife, in a Chicago Bulls sweat jacket and with a towel around her neck, bounded down the corridor. Nuala rarely walks, save when she is on public display. She bounds.

"Dermot Michael Coyne! Why didn't

you come down to the exercise room and meself wondering what had happened up in Winnetka? Just sitting here lollygagging while I'm losing me mind!"

"Just keeping the rules."

Needless to say I had anticipated this encounter.

"What friggin' rules!"

"The friggin' rules which says I may not come into the exercise room when you're working out because I'll ogle you and distract you from what you're doing."

"EEJIT!" she shouted. "You know there's exceptions to all the rules."

"Indeed, when the legislator makes exceptions. But I'm not the legislator."

"You're a gobshite too." She leaned over me and kissed my forehead.

I held her close.

"Dermot, I'm all sweaty and I smell! I gotta take me shower!"

"That can be arranged."

She pulled away from me.

"Tell me what happened!"

So I relayed the story of my visit to SS Faith, Home, and Lincoln Aviator and my conversation with Mike Casey.

"Well," she said with full authority, "I'd say that little bitch is getting what she deserves and probably loves it too."

"I thought such a relationship with a wife might be very interesting . . ."

She hit my arm, not too hard!

"Well, you'll never have it with this wife!"

"I have resigned myself to that truth."

"Have you now and yourself with your dirty male thoughts."

"Their neuroses complement one another. So it's a functional if immature relationship."

"Until her spiritual director at Opus begins to ask questions about her sex life."

"He won't, not as long as she keeps producing children."

Nuala Anne's fist rested against my arm, now affectionate. She was losing interest in our banter — which meant she was thinking.

"A terrible lot of tragedy in a single family, isn't it, Dermot love?"

"Terrible altogether."

"No affection at all between father and son and probably not between husbands and wives either."

"The human condition," I said, no other cliché being immediately available. "Do you have any insights yet about which way we're going?"

"It's still awfully vague, Dermot love."

She had now used that title for me twice.

That meant we would surely make love that night.

"Do you think that John and Estelle are passionate about one another?"

"Sure, are they never! And themselves having a hard time keeping their hands off one another. 'Tis a terrible thing altogether when women are so openly seducing their husbands. No shame at all at all."

Her fist became a gentle hand caressing my arm.

"You know what I'll be after doing tomorrow, Dermot love?"

"Something wicked, I bet?"

"I'll be riding down to South Michigan Avenue to see Madame and herself reprimanding me for not practicing enough and then . . ."

"Then?"

"Then won't I walk up to the Four Seasons and have a bit of chat with Estelle Curran and then . . ."

"Then?"

"Then I'll go over to the Hancock Center and swim a mile!"

"Brilliant! So we better do that shower now, so you'll get a good night's sleep."

"And meself wondering why you've been taking so long!"

As Nuala herself said, it was great craic.

18

At my family's home there was another mysterious letter, from the equally mysterious John Peel. It instructed me to attend him at a certain abandoned warehouse at Marshalsea inside Dublin. I borrowed one of the family steeds and rode over to the warehouse. To my astonishment it had been converted into an armory, though perhaps I could better describe it as an arms factory. Bob stood at a table in the center of the floor, giving orders, making decisions, supervising the work. Some men were making pikes with collapsible handles that could be hidden under cloaks, others were mixing the materials for the making of gunpowder, still others were working on rockets, a few were oiling blunderbusses and muskets. One man was carrying containers up a decrepit staircase to a second-floor storeroom.

"Do you like my little depot?" Bob asked me with the faint blush that was typical of his character.

"The men of '98 had nothing like this."

"No indeed. If they had, perhaps we would not be here now. We must, however, content ourselves with avoiding their mistakes while trying not to make too many of our own."

"You sound pessimistic."

"Not in the least. I am excited about the possibilities of victory, but many things have gone wrong . . . You have called upon Miss Curran."

"Yes indeed, and was spied on for the length of my stay by her smelly fool of a father."

"You must not be harsh on him. He has done much good work for the cause of Ireland. He does not believe that the people of Ireland are ready for another bloody rising so soon after the last failure."

"It is not clear to me that they were ready for that one either."

"Perhaps you are right. Those who win write the history, do they not? One cannot expect that all the people will be on the side of freedom. However, one needs only a small percentage of brave and hardy men. When the green flag flies over Dublin Castle and the city is in the hands of the Irish army, the rest of the country will celebrate our victory and support our cause. We are the saving remnant of the scripture . . ."

"And your friends in France?"

"My brother still thinks they will arrive and in great strength in early August. We will have to rise earlier to assure Bonaparte of our seriousness."

"That's a change of strategy, is it not?"

He lifted his shoulders in a negligent shrug.

"Sometimes commanders must improvise."

"I understand."

"Did Sarah seem well?"

"The very picture of health . . . a bit anxious perhaps . . ."

"That is understandable . . . I have been able to visit with her a few times."

"Is that altogether prudent?"

"She will be my wife . . . Surely I am entitled to an occasional risk in the name of that future relationship . . . I am concerned about her health. Only Richard of all her siblings is still alive . . ."

Some readers of this little memoir will wonder if Robert Emmet and Sarah Curran had not already acted as husband and wife with one another. Let me put your minds at rest. Bob was that rarity in the Ireland of thirty years ago, a devout Protestant with the highest of moral ideals. Sarah was an inexperienced young woman. It is absolutely unthinkable that they would have anticipated their formal marriage. Nor would he have taken the risk of marrying her secretly and leaving her as the unprotected widow of a revolutionary.

"August?" I asked.

"For the Rising?"

"Yes."

Again the meek little shrug.

"Perhaps . . . There is pressure to move it up several weeks. I resist this, but our men are restless and impatient."

They were all mad, I thought. The French were not coming. Only Wexford and Kildare would send many troops. It would be a fiasco.

At the end of the day it was a fiasco. But for a few moments on that night in July it appeared that the Rising might have a chance of victory.

"The Castle does not know about this depot?"

"They have not the slightest idea of its existence. Their spies are lazy and their leaders complacent. They make our work easy for us. Nor are we without resources of our own."

"You have spies in the Castle?"

"I didn't quite say that," he said with a wink.

"Irish spies, spying on the English. That would be an interesting innovation, Bobby."

He shrugged his shoulders again.

"You will be back in Dublin in June?" he asked me.

"For several days . . . Then I must go to Wexford Town to work with my bishop."

"He is more sympathetic to our cause than others, I understand."

"Not unsympathetic surely, but he does not want to see more bloodshed."

"Neither do I . . . In any case, should you want to see me then, it might be unwise to seek me either here or in the house at Harold Cross. There is a little villa at the end of Butterfield Lane in Rathfarnham that is my sanctuary. If I am there, I'll be delighted to offer you a small drink in which we can drink a toast to the Republic of Ireland."

We shook hands.

"Remember to take care of Sarah to the extent you are able."

"I promise."

I don't know what I meant by that promise when I made it. I still don't know.

Back at home, I reflected on Bob's mood. I thought his prediction of victory was only a ritual. He knew that they would lose on the first day. They would not capture the Castle, much less drive the English out of Dublin. Bob was prepared to die, a death he would offer for the future of Ireland. Sarah? He would die with her name on his lips. He was nonetheless a clever man. He would know how to exploit his death for his cause in ways that neither Tone nor Lord Edward would have imagined. He would not be a silent martyr. And poor, lovely, innocent Sarah would be part of his legend.

Several days later, his "depot" blew up. Later I would learn that one of his toy rockets had detonated. The Dublin papers reported it as a fire which was easily extinguished. It seemed unthinkable that the Castle did not realize that a revolution was near at hand. In the event they did not, so confident were they of their hold on Ireland.

"You read about the fire over in Marshalsea?" my father asked me at breakfast the next morning.

He was in complete sympathy with any movement which would drive the English out of Dublin. However, he lacked confidence in the United Irishmen, a stand with which I could not argue.

"I did," I said. "Sounded a little odd."

"I think your friends the United Irishmen might be at it again."

"Does the Castle think so?"

"Lord Hardwicke and Mr. Wickham are good men, sensible like Cornwallis and Castlereagh, but not nearly as intelligent. If Lord Charles were here, he'd smell the gunpowder in that explosion and anticipate. Stop the nonsense and save a lot of lives."

"It certainly would."

"Some of my friends say that young Emmet is one of the leaders . . . He's a friend of yours, isn't he?"

"I thought he was still in France with his brother."

"That's what everyone seems to think . . . Could he lead a rebellion?"

"You've met him, sir. Did Bobby strike you as a leader of a revolution?"

He laughed.

"Hardly, meek-looking little creature. Strong voice and persuasive, still . . . Dan O'Connell says that we will earn home rule eventually, but only by peaceful means . . . What do you think?"

He asked me my opinion often, much to my surprise.

"I don't take to the man, but he's probably right."

"If young Emmet should lead a rising, would you go out with him like you did last time?"

"I didn't go out the last time, sir. I just watched."

"If they caught you, they could have had you up for just watching."

"They didn't, sir. If there should be a rising, even one led by Bobby, I wouldn't even watch."

He considered my face carefully.

"I'm very glad to hear that."

I would watch, of course, but from a safe distance.

What if Sarah should summon me for help?

That was another matter entirely. However, my father hadn't asked about Sarah. I assume my mother, one of the best sources of information in all of Ireland, God bless her, would have told him about Sarah. I did not know.

Should he have asked I would have said I was committed to the priesthood.

Which I thought was the truth.

In Carlow there were only the vaguest of rumors about some of the men "going out." Most of my classmates thought it *would be absurd to try so soon. Others said that if the United Irishmen did not strike again, there would not be another chance for a half century. Very few of us, however, had any question about the morality of more bloodshed. The English and the Protestants ought to be driven out. They did not belong in Ireland. I mentioned Dan O'Connell's thesis. My friends dismissed him as a Kerry sheep thief and a bog Irish gombeen man.*

— 19 —

I wore a dark brown suit for me visit with Stelle Curran. It was too dark for April. But Chicago weather in April, I had discovered since I had come to Yankland, was always too dark for April. As soon as spring took a definitive bow I would turn to light blue, lime, or white suits. I love to stroll down Michigan Avenue in a white suit as early in the year as possible because it reveals the optimism of me nature. In me white suit people would never think I was one of the dark ones.

Didn't she outdo me altogether with a light blue jersey dress with a wide white belt and a white collar? It was not the kind of dress that she picked up at Filene's Basement either. Her ash blond hair was perfectly coifed too in a neat little helmet. I felt like I shouldn't be in the same room with her.

Me husband was right, as he always is about such matters: her body was the sort which would give men of any and every age lustful thoughts. I resolved that I would look like her when I was in my middle fifties.

We were perfectly friendly to each other, though she was guarded, never having encountered one of the dark ones in a tête-à-tête. I was a lot more at ease. She told me to call her Stelle, which was her favorite name. She asked to see the pictures of my children she had not met.

"My he looks like a splendid little boy."

"Wonderful altogether, just like his da— a quiet, thoughtful kid who is interested only in drawing and soccer."

"And what a gorgeous little redhead. I imagine she's very sweet and considerate."

"Sure that's what she wants people to think. Isn't she a troublemaker just like her mother!"

"And you fight a lot, just like my daughters and I used to fight?"

"The daughters always win!"

"They do indeed . . . Now, Nuala, you have some more questions you wanted to ask . . ."

Room Service appeared at the door of their elegant three-room suite with mid-morning tea and scones.

She poured the tea and offered me a scone, which I did not refuse.

"Well," I said nervously, "I have the feeling there is something more you want to tell us about the explosion."

She sat up straight and rigid, like she was going to argue. Then her shoulders slumped her eyes filled with tears and she began to talk, almost in a whisper.

"I've never told anyone this before, except my priest and my psychiatrist, but the little boy we lost, Brendan, was the child of an incestuous union with my father-in-law. I don't know how this would account for the explosion, but I feel I must tell you."

"Oh, Stelle!" I cried out.

So we both had a good cry, repaired our faces, and she went on.

"It was 1981. I had married at nineteen and given birth to five children in nine years. I had been raised in an old-fashioned Catholic family. You knew almost nothing about marriage or sex and had as many children as you could. Moreover, you were to be a stay-at-home mom as we call them now and take care of all your children even if you had help. I had to give them my full attention, all day, every day. I put on twenty-five pounds and became fat and frumpy, or so I thought and I think John thought too. I was smoking too much, drinking too much, crying too much, and feeling very sorry for myself.

"I didn't get much out of sex. There was nothing in my background to lead me to expect much out of it. I permitted Jack to make love to me whenever he wanted and sort of pretended to enjoy it. He didn't know much either and after a while he didn't ask very often. He must have wondered what happened to the beautiful, bright-eyed woman he married, just as I wondered what had happened to the gentle, loving man I had married. I'm sure he fooled around, what man wouldn't? I didn't ask, I didn't want to know. And he never told me. I was only thirty-one and I was a washed-up hag. Yes, I was making a little progress on my degree from Barat and had learned how to cook. I had even become good at it. But I knew I was finished. I might as well be dead."

I felt the cold gray mists over the Lake slip into the suite and creep all around us. The hell she had endured was threatening both of us. She couldn't see the mists of hell, though I could. We both felt them.

"But you turned your life around, didn't you?"

"Did I, Nuala Anne? I guess I did, but it got worse before it got better. And sometimes I think I'll never get over it. In the winter of 1981 John rented a condo for us down in Ocean Reef, just down the street from Long Tom's. The idea was that I would get away from the children for a couple of weeks and we would renew our marriage. I was a nervous wreck away from the children and utterly uninterested in renewing the marriage, which I thought was finished forever. We made love a couple of times, but they were lackluster, pro forma exchanges. John got the message. After the second week, he had to hurry back to Chicago. I was sure that there was another woman waiting for him."

"Do you know that for sure?" I asked as gently as I could.

"No, I don't. I was convinced of it then, but my mind was a wreck and I couldn't think straight. At this distance, after all that has happened, it doesn't matter . . . It was, nonetheless, heartless and cruel of John to leave me there alone, even if he did phone several times every day. Long Tom was sixty-one then, thirty years older than me, a strikingly handsome male — still is as a matter of fact. When John and I were dating he always looked at me with an appreciation that seemed to me then was inappropriate — like he was undressing me and liked what he had discovered. Men look at women that way. It had happened to me before. I paid little attention, sometimes I hated it, sometimes I liked it, depending on the man. But from my father-in-law, it seemed, well, offensive. I was surprised the first time I saw a picture of Elizabeth, John's mother as a young woman. She looked a lot like me. I wondered if John fell in love with me because he was marrying his mother. I never asked and now never will because it doesn't matter."

"I think I look a lot like Dermot's mother," I said softly.

"Long Tom never stopped it. He always undressed me with his eyes when we were together. He had a secret little smile that I alone seemed to see. I was offended as you can imagine, but also just a little flattered. He was a war hero, tall, strong, competent, and with a lot of charisma. I could never understand why he didn't remarry. I never thought that . . . Let me correct that in the name of honesty. I never permitted the thought that if I were alone in our condo, he might come calling. It was one of those daydreams that you always deny because they are so totally improbable . . . Am I shocking you, Nuala Anne?"

"Only with your honesty and courage."

"Well, he did come calling the first night John wasn't there. You must understand, Nuala, that I was half-drunk, frustrated, angry, disappointed. I don't say that I didn't know what I was doing, because I did and I liked it, but it seemed then and it seems now that I enjoyed it."

"He raped you!"

"Every night while John was away, six nights in a row. Is it rape when the victim enjoys it and looks forward to it again? The first night I was lying in bed in my panties, drinking Scotch, too much of it, trying to read a book, feeling sorry for myself. He opened the door and looked at me and laughed. I knew what would happen. I knew I should resist him, but I was quite incapable of that. I pushed him away. He merely laughed at me. He laughed most of the time he was making love. We never said a thing to each other."

"Poor Stelle."

"Poor Stelle indeed! I still have nightmares, terror dreams, and wake up in a cold sweat. Even now the dreams are awful, but not without pleasure. Those five nights were the best sex I had — until then. I was a victim of my father-in-law, but the pleasure of victimhood was unbearably sweet. Long Tom knew how to love a woman, how to push all the right buttons, how to wake up desire . . . He was a master of the game."

She continued to weep, caught between humiliation and pleasure in her memories.

"I suppose I could have called John and told him that his father was half raping me. I thought of that several times, even picked up the phone to dial the number, but I was afraid . . . Afraid of everything, afraid that he would visit me again that night. And to be honest that he would not visit me."

"A jumble of fear and guilt."

"A lot of fear, the guilt came only later. Then John came back and his father left me alone. His little smile, just for me, said I've had you, whore, and I know what you're like. It was hateful. I hated him for a long time. Now I feel sorry for him. Poor, wretched, fouled-up man."

"I shouldn't wonder."

"Two years ago, when we went down there at Easter, he whispered in my ear, 'I'm sorry. Please forgive me.' "

"And you said?"

"I told him that of course I forgave him. He's an old man with lots of regrets . . . When he was raping me, he called me 'Liz' several times. He confused me with his wife."

She paused for a moment. I tried to figure out what to say. My customary glib Irish mouth couldn't form a word.

"I should tell you, Nuala Anne, that when I was in eighth grade, my father groped me several times. I told him to stop or I would kill him the next time he tried. He knew that I meant it because I had a knife in my hand."

"God preserve us," was all I could say. "You're a desperate woman . . . that means a good and brave one."

"I don't feel that way just now . . . Yet it is good that I talk to someone whom I like and trust."

"I'll only tell me Dermot . . ."

"I understand that, it's the whole point isn't it?"

"So after we returned to Chicago, in a blizzard of course, I turned up pregnant. I hated the pregnancy. I hated the bastard inside me. I hated the thought of another child in my already child-crowded life. I asked God to take the child from me. I made an appointment with an abortion counselor. I couldn't do it. But then as I could feel him kicking inside me, I changed my mind, as mothers do. I wanted him. I loved him, no matter who his father was."

"Your husband might just as well have been the father . . ."

"But then why would God punish me by taking Brendan away from me?"

She's breaking down completely. I have to do something.

"That's not my God, Estelle Curran, and it's not your God either and you know it."

Her sobs turned to laughs.

"Of course, it's not. I know better now. I'll never know this side of heaven who was Brendan's father and there it won't be important, will it? . . . We loved the tiny mite so much. John and I came together to try to keep him alive. The doctors said that it was at best a fifty-fifty chance and that he would have substantial life problems. You, of all people, know what we went through. I baptized him. We told the doctors to do everything they could to save him. They shook their heads but said they would. I believed them. They asked about the 'DNR' instruction — how did you handle that?"

"We agreed to that. Father George — Dermot's brother the priest — said that was the correct decision. It never quite came to that, thanks be to God."

"We were there in the Neonatal Intensive Care Unit and we could see him dying. He just couldn't breathe. The resident, who was very sympathetic to us, said there was nothing more we could do. So we said a decade of the rosary. At the third Hail Mary, our poor little Brendan went home."

"And is up there watching you today and himself very proud of you."

"I believe that," she said with a sigh. "I don't always feel it but I always believe it . . . Don't worry, Nuala Anne, I'm through crying. Thank you for helping me to relive the worst time in my life."

"Did it get worse after Brendan died?"

"Oddly enough, it didn't. I was determined for his sake to remake my life. I already had a good priest, I got myself a good psychiatrist, a good sex therapist, a good nutritionist, and tried to put myself back together again. I went back to school full-time, I lost thirty-five pounds — the last five are the hardest and I still struggle with them — I founded my catering business and I fell in love with my husband again and he with me. Maybe I should say we fell in love with one another for the first time. It's lasted, gets more intense rather than less."

" 'Tis obvious to anyone who sees you together. He looks at you the way me Dermot looks at me."

"It took two years to re-create me, or to create me for the first time. It still seems tenuous. I see my psychiatrist every week and my priest once a month. And I pray that I can hang on. So far I have."

"And your man supports you?"

"Oh, he does. He doesn't understand but that doesn't matter because he loves me. We drink only a glass of wine at dinner, we stay in condition, we read the same books, play the same sports. We try not to worry about the past. He certainly doesn't fool around anymore, if he ever did, and that doesn't matter now."

"He'd better not."

"That's what he says. Recently a friend of ours acquired a trophy mistress. John said to me, 'I don't know how he does it. One passionate woman is almost too much for me.' "

"Sure, isn't he the darling now!"

That nine-fingered shite hawk Dermot Michael Coyne has never said that to me. He'd better say it soon.

"Now you want to ask me whether I know anyone or any reason for blowing up our house. After what I've said you wonder whether it might be something that Long Tom Curran might do. He stands to make a little money from the mortgage he still holds. But it's trivial to what he has. He has, I think, always resented my John who he sees as more successful and more respected and has a wife who is still alive. Looking back on our interlude, I think he was punishing me and punishing John even more. Perhaps he counted on my telling John. I don't know what would have happened, which is one of the many reasons I've kept quiet about it and always will."

"Hating you, hating your husband, and in his twisted mind still loving his wife."

"And in his own twisted way even loving me . . . It took me a long time to think about that, but it may be true. That doesn't matter anymore either."

"It might matter," I said with more wisdom than I thought I possessed, "someday when you're standing at his deathbed, by yourself for a few moments, and himself unable to talk."

"I might even say that the whole thing forced me to turn my life around and become an adult."

"Indeed, it might."

"I think we ought to have a glass of sherry before you go."

It was very good sherry.

"So might Long Tom have ordered the destruction of the house in which he lived with Elizabeth for many years and without her for many more years? You must remember that he went through great agonies out there in the islands when he was just a boy. He never recovered from that anger. No telling where it might go and on whom it might fasten. At this stage of his life he's mellowed enough that the anger seems gone. Honestly, it wouldn't make sense, but Long Tom never made sense. I just don't know."

Neither did I.

So I walked across the street to the Hancock Center, joked with the doorman, and rode up to our little love nest, took off my clothes, and put on one of my more modest bikinis — me Dermot likes to shock the uptight and deadly serious people who use the pool. Speaking of that gobshite, he should have been in the apartment waiting for me. I hadn't suggested that he join me, but it was certainly implicit in what I said about me plans for the day.

So I said to hell with him — well, it was a little stronger — and put on a robe and clogs and went down to the pool. I had it all to meself, so there was no one to grade my dive as I went in.

I was angry at all men. Long Tom

Curran was a vicious bastard for raping his defenseless daughter-in-law, no matter what he had suffered in the war, no matter how complex and mixed his motives, and no matter how it was somehow all ink for God's drawing with crooked lines.

I was also furious at Dermot Michael Coyne for not being there when I needed to talk to him. Frigging gobshite.

Then suddenly a huge creature dove into the pool next to me.

"Dermot Michael Coyne," I shouted, hugging him, "where have you been and meself needing you."

— 20 —

Marie Therese Curran filled the office with her height (five-eleven, I guessed), her beauty, and her obvious intelligence — Estelle's daughter with a lightning mind. It was a small but very plush office in a large and very plush venture capital firm in the 333 South Wacker Building.

As I tell me wife, I'm not threatened by tall women or intelligent ones or I never would have married her. Yet I could not imagine Marie Therese strolling down the Magnificent Mile against the spring winds in Nuala Anne's floral print dress.

She shook hands with me and apologized for her office.

"Someone that's only twenty-three doesn't merit this office. However, I have persuaded my bosses that I'm a mathematical whiz. It was fairly easy because they are illiterate when it comes to numbers."

"Venture capitalists don't know numbers?"

"What they do is mostly instinct, like

commodities traders. My numbers are a reality check on them. Sometimes."

"I was a trader once, but gave it up."

"Too many mistakes?"

I love to answer that question.

"One big mistake that earned me a million. Then I quit."

"We should be that lucky around here." She laughed, a big hearty laugh.

Then her facial expression turned serious. Time for getting down to business.

"When you talk to Marti and Jack she may give you the wrong impression. She will suggest that after I finish law school the two of us will take over the firm and call it Curran and Daughters. She is an imp. Mind you the idea is not unattractive. We would surely be successful. But there are enough conflicts in the family past without adding more. It's true I'm going to law school, but I don't expect to practice law. As the cliché puts it, there are already too many lawyers. Neither of us have any serious intention of joining the firm, much less trying to take it over. I wanted to assure you of that."

"However, such a putsch would certainly be successful."

"Neither of us have any doubt of that." She grinned. "But we couldn't do that to our siblings. They're interviewing young women now, even Dad says they have to integrate. About time."

Her height and her brisk manner did not diminish her attractiveness in the slightest. Despite Nuala Anne's warnings, my eyes began to do their subtle work. I forbade them from continuing.

"You speak of conflicts in the firm?"

"Mostly in the past, Grandfather and Dad worked together with considerable success, but they did not get along personally. Grandfather, as you may know, left the family to join the army and became a prisoner of war in the Philippines. When he came home he drove Great-grandfather out of the firm. The strains now are not as serious, but they are there."

"Ah?"

"There are differences of personality, mostly involving Trevor, who finds the others in the firm, how should I say it, flighty. He is also ill at ease with the new associate who is gay, though that may be the result of his wife's endless complaints about the associate. She is a religious fanatic and somehow believes that his presence will corrupt her children, though they have no contact with the firm. In Annette's world virtually everything is a threat to the purity of her children, or her 'kiddies' as she often calls them."

She didn't like Annette very much. However, the image of Annette's causing a crisis in the firm through her husband seemed far-fetched. Trevor, it had seemed to me, was skillful at fending off his wife.

"Do you think she will create major crises in the firm?"

Marie Therese hesitated.

"Tensions, yes indeed. Crises, as in earlier years, probably not.

"Now," she continued, "as to the matter at hand, I am convinced that we have to look back into the past of our family. None of us would want to harm any of the others. For siblings we get along very well. We adore our parents. We even like our in-laws, well, except poor Annette. Grandpa has seen too much and suffered too much, but he's an old man now, practically dying. He could not have created this fairly elaborate conspiracy, could he? So we must look outside."

"That's not an unreasonable position."

"So I decided to do some research, since researching is my business. Using a number of databases that are not, ah, readily available, I have come up with three instances where the firm could be seen as

harming someone. The claim would be unfair, but it still could be made."

"The cops wouldn't have access to these
databases?"

"Some of them, of course, but not
enough to create the profiles I have put together. There are three individuals in this
city, not entirely of sound mind, who
might harbor deadly thoughts towards us."

She passed three folders over to me.

"The first one is a certain Ms. Germaine
Livermore, a woman in her middle forties,
with considerable experience in such ventures as artistic dancing and exercising on
the streets. She was known by the professional name of Sunny — with the U —
Christian, a very inappropriate name. She
persuaded one of her clients, a Mr. Samuel
Connors, to make an honest woman out of
her. I have no doubt that she was sincere in
this persuasion, though he was twenty
years older than she was. They married
and lived together for ten years, apparently
with some contentment. Mr. Connors had
three children and a wife who had deserted
him. These persons were named in his will,
which was prepared by the firm, as his heirs.
He made no attempt to change this will or
to make any provision for his second wife.
Unfortunately he died in his late fifties of a

massive heart attack. Ms. Livermore or Ms. Connors as she was then, challenged the will on the grounds that he had made promises to her in the presence of witnesses. Naturally Dad did not take the case. However, he did testify that the firm had done Samuel's tax and inheritance work for many years and that he had never even mentioned the fact that he had a second wife. Naturally, Ms. Connors did not have a case. However, the lawyers for the first family advised them to make a moderately generous settlement on Ms. Connors. They stubbornly refused until it was pointed out to them how much they would stand to lose in prolonged litigation. They grudgingly agreed to a settlement. Negotiations were acrimonious. While the settlement was more than enough to maintain Ms. Connors for the rest of her life, she felt that she had been cheated and demeaned and made some unfortunate comments about revenge. She is now in a relationship with a certain Gilberto Juarez — or so he calls himself — who is a very important personage in one of the Hispanic drug gangs. Finally, her fury has driven her several times to seek psychiatric help. I don't think that the firm could have assembled such a dossier, do you, Dermot?"

"What did you find out on me?"

"Only the very best, Dermot," she said smoothly. "And Nuala Anne's charitable generosity confirms that she is the wonderful human that she seems to be."

I don't even know how much Nuala Anne gives to charity!

"I would like to stress that while some of this information is not on the public record, I obtained it all legally."

"Naturally," I said, somewhat shaken.

"You can share the information with the police and of course with your wife, but don't give the police the dossiers or tell them how you obtained it."

"My lips are sealed."

Who needed spies these days?

"The second file is a certain Herbert McNeill, a very angry African-American gentleman who unfortunately had to do time at the Joliet institution for income tax evasion. He owned — and still does — a string of clothing stores in the African-American neighborhoods. He made quite a bit of money and concluded that he needed good tax advice. He consulted my brother Trevor, who carefully prepared his returns for three years. Unfortunately for Mr. McNeill, he did not share with poor Trevor — strike the word 'poor,' that's the way we talk about him for obvious reasons — information about all his sources of income, some of which seems to have been from laundry work — of money, not garments. He did not disguise this income very carefully and lived a lifestyle much more luxurious than the tax return suggested was feasible. So he was indicted, convicted, and sentenced — and also fined. Irrationally he blames Trevor for failure to prepare an adequate return and cannot understand that such a return requires accurate listing of sources of income. Since Trevor has no source of information in the African-American community, he has no knowledge of this rage. It is not clear to me that Mr. McNeill is smart enough to organize such an elaborate conspiracy like blowing up River House but he has friends who are."

"Even your family's kind of law turns out to be very dangerous?"

"Only when it is unfortunate enough to encounter the random sociopath . . . The third case is more interesting. The gentleman in question is one Paul Barnabas McGovern, a sometime successful tort lawyer who by the way lives in the Lincoln Park District, not far from River House or from your home, as a matter of fact. He made considerable sums of money for himself by settling cases with insurance companies for sums that may not have been equitable for his own clients. In this profession he was known as 'Settle Now' McGovern. Some of the other members of the tort bar argued that they could have obtained far more for the clients — and of course for themselves, but they would have had to prepare to go to trial. The insurance companies knew that if Mr. McGovern was involved, a trial would not be necessary."

"Nice man."

"Indeed yes. As his career and income advanced he seems to have acquired the notion that he was the greatest lawyer in Chicago and should be elected president of the Chicago Bar Association. He rallied a group of colleagues and friends to advocate his cause. Some of them, it was later alleged, had received financial considerations from him for their loyalty. It was of course a hopeless cause. Lawyers often find it easy to hold their noses in the presence of such a man, but there was no way they would have elected him to represent the legal profession in Chicago. Moreover, the media found him an easy target for their attention. Some of the cartoons of him were, quite frankly, scurrilous and very funny. Moreover, the most appealing of the other candidates was Thomas Fitzsimmons, a man of impeccable integrity and good friend of the Curran family — fellow admirers of the Society of Jesus. Dad backed him vigorously, as he would have even if Paul Barnabas McGovern had not been running.

"Well, as you may imagine, Mr. McGovern was roundly rebuked for his presumptions. He did not accept defeat lightly. He attacked all those who had opposed him, Dad being his main target. He promised that he would get even with all of them. He retired from the practice of law and sealed himself up in his Lincoln Park citadel. He fires off letters of complaint about homosexuals, abortionists, immigrants, adulterers, fornicators, and other varieties of sinners to every Chicago publication. He remembers enough law to avoid libel actions. The media use his tirades because they're always good copy. He even appears on some television talk shows when they're looking for a conservative voice that does not have to appear as sane. He is also an active, if secret, informant for the Department of Homeland Security. He or those who work for him are active in hunting down suspicious immigrants especially if they live in the near

North Side neighborhoods. He has a particular dislike for immigrants who have achieved some sort of success in American society. He apparently takes delight in breaking up immigrant families."

"Well," I said, "a thoroughly evil man."

"He is not known for blowing up homes. However, it is believed that he is becoming more bitter and more angry with each passing year."

We had one of Nuala's spies!

"Thank you very much," I said, rising with three dossiers in my briefcase. "I'll pass them on to my wife and summarize them for Commander Culhane."

Her lovely face twisted into a worried frown.

"Tell Nuala to please find the criminals. We are terribly worried about Mom and Dad. We love them so much. This has been a shattering experience for them."

I rode down the elevator to Wacker Drive and considered what a good spear-carrier would do next. First thing he would do would be to call John Culhane and summarize the dossiers for him.

"Those are very interesting, Dermot. We'll look into them at once. I note that all these possible suspects have at hand motives to cause trouble for the Curran family

299

. . . Where did you find out about them?"

"From a database."

"May I ask which database?"

"I don't know and I didn't want to ask."

"They'll be on one of our files, likely enough. But they won't have all that detail. Everyone is in the cop business these days. I wish we could buy into some of the others. Maybe when I retire . . . Anyway, thanks a lot, Dermot. I'll get back to you."

Information overload, I thought. Everyone knows something about everyone else. Nuala is right. The spies are everywhere. I needed a nap, just like the tiny one.

Instead of napping, however, I rode back up the elevator to the heights of 333 Wacker to the law offices of Stone, Hurley, and Levi — the middle name of which was my sister's long departed father-in-law. Both Tom and Cindy claimed that they had inherited the title.

I had to wait a quarter hour before my sister could squeeze me into her schedule. Her assistant frowned when I confessed I did not have an appointment.

"Dermot! What a pleasant surprise!"

She really didn't mean it.

"Would it help your case against the government of the United States and its various agencies if you knew that a certain

Paul Barnabas McGovern was a secret Homeland Security spy on the near North Side?"

Her eyes brightened with the gleam of battle!

"Would it ever! Are you sure?"

"I'm sure all right. No proof."

"No need of proof," she said, grinning impishly. "I'll subpoena him and them all on the spot. Even if he won't talk and they back him for national security reasons, the media attention will put him out of business . . . How do you know?"

"Information received."

"Not from one of your wife's trances, I hope."

"Nuala Anne doesn't have trances. And, no, she is not my source."

"You're lucky to have her, Dermot. I hope you know that."

"I've heard that remark often."

She leaned back on her desk, pleased and complacent, thinking already of the first document she would dictate.

"Dermot, this is wonderful news. Thank you very much!"

"Have fun with it!"

"I will . . . Say hello to Nuala."

I descended to the main floor and marveled once again at the so-called winter garden in the lobby. It reminded me of nothing so much as the ruins of a German factory destroyed during the war, which the local greenery had invaded.

Out on Wacker Drive my cell phone rang.

"Dermot Coyne."

"Jack Curran, Dermot. There's been another attempt on my parents, a car bomb in the Four Seasons parking lot."

"What happened!"

"Mr. Casey's men found a bomb in their car! In the Four Seasons parking garage. They're evacuating the building. The police bomb squad is on the way!"

The garage is a ten-story building, for public parking as well as for hotel guests. It is part of a single structure, including the hotel, condos, and a multilevel mall. Evacuating it would be a huge mess. An explosion inside. It could be like the first World Trade Center blast.

We were up against big-leaguers who were playing hard ball.

— 21 —

I returned to Dublin briefly in June. I had made up my mind. Father was right. I would be pushing my luck too far if I became involved in Bobby's frivolous rising. Even if it were successful, which I doubted, I wanted no part of it. As for Sarah . . .

She was his woman. Or he thought she was. And if he were killed . . . Well, I'd see what happened then.

You can see that, close as I was to the priesthood, I was still having doubts.

I spent some of my summer in Wexford again to work for the bishop.

"Is there going to be another rising?" he asked me.

"I suspect so. Don't worry, I won't be a part of it."

"Will it fail?"

"Almost certainly . . . There's even less support for it here than there was in the '98."

"You may remember that there was a lot of support here in '98."

"You think, Bishop, that Wexford would support it again despite the terrible losses the last time?"

"Some will, probably not enough . . . In a way that's a shame."

A radical thing for my bishop to say.

I would later learn that in Dublin there were conflicting arguments. Some of the leaders — including I suspect Bobby himself — were uneasy. Promises from the different counties were weak. Kildare and Wicklow would surely send troops, Wexford probably. The rest of the country was quiescent. Thomas Russell, the leader of the United Irishmen in Belfast (and like Bob a Protestant), was confident that the Presbyterians in the North would rise, but admitted that anti-Catholic sentiments in the North were increasing. Arms were in short supply. All they really had were pikes. Very few muskets and blunderbusses were available.

However, a large French fleet had definitely left Brest according to Arthur O'Connor, and Bonaparte was waiting for a show of strength from the Irish.

In fact, as I've said before, the fleet that had left Brest slipped through the English blockade and headed for the Mediterranean. Bonaparte did not trust the Irish any more than they trusted him. On the strength of this rumor, the more hot-headed leaders insisted that the Rising be brought forward to July 23. Preparation for a rising leads to anxiety and eagerness — let's do it and be done with it. It also leads to a disposition to accept any wild rumor. I would have hoped that Bob might have resisted such panic. I'll never know this side of paradise. (Yes, I believe that Protestants go to heaven. I look forward to meeting Lord Edward and Wolf Tone and Bob Emmet in the world to come).

(And Sarah too!)

Bob later wrote from jail to his brother Thomas that there was little chance of stopping the Rising at the last minute. The Kildare men were out for only three days. Indeed at 7:00 in the evening some of the Kildare men left.

So they went ahead. The Rising was timed for 9:00 at night, still twilight in midsummer. By 7:00 it was apparently clear to Bob that the Rising was doomed. They would have to make a brave show of it, then retreat to the mountains.

In his full green uniform he boarded a carriage and rode to Dublin Castle, where he would meet with a force of three hundred men who had marched up from Coal

Quay on the river. To his astonishment the Castle gates were open. If the men from Coal Quay had appeared on Thomas Street then, they could have seized the Castle and raised the green flag over it. The English were completely surprised. A disorderly revolution, little better than a mob, battled with a disorganized government. The outcome could have gone either way.

Bob returned again to the Castle with a small group of men, but the gates were closed and locked by then. The mob that had gathered at the gates succeeded only in piking Lord Kilwarden in the groin, leaving him to bleed to death. He was the judge who issued the writ that sought to save Tone. The mob had killed a man who was to some extent sympathetic to their cause.

Bob, having lost complete control, then withdrew his forces back into the mountains, where he had hoped to go if there had been a chance to postpone the Rising at the last minute. The battle in Dublin, now completely disorganized, went on for the rest of the night, until the English forces finally managed to get themselves organized. The Irish fighters gave a good account of themselves, much better than anyone had expected.

Some say even today that it was a foolish, childish rebellion led by an immature and romantic young man. They blame Bob Emmet for being a fool.

My opinion, for what it's worth, is that even if the expected fighters did not arrive, there still was a chance of victory. The Rising had been well planned and, unlike its predecessor, achieved complete surprise. The Castle spies had been fooled this time. The failure was ultimately the result of a complete breakdown in communications, a phenomenon which affects all wars. Bob was naïve to assume that plans organized before the Rising would work during the confusion of battle. To me it seems that the open gate of the Castle stands as a sign of what might have been.

Should Bob have anticipated the communications problem? Certainly he should have, but that was not a lesson he could have learned from the '98, which never was that close to victory.

Communications between Wellington and von Blucher were nonexistent at Waterloo. The latter appeared with his Prussian troops on the field of battle at the very last minute. The first message the Iron Duke received was when he saw blue-clad soldiers emerge from the forest.

Bob should have stayed in the mountains. He might have eventually escaped and joined Thomas and his family in America. But he moved back and forth from the mountains to Rathfarnham. I suspect that the reason was Sarah, whom he was trying to persuade to accompany him to America. I think she would have joined him if she had not been so afraid of her miserable father.

"My wife is here?" I asked the doorman.

"Yes, sir, Mr. McGrail."

"If she tries to leave, tell her to go back upstairs and wait for me."

Delaware and Michigan Avenues were swarming with people, the curious, the evacuated, the investigative. Fire trucks, police cars, battered Chevies which had "Feds" stamped all over them were everywhere. I finally found a sympathetic-looking African-American woman cop.

"Superintendent Casey."

"I'll get him right away, sir."

Mike might have more clout than the current superintendent. After all, he dispensed part-time jobs.

The police were herding people away from the building, mostly north towards the Lake. Panic hung thick in the air, but people were reluctant to leave.

We went against the flow of the crowd. Mike's name was the magic that got us through to the elder Currans, who were standing relatively close to the building but across the street on Michigan. The little Archbishop and Father Rory were with them.

I shook hands, hugged, commiserated. The Currans of both generations looked badly shaken, as well they might.

Mike explained the situation.

"My men always check out the cars of clients, just a glance. They spotted the bomb. It was small. It would have destroyed the car and its occupants and any cars in the vicinity but not the building. They alerted the department. We now have every investigative force in the world swarming around here. The bomb squad is upstairs, seeing if they can disarm it on-site. Probably they can."

"This is unacceptable in our parish, is it not, Rory?"

"Nothing can happen here without your permission, can it, Blackie?" Father Rory laughed.

"Patently."

"Your wife and I had a wonderful talk, Dermot. She's a remarkable young woman."

"I never said that she didn't have some remarkable qualities, did I now?"

Why didn't she know about the bomb?

Because she knew Mike's guys were on the job.

I stepped away from the Currans, took out my cell phone, and dialed my friend and grammar school classmate Alfie.

"Alfie, Dermot."

"Hey, Dermot."

"Hey, Alfie."

"I'm watching this stuff on TV. They say the bomb squad is up there disarming it."

"You saw what went down the other night up on Webster and the River?"

"Yeah, a real shame . . . national landmark like that."

"You hear anything?"

"Out of curiosity I asked some of my friends to ask their friends if they knew about it. The friends of the friends are very upset. Chicago is becoming a lawless town. We can't let things like that go on."

Not unless they had approved first.

"Are they looking into it?"

"I hear that they are. They won't like what's going down over there, not at all, right out on the Magnificent Mile."

"Yeah, well thanks, Alfie. Let me know if you hear anything."

"Dermot, you got it . . . hey, that last book of poems was wonderful. So was the

311

record with your wife singing them. Great stuff."

Connected people who read poetry? Why not?

"Your friends out on the West Side are troubled by this stuff," I said to Mike Casey. "My source will be back to me."

They weren't his friends, of course, and most of them didn't live on Taylor Street anymore.

"They would be. Outsiders aren't supposed to trespass on their territory."

"Not without asking their permission."

"They wouldn't give it."

"My source said that they thought Chicago was becoming a lawless city. Poor police force I suppose."

Mike laughed sardonically.

"Not like the old days when they owned us."

A cop in protective armor emerged from the hotel and raised his thumb.

"All clear," someone said on the PA.

Everyone laughed with relief, the Currans louder than the rest.

Annie Reilly emerged from the crowd.

"Let us take you to dinner . . . you too, Archbishop Blackie."

"We would like to talk to you, Mr. Curran," said the leader of three suits who were approaching them.

Bureau.

"Tomorrow morning," Mike Casey said.

"Sir . . ."

"I SAID tomorrow morning."

The suits were left holding their warrant cards in the wind coming down Michigan Avenue from the Lake.

Much later Nuala and I were lying in our bed in the studio, covered with a sheet for modesty's sake.

She was sleeping soundly. She had insisted on telling me her whole story before we went on to other matters. I was also told that I was totally irresponsible for not calling her to tell her that I would be late — even though she had not warned me that she would be waiting for me.

Then we went on to other matters.

I woke her in time for the five o'clock news.

Mary Alice Quinn began by announcing that a fear of another 9/11 attack had hit the middle of the Magnificent Mile.

My wife, still covered chastely by the sheet, cried out in dismay. She did that several more times as the story continued. At one point, just before the all clear was announced, she saw me at the edge of the frame.

"Dermot, 'tis yourself!"

" 'Tis!"

Police officials made their comments. Politicians promised that such threats were intolerable. Young Jack Curran, spokesperson for the family, warned with passion in his voice and fire in this eyes that if the family had to do it themselves, they would protect their parents.

"We will not tolerate this vile plot against my mother and father. We will fight with all our power to bring the criminals to justice."

"There's Blackie!"

" 'Tis, with young Father Rory, with whom he is apparently working."

Then Blackie, who disappears quickly, vanished.

Mary Alice concluded the story.

"The scare this afternoon was caused by an apparent car bomb attached to the car of Mr. and Mrs. John Curran, who were staying at the Four Seasons after a bomb blast last week destroyed their home on the banks of the Chicago River. Someone obviously wants to kill Curran, a prominent Chicago lawyer, and do it as spectacularly as possible. The question now is whether Chicago police will be able to protect the Currans from these mad bombers."

314

Me wife fell back on the bed.

"That was right outside the window in the swimming pool."

"Woman, it was and yourself clueless."

"Well, I didn't need clues now, did I? Didn't Mr. Casey take care of it all?"

"He did, now get up and dress yourself. We have a dinner reservation at the Cape Cod Room."

"Dermot, call home and see how the kids are!"

So I called home and found out the kids were fine. I reported that we'd be back after we had our supper.

"Take your time, Da," Nelliecoyne said. " 'Tis good for you and Ma to get out sometimes by yourselves."

What did the little witch mean by that?

Better that I not ask.

After we had our Bookbinder Soup (with the sherry) and ordered our crab cakes, we settled back in the warm comfort of the dining room and began to compare notes. The room looked like a restaurant on the Cape, but only if you'd never been inside a real Cape restaurant. The version at the Drake Hotel was much more elegant.

"Someone thought they would be in the house on the night of the explosion," me wife said, "and knew where their car was today. Someone with pretty good spies."

"In the family?"

"Who else, Dermot Michael?"

"I have a hunch you're the first one who has thought of that. . . . What did you think of Estelle's story?"

"Don't I believe every word of it and herself being a great brilliant woman. Still."

"Still."

"Ah?"

"You sound like Blackie . . . she may not have admitted it to herself and that's all right, but I wonder if there was not some attraction for her in forbidden fruit, if you take me meaning?"

"I take your meaning."

"It probably doesn't matter. Her rebound is brilliant altogether. Great strength of character like."

"Will the character stand up under her current stress?"

"Fair play to you, Dermot Michael. She's an intense woman, just now on the edge of volatility, if you . . . But I've already said that, haven't I now? Isn't she just like our tiny one?"

"Estelle Curran is like Socra Marie?"

"Didn't Dr. Foley at the hospital say Socra Marie had a very strong will to live and that's why she didn't die half a dozen times. Stelle has a strong will to live, that's why she bounced back so fiercely. Just like our tiny one always bounced back."

"Fair play to you, Nuala Anne. I think you're right, as always."

"Och, Dermot, don't you make me blush . . . better that you say 'most of the time.' "

"Who would know where they're staying?"

"Wouldn't the whole family know? If the spy is one of the family, it could be any of them."

"But how many knew they were leaving for Europe?"

"You might be able to find out when you lunch with Jack and his wife tomorrow. Now didn't he sound like someone right out of Bobby Emmet's time on the telly?"

"Not as pious as Emmet and not as judicious in what he said, but, yeah, maybe someone out of that world, like the priest, whose name we don't know."

"Sure, isn't Bookbinder Soup wonderful?"

" 'Tis."

She was quiet for a moment.

" 'Tis strange, isn't it?"

"Two feisty Irishmen with all the skills that your litigators should have and themselves working for John Curran."

"Three . . . John Curran himself."

"Ah, no. He didn't want to become like his father. That is a strange combination altogether, isn't it, Dermot Michael? What do you think John would do if he knew his father raped his wife?"

"Kill him?"

She was quiet for a moment.

"I don't think so, but he'd get him one way or another."

"Maybe Long Tom didn't care?"

"Just think about it, Dermot love. Suppose you resent your son, because he's had an easy life and you've suffered under your own father and fought through torture and prison and four years of war and you envy him his beautiful wife. 'Tis a brilliant thing to take her, isn't it now, and yourself loving every second of it."

THE WOMAN HAS A DANGEROUS IMAGINATION.

You just figure that out?

"I suppose so."

"And every time you see them together you can revel in what you know and what you've done. That's a bad man."

"So as you're getting old and near death, you decide you'll have one more ultimate triumph over them?"

"What good is it if they don't know it's you? At least one of them has to know."

"So Long Tom may not be the criminal?"

"I didn't say that, did I now, Dermot love?"

"You're just not convinced?"

She was wolfing down the crab cakes and au gratin potatoes.

" 'Tis all right for me to eat this delicious supper. Best fish dinner since I left Connemara. Didn't I have a lot of exercise today, one kind or the other?"

"What, by the way, did Madame have to say to you?"

"Wasn't she pleased with me for one of the first times ever? . . . No, Long Tom is a bad man with a lot of hatred stored up in him. He's probably killed a lot of people, but I'm not sure he'd try to kill his son."

"We don't have any evidence anyway."

My cell phone rang.

"Hey, Dermot, Alfie."

"Hey, Alfie."

"My friends tell me that their friends are really furious. The bombers are guys from out of town. Latins of one kind or another. They have no respect. My friends hear that their friends intend to find out who they are and either take care of it themselves or inform the police."

"Isn't that second option a little unusual?"

"Nah! My friends' friends say that sometimes that's the cleanest way to do it. Then they don't get blamed."

"Cool, Alfie."

"Yeah, I thought so too. Hey, Dermot, tell that beautiful wife of yours that my whole family really digs her last record."

"She'll be glad to hear it."

"Alfie," Nuala Anne said as she dug into her second crab cake.

"Yeah, he says to tell you that he and his whole family really dig your last record."

"Isn't that sweet of him? Is he a bad man?"

"Made man? Killer? Not at all. He's a spokesman, passes on information for the outfit, but only what they want passed on."

I told her his message.

"Will they do it?"

"Sure. They have been treated with disrespect. Also they fear that they might be blamed, if not by the cops, then by the media. Two will get you five that the suits will be hinting tomorrow that it was an organized crime hit."

Nuala nodded slowly.

"I want the bread pudding for desert, Dermot Michael . . . Still it's strange them two feisty Irish lawyers are working on matters that are not exciting. I wonder why

. . . Maybe John Curran is some kind of magic person. Well, I'll find out when I see them tomorrow."

First I heard that John Curran was too important for the spear-carrier.

— 23 —

"You can pick out the great Irish litigators in the courts easily," Gerry Donovan informed me. "They're short, overweight, drink too much, and you think that when they were younger they wore baseball caps backwards."

He was a little above medium height, freckle-faced, with closely cropped brown hair and brown eyes that danced with mischief. A green hat and he would have been the perfect leprechaun, a role he had played, as it turned out, for the Notre Dame football team.

"Well you're not overweight," his wife said, patting his arm. "And I won't let that happen."

She was a gorgeous, statuesque blonde, a younger version of her mother. I had taken them to lunch at the Chicago Yacht Club, where the grass was green, the trees still barren, and the Lake still a dull gray. A few early boats were anchored at their moorings — April the cruelest month of the year at the CYC.

They were two light-hearted kids, just touching thirty, the age when late adolescence is supposed to end.

"So, yeah, I'd like to buy one of those Yacht Club hats and wear it, backwards, of course, the next time I go to court. Get one for Jack too. It'd create quite a scene. We'd be held in contempt but the judge would have to vacate the order when we explained that it was a repressed impulse from our days in the bar and not at it."

"Now ended," she said, consuming him with an affectionate smile, "permanently."

"What man in his right mind would want to go to a bar with a wife like you waiting at home and two marvelous kids who are always quiet and obedient and reasonable."

They both were of Nuala's cohort, and a few years younger than I was. He did wills for his father-in-law's firm. She was a stay-at-home mom who wrote articles for computer journals and attended creative writing classes at a community college on the North Shore.

"But you're not a litigator, are you?" I asked.

"Jack and I are both apostate litigators . . . Gerald the Apostate, has a nice sound to it, huh . . . We like the peace and quiet of Curran and Sons. When we need someone to appear in court one or the other of us goes over . . . Sometimes we send the boss if it's a simple case . . . We both have beautiful wives. I have young children and he will soon . . . We get our jollies out of arguing with each other and our wives and our kids. John Curran has the right idea. There's no reason that the practice of law should be a rat race."

"You both lose the arguments with your wives," Deirdre said.

"Well, we let them think so anyway . . . It's not whether you win or lose . . ."

"It's how absurd your argument can be."

"That's called litigation!"

"Did you talk the other night about John Philpot Curran? You know anything about him?" he said, abruptly changing the conversation.

"Just a little."

"I'm interested in the '98 and the '03. Crazy men, but very brave. Philpot Curran was a brilliant lawyer, but a nasty man, don't you think?"

"I agree completely."

"Gerry knows a lot of history," his wife said admiringly.

Please God don't let that admiration die out.

I changed the subject back.

"No women in the firm?"

"They thought my little sister-in-law Marie Therese would join up, someone to clean up the wastebaskets at the end of the day. But she wouldn't do it. She knew that she'd have to make them work and that would be boring. So she's into venture capital."

"She'd take over the firm." His wife giggled. "Smarter than any of the men in the family."

"She's a genius, Derm, and ambitious, two negatives for our firm . . . Besides poor Trevor provides all the serious we need."

He rolled his eyes as he mentioned his brother-in-law's name.

"That wife of his," Deirdre commented, "is a bitch plus. Always quoting her Father Charles, as if the Pope worked for him . . . And you must take my husband with a grain of salt, Dermot, a whole sack of salt. They're good lawyers, they work hard, and they earn lots of money. They're just dropouts from the guild."

"Far be it for me, a frequent dropout from the poetry guild, to be critical . . . Now tell me. Who blew up the old home?"

"And almost incinerated a large chunk of Lincoln Park West," Gerry added.

"We talked about it on the way over here," Deirdre said, eating a small slice of the omelet she had ordered at my recommendation. "We can't figure it out. Trevor thinks it was the developers. Gerry says it must be someone who is angry because they think the firm let them down. Jack says that it was clearly a Mafia hit because we weren't paying protection money, but he's not serious. Daddy thinks . . . I'm not sure what he thinks. Maybe someone who hates him and wants to kill him. He suspects they'll try again."

"And what do you think, Deirdre?"

"This is one of the rare instances where I agree with my dear husband," she said again with the same maternal smile — tinged with erotic desire — that she used whenever she spoke of him or to him.

She ran the show, no doubt about that. Did he realize the kind of trap he had entered when she seduced him into her bed? Probably. Probably he liked it.

You're a hell of a one to talk, Dermot Coyne.

Shut up! I'm working!

"We work with issues that involve a lot of money, tax payments, inheritance, property transfers, investments. We earn a lot because we have a reputation of being foolproof —

We don't make mistakes. Sometimes our clients think we have. So they sue us. We have two suits pending against us, both about wills, brought by those who think we helped to deprive them of their inheritances. But neither plaintiff is the kind of person who would even know how to put out a contract. Yet there might be someone out there we don't know about . . ."

"That's why Mom and Dad have hired that nice Mr. Casey to provide security for all of us. It seems silly to me, but I guess there's no point in taking chances . . . They are two wonderful human beings. I don't see why anyone could want to kill them."

"Except for Trevor, and he's basically OK, they have produced wonderful children, present company included. Just good people, maybe they don't know as much history or theology as they think they do . . ."

Deirdre had patted her husband's thigh as he praised her.

My wife would never do that.

THE HELL SHE WOULDN'T!

"I know it's a vicious, crazy world out there, Dermot, filled with evil people, but I can't imagine . . ."

"Your grandfather is a strange man, Dee Dee."

"Moody and unpredictable. But he's had a hard life. I don't think he hates any of us. After what he went through in the Philippines . . ."

"Bataan Death March . . . I agree that he's had a hard life. Sometimes he's very genial, sometimes not."

Her hand is still on his thigh even after he corrected her!

LOOK WHO'S A PRUDE ABOUT PUBLIC AFFECTION.

"Yet he might have enemies . . ."

"I'm sure he did. He was not like Black Bart, but, I am told, he could be pretty ruthless. Yet he's in his eighties. Most of his enemies are dead. Why go after his family at this late date? It's a possibility of course. Someone should ask him. Yet I think it would be a dead end."

"He was supposed to be quite a lady's man in his day. Do you think there might be another family lurking somewhere?"

Deirdre considered that possibility.

"He's certainly a lady's man. I don't particularly like the way he drinks in women, myself included. I'm sure he's not been celibate these thirty years in Ocean Reef. Yet he doesn't seem to me, for whatever my instincts are worth, to be the marrying kind."

"Bed them and leave them," Gerry said. "Not a nice man at all. Maybe never grew up."

24

"I tell my wife, Nuala Anne, that we all have to die sometime," John Curran said to me. "She agrees, but she says it would be nice to live long enough to watch our grandchildren grow up."

We were sitting in his elegantly furnished office halfway up the LaSalle Bank Building, which me Dermot tells me used to be called the Field Building and was the only skyscraper built during the Great Depression.

"The Field Building, not too low, not too high," me Dermot says, "is the perfect site for a very successful boutique firm concerned about its image. One Eleven West Washington would suggest it wasn't all that skillful and Sears Tower or 333 South Wacker would indicate that it might not always be that discreet. When you get inside the office, you will find it very well appointed, quiet, restrained elegance. John Curran knows how important image is in the law business."

Me good husband has an amazing collection of useless but interesting information. That comes, I think, from reading too much, especially when he should have been studying in college. I like him the way he is still. He was certainly correct about the appointments in the law offices of Curran and Sons.

Besides, he had the good taste to marry a foul-mouthed fishwife from the Gaeltach, didn't he now?

In defiance of the gray skies and the promise of rain, I had donned my mint green suit, which was out of place in a law office. I did it deliberately. I'm Nuala Anne and I can dress however I want!

The reassuring solemnity of the law offices of Curran and Sons was marred that day by the presence of phalanxes of police officers, some of them working for Mr. Casey, and men in suits, as me Dermot calls the Feds. I had given them all dirty looks as I explained who I was, in Irish of course. Finally, young Jack Curran had to come and rescue me.

"What," he asked, his impish eyes twinkling, "if one of them had been able to answer you in Irish?"

"Fair play to them," says meself. "They could have arrested me as an IRA suspect. They can't deport me anymore."

He thought that was very funny.

"If I had to face that sister-in-law in court" — he had laughed — "I'd resign."

"It would be the wise thing to do."

His father, however, was not in such a playful mood.

"All this attention," he had begun, with a wry grin, "will not help our business. Would you trust your will to a firm that almost blew up twice?"

"I would," I had replied, "especially if they were smart enough to survive. I'd figure they were very 'cute' indeed, as we say across the sea."

Then he began to talk about his wife, who was clearly the favorite subject of his conversation.

"Estelle," he told me, as if in confidence, "is a remarkable woman. When I married her, she was a child. So was I, as far as that goes. We both had a lot of growing up to do. She was in her thirties when she blossomed. I'm not sure I've grown up yet. She had a very difficult childhood. I think she married me to escape from her family. In part anyway. My childhood was no picnic but it was a lot better than hers. For the first years of our marriage she had to try to catch-up with me. After that I've been the one who's played catch-up. I admit that it's kind of fun chasing after a woman like Estelle."

His face softened and his eyes glowed. I wondered if me own man ever felt that way, except maybe when he was starting to ride me — a terrible thing to think. Especially since it isn't true!

"Wouldn't she be enjoying it too!"

"Ah, Nuala Anne, aren't you the perceptive young woman! Still, she's very vulnerable, though one wouldn't notice it."

"Only if one were blind," says I, reverting to me fishwife self.

"Her personality is pasted together, understandably. Stress and strain threaten it. She's threatened now."

"Och," says I like I was Sigmund Freud hisself, "a woman can be vulnerable and tough at the same time. That one of yours is as tough as they come. She has a powerful will to live."

He cocked his eye at me and smiled.

"Takes one to know one, I suppose."

Didn't me face grow very warm just then? So I didn't say anything at all, at all.

"I can't figure out for the life of me who would want to dispatch us so violently. None of us have serious enemies. In our kind of law we don't make serious enemies.

The Feds are talking about the mob being involved. We don't deal with the mob. If one of them came in and asked us to help with their taxes, we'd argue that our platters were full. But they wouldn't come. They know who and what we are and they go to their own anyway. I know some of their lawyers, but only on a nodding basis. Why would they go after us? We don't own anything in Las Vegas."

"It's not them fellas," I said.

I almost called them gobshites, but the atmosphere was too dignified for such Irish terms.

"Are you sure?" he asked, his eyes widening.

"I am . . . Could it be an old grudge from the past?"

"From my father's day or my grandfather's? Perhaps. They certainly made their fair share of enemies. But they're all dead as far as I know. Maybe their children would want some revenge, but why now? It's been a long time."

"They didn't get along very well, did they?"

A pleasant-looking matronly administrative assistant brought in a teapot.

"Would you pour for us, Nuala Anne? The Irish always do it with so much more grace."

" 'Tis because we had nothing more to do with our time than be graceful," says meself.

He was pleased with me grace, I could tell by the look in his eyes still. He was thinking of another graceful woman, which was fine with me. A man drinks in another woman with his eyes, not because he really wants her but because he wants another woman who isn't available at the moment.

"Black Bart and Long Tom did not get along at all. I think that Dad found it hard to be a father because he had no one to imitate. He joined the army in the late thirties to get away from his father, whom he described often as a lecherous old crook, not inaccurately from what I've been able to gather. Yet when Dad graduated from Loyola Law after the war Bart knew it was time to transform the firm. The rules were changing, the implicit rules about what you can get away with in this city and what you can't get away with. He and Dad fought all the time about how to do it and Dad usually won, though, from what he tells me, Bart would claim credit."

"Your grandfather fooled around?"

"Constantly . . . Dad didn't like it but didn't try to stop it."

"How did you get along with your grandfather?"

"I might just as well not have existed. He wasn't rude, he wasn't crude. I just didn't exist."

"That bothered you?"

"Yes it did, but Dad was easy to work with most of the time, so it wasn't so bad . . . . Occasionally when Dad went into his moods, war stuff I guess, he would explode. Never at me, never at Mom — he would have been afraid to do that — always at Granddad. Those were scary times. He'd get drunk and curse and fire people. Mom would straighten him out. He wouldn't apologize, but he never complained when I rehired the people he had fired."

"Your family life must have been difficult?"

"Not when Mom was alive. My mother was a wonderful, patient, loving woman. I learned a lot about women from her, though probably, given my life since then, not enough. She wasn't very good at expressing affection, which made it unanimous around the old house on the River."

"Both your father and your grandfather left the firm, didn't they?"

Wasn't I trying to get at their family life, which did not seem to have been very good? I couldn't get it out of me head that there was something back there that might be at the root of the problem.

"Bart walked out one day after one of Dad's explosions. I was working there as a clerk. Dad called him every foul name I had ever heard, most of them probably applying. Bart told him to go kill a few more Japs and get it out of his system. Dad tried to strangle him. Joe McArdle, a partner in those days, and I pulled him off. Bart walked off and never came back. His lawyers cut a very hard bargain with us for his share of the firm. Unfair, I would say. But Dad gave him whatever he wanted, he was so glad to be rid of him. There were undercurrents beneath undercurrents in the office till then. After Bart left, Dad smoothed things out and our billings grew rapidly. He was a hell of a good lawyer, still is, I suppose. Never blew up at me. Went out of the office and had his tantrums. I don't know who he might have offended during those times. Then my mother and grandfather — Elizabeth and Bart — died in the same year. Dad told me suddenly that he'd had enough Chicago for one lifetime and wanted to move to Florida. I could take over the firm if I wanted it. I was in my early thirties with a couple of kids and an unhappy wife, but I didn't want anyone else to buy it. His price, unlike his own father's price, was very reasonable, given inflation. We signed the deal, down payment and long-term note. We shook hands and he left the office, never to return. He flew to Florida the next day without saying good-bye and never came back to Chicago. We bought a condo near his, not nearly so elaborate and see him sometimes when we are down there."

"Sometimes?"

"Some years he's away. Some years he didn't want visitors. I think all the little kids got on his nerves, though he was always charming to them . . . You have to understand, Nuala Anne, that we Currans are long on charm and long on moods. I was too until Stelle cured me of them."

"How did your father get along with her?"

"He told me not to marry her because she was an emotional mess. He was right, but I'm happy now that I ignored his advice. He is always polite and courteous to her, just as he was to my mom. She doesn't much care for him."

"You have paid off the loan to him?"

"Rather easily because of the Jimmy Carter inflation. We didn't pay off the loan on the house. It was too small to bother with. He had plenty of money when he left Chicago and still has, I'm sure. He didn't stand to gain much when River House blew up . . . I can understand the reason for your questions, Nuala Anne. Indeed they are very perceptive. My father and grandfather were unusual characters. Heaven only knows what mischief they may have done in their lives, either here or in Ocean Reef, how many women one or the other may have seduced. We may well be paying a price for their misbehavior . . . I'm inclined to think they covered their tracks pretty well. I've told Commander Culhane about them. I expect that he's checking with the Florida police."

"Do you think he remarried?"

"Not to my knowledge. I suppose that there would be records if he had. He was only a couple of years older than I am when he went to Ocean Reef. He was a big handsome man with a romantic history and, as I've suggested, the dangerous Curran charm. Many women, even much younger ones, would have found him irresistible. My hunch is that after Mom's death he was not interested in another marriage."

"Wouldn't he have been a dangerous predator then?"

He pondered that question with an expression of pain.

"I wouldn't say that. I try not even to think about it. But you're right. I think he might even enjoy preying on foolish women, still avenging himself on the Japanese. I doubt that there are heirs down there. If there are, they are entitled to his money. We don't need it and probably wouldn't take it under those circumstances."

"No reason, though, why they should seek to kill you?"

"Only for revenge of a sort. The police will have to sort that out."

"You reported the attack on River House to him?"

"Certainly . . . He just laughed and said the old dump should have been blown up long ago."

"And the second attack?"

"He kind of snorted and said I'd better be careful."

"So there was not much love between you and himself?"

He paused to consider that question as I refilled his teacup.

"A man always wants his father's affection and respect, I never received much of either. Still, I loved him. I respected what he had done with the firm. I respected his heroism during the war. His Medal of Honor was one of the priceless things lost with River House . . . We Irish are not much good at expressing affection. I think I've learned something about it, especially from Estelle."

"And your relationship with your own kids?"

"How can one tell that. Our kids all seem happy. Trevor is a little strange. No one likes his wife. But he does his thing here at the firm and makes no trouble as long as we leave him alone. He's very good at it. Jack is an imp, but a very bright imp, as you may have noticed. He pays me the great respect of making fun of me. He's a dead ringer for Bart, his great-grandfather. Except the mischief in his smile is not mean. So for that matter does my son-in-law Gerry Donovan make respectful fun of me. He figures quite correctly that I enjoy it. It makes for a happy office. They both seem to be proud of my legal abilities, as I am of theirs. Deirdre is her mother all over again, though much more of an adult than Estelle at the same age, something that Estelle tells her often. Deirdre refuses to believe it."

"And the two younger ones?"

"Marie Therese is the brightest of all of

us. She's gone into investment banking to prove she can do it. She's also going to law school at night. We hope she joins the firm, but, being who she is, she will only after she's proved her worth."

"Fair play to her," says I.

"You Irishwomen always stick together!"

"Only in self-defense."

"Father Rory?"

"He's the most mysterious of all. It was his decision to be a priest. I had hoped he'd be a Jesuit, but he decided against that. So we sent him to the North American College. He led his class and was ordained in Rome. I began to hope that he might become a bishop, maybe even an Archbishop here in Chicago. The city needs new blood after all these years of Sean Cronin, who has not been the leader he might have been."

Only with great difficulty did I refrain from rising to the defense of my Cardinal Sean.

"And the Cardinal resists continuing his ecclesiastical career?"

"He seems to think that Father Rory needs more seasoning, whatever that means. So he's sent him to the Cathedral to work for that truly strange little coadjutor Archbishop."

"Ah."

"I don't know what to make of him. Sometimes he disappears like he's not even there."

"I've heard that said of him."

Blackie Ryan is the only detective in Chicago who might, mind you I say "might," be better than I am.

"Father Reide says he's a brilliant philosopher, but I detect no signs of it."

"He and Father Rory do not get along?"

"Quite the contrary, they seem to get along just fine."

Good for Father Rory, I thought to myself. I wanted to be there at the next family dinner where Blackie would be present and dominate in his own ineffectual little way.

That reminded me of my final and most important question, which scatterbrain that I often am, I almost forgot. Me Dermot would be very upset with me if I had.

"Your trip to Cortina was a bit of a surprise to the family was it not?"

"Well, it was a surprise to us. Father Rory called us from Rome with the news that he had been assigned as Associate Pastor to the Cathedral and that he would have to postpone the College of Ecclesiastics for a year or maybe a couple of years."

"He seemed disappointed?"

"One can never tell with Rory. I was certainly disappointed. Estelle was less so. She told me that it was foolish to think our family could take over the Catholic Church, and not worth the effort anyway. Father Rory said that he had heard the skiing was still excellent up at Cortina and suggested we come over for the weekend. We both thought it was a good idea, for perhaps different reasons. So we made reservations and flew over, thanks be to God. Otherwise, we would both be ashes."

He shivered, as well he might have.

"Sure, you wouldn't be leaving without telling your family?"

"They all thought we were going to have a quiet time at River House over the weekend. However, when we change our plans, we always notify them, beginning with the oldest that's available. He or she is supposed to call the next oldest and so on down the line. I phoned Trevor from O'Hare. There was no one home, so I phoned Deirdre and asked her to pass the word on to the others."

"So, if someone had access to your plans before Rory called, they would not know, unless they were part of your family or your travel agent, that you would not in fact be in the house."

He sighed, not nearly as loudly as I do or even as me man does when he's making fun of me. I like it when he makes fun of me because it means he loves me.

"That's what worries me. The bomber believed we were in the house. Indeed earlier in the week we had planned one of our family dinners, but we canceled it because Stelle and I needed some time alone, either in the house or somewhere else if the opportunity arose. So the bombers might have thought that all of us were there . . . They were doubtless surprised to find out that all they got for their troubles was an old house. Our angels were working overtime."

I found myself fading, not sure what question to ask next. I had collected a lot of information about the family problems of three generations of Currans. I wasn't quite sure what it all meant. I wondered if John Curran was filtering it all through his own perspective. Yet it did seem likely that he and Estelle, after their second love affair had begun (and maybe before), had begun to break the cycle of pathology that had haunted the Currans for a century. None of this gave me any clues that would reveal who had driven the car bomb up to River House.

Or maybe it did. I sensed that I had missed something, but I couldn't put my finger on it.

I thanked John Curran for his patience and assured him that everything would be all right. Weren't we working for his angels?

He was polite and as always charming but I could tell he was doubtful.

You blew it, Nuala Anne, and yourself a friggin' eejit. You should have left this part of the job to poor Dermot, who is good at it, much better than you. He'd remember every word of the conversation with John Curran and I was confused about what he had said and what I was reading into it.

You're a focking gobshite and yourself thinking that, because you enjoyed your little tête-à-tête with himself, you can carry the spears as well as pick the insights out of the air. Spear carrying isn't easy and you should let Dermot do it. You didn't have a clue all morning. Sure, maybe you're not so fey anymore. That would be all right too if you weren't trying to save lives. Should someone kill the Currans won't it be all your fault?

Outside the rain had stopped temporarily but weren't the clouds still streaming towards Lake Michigan the same way they'd come up over Galway Bay. Crowds of people were rushing into the buildings, like bees trying to return to the hives when the light was fading at the end of the day. I glanced at my watch. One-fifteen already. Late lunch hour crowd.

The lawyers would still be lingering at the bar association talking their usual bull shite. The commodities traders would be dashing to Traders Inn for their first drink of the afternoon. The movers and shakers would be taking their time over at the Chicago Club because no one checked out the time they came back from lunch. I was getting to know Chicago pretty well.

I removed me cell phone from my purse. It was blinking. A call I'd missed. Maybe kids were sick . . . Maybe there was something seriously wrong with the tiny one . . .

I pushed the voice mail button.

"Hi, Nuala, Peter Murphy here. I thought you'd like to know that the li'l critter came right on time — 12:15 p.m., Thursday afternoon like you said. He and his maw are doing just right fine. Easy delivery, if there are such things. No need for the Caesarian like we feared. We're calling him Johnpete like we'uns planned."

Wonderful! I knew my prediction was right. They always are when it comes to babies. So I was still fey. I just shouldn't try to be better at Dermot's work than he is.

I pushed the "return call" button.

"Peter Murphy."

" 'Tis meself. The blessing of God the Father and God the Son and God the Holy Spirit be on all who live in your house and Mother Mary too."

"Thank you, Nuala. We need the blessing with two little critters living in our house . . . Hang on, Maw wants to speak to you."

"Li'l varmint right cute . . . a-thinking we keep him. He came out real easy. Nice li'l polecat . . . Now you stop your cryin' . . . I don't wan you a-weeping and sobbing at the Popish Baptism, you bein' the god-mother and all."

We both cried of course. Then I let her go back to sleep.

Nice going, I told Herself. The species goes on.

Then I called me Dermot.

"Coyne."

"Didn't the li'l varmint come right on schedule."

"Your schedule, you mean?"

"Ain't any other. Everyone is fine. I'm the godmother."

"Well, he'll be a shunuff Popist, that's fer sure."

"Dermot, I'm sorry."

"What did you do now?"

"I usurped your job. Spear carrying is tough."

He laughed and laughed and laughed.

"I don't have a memory like yours. I wasted the whole morning."

"We'll talk about it when we both get home. I had a most entertaining morning. I don't think I learned much."

For five minutes even my mint green suit didn't stop a cab. I was polite to the cabby just the same. Hooray for you, Nuala Anne, you're a citizen now but you're still not a rude Yank.

Then I remembered that I hadn't much progress on Nelliecoyne's First Communion dress. I should not have promised to sew it meself. That was something else I wasn't good at. And when would the Baptism of the li'l critter be? That would snatch another precious day out of my schedule.

25

"Your wife and my father were oozing charm all over the floor when I left the office," Jack Curran told me. "She'll win of course. She talks funny. Funny-talking charm always wins."

"The fact that she is totally gorgeous," his wife Marti added, "gives her an extra point or two."

"It wouldn't make any difference without the brogue, would it now, Dermot Coyne?"

I sighed, as close to the Galway sigh as I could get. "It would not and herself able to switch from Galway to Dublin and back in a single sentence."

We were sitting in the back corner of Pane Caldo, a small, almost secret, restaurant on Walton Street. Marti, a public defender, with red face and flaming red hair, was wearing a skirt and blouse and a raincoat. She was from the South Side, which is not a mortal sin, at least not when you're as pretty as she is.

"We Currans have been charming lawyers for more than a century, charming drunks, charming lechers, charming crooks, charming scoundrels. It's a great tradition, but I'm afraid my dad is not keeping it up."

"Oh?"

"Yeah. He's charming all right but he's a good man. That's against the family rules of men like Black Bart and Long Tom, my illustrious grandfather. He is an evil man, not necessarily a failing in a lawyer. John and Stelle are both good, though I suspect they didn't start out that way. I've never been able to figure out which one seduced the other down the path of virtue."

"Not just nice," Marti chimed in. "Nice is discount store good. It's cheap grace. You gotta work at being good. My husband, for example, is certainly nice and he'll be good someday but he'll have to work on it."

"I suppose it has a lot to do with their sex life, which embarrasses us children. Your mother and father are not supposed to be into sexual love. In fact, the legal profession cannot really tolerate it. A lawyer can have sex, even sexual relations, but sexual love, that takes too much time and energy away from the job. I suppose his colleagues let him get away with it because they are glad that he's not evil like Black Bart or Long Tom."

"Sexual passion does not cause a good marriage like most people think," Marti said. "It results from it. You want good sex, you gotta be good to your partner all the time. A guy says, I'd be a great husband if only I could get good sex every once in a while. I say to him he's an idiot. He'd get good sex if he were a good husband. Right, Jack?"

She nudged him with her elbow, very tenderly.

"As always."

Were these two brats for real? Or were they castoffs from Second City?

"All this talk about flying over to Cortina to boost Rory's morale is hooey. They had been planning to spend the weekend in bed. Then they decided that it would be more fun in a ski resort in the Alps where you could ski in the morning and then crawl into bed after a big lunch and a bottle of expensive wine and screw all afternoon. That's the way they are. Can't knock it."

"And since they're both more than nice, they'll be only too happy to take care of our kids when we go over there in a couple of years."

"Did you get the message about them leaving for Italy?"

"Sure Dede called me. I passed it on to Marie Therese. It's the family system."

"Some people," Marti continued the riff, "rare, I admit, are good but not nice. Take your sister Cindy. She's certainly a good woman, really good, but nice? That she hasn't got. That's why she's such a good lawyer. I bet she is mildly amused by the fact that you write poetry, but has never read it."

This combo could prove dangerous.

"Women lawyers," Jack commented, "cannot afford to be nice. It's against the rules. When this redhead and Marie Therese take over the firm — Curran and Daughters — they'll infuse a lot of tough, competitive, hardheaded machismo in it. They'll dump the rest of us not bringing in enough business to justify our overhead."

"For sure. We'll hire five associates every year out of law school, not pay them much, make them do all the work, then dump them after six years while we eat bonbons and go to spas. We'll say they don't quite fit the image of the firm — too aggressive."

"Women are the only hope the profession has of retaining its fabled machismo."

The talk ended while the waitress brought our pasta.

I knew where I was — at an improv company featuring G. K. Chesterton and Oscar Wilde.

"Anyway, because Dad is so good, I work at the firm and talk all day long, which drives my poor brother Trevor bonkers, but he never says anything. That's not really even nice of me. But at my age, you can't be nice all the time."

"You're too hard on yourself, love. You do talk a lot, which is harmless if sometimes mildly annoying. But you also say things, which is harder to ignore. Anyone who's been to law school can babble. But if someone says something, then he's likely to be trouble. He thinks, and that's really dangerous."

"We have too many thinkers in the profession," Jack said. "Most of them are judges and they're convinced that they're wise. They get away with it because counsel is usually smart enough not to make fun of them . . . And you wouldn't want to go to bed with a real thinker. I mean you'd be trying out all your foreplay tricks and she might say something instead of babbling. You have a thinker on your hands. What do you do then?"

"Punt," Marti suggested. "Good lovers have to pretend that they're shallow."

"So as you can see, Dermot, Mom and Dad have done a pretty good job on the family despite the fact that they're both good. Good parents usually have bad kids. Childhood was too pleasant. Bad parents usually have bad kids too, but sometimes good kids. Look at Dad and Long Tom. None of us, as far as I know, are up for an indictment. All of us are at least nice some of the time. Dede and Gerry are partway into goodness. They've done pretty well on in-laws too."

"Except for that tight-assed little bitch Annette," Marti snapped. "Looks down on all of us because we don't have spiritual directors."

"Annette knows she's good because Father Charles has told her she's good."

"She's a dark shadow on your parents' golden years."

"Someday Trevor will have to order her to leave Opus. That'll be a tough decision. Opus tells her that she has to obey her husband always, but it also tells her this time she can't obey him."

"We shouldn't enjoy that, Jack," Marti admonished him. "It's not nice at all."

"You see my problem, Dermot, we decide that I'm nice some of the time and my wife uses that to push towards being good."

"Wives always push their husbands, Jack," I said, getting into the flow, "more often then not away from good. You and I are lucky we have the other kind."

They both howled at that epigram. I was part of the game.

"Just the same, Dermot," Marti turned serious for a moment, "Stelle and John are wonderful people. I'm lucky that they let me into their family circle."

"No choice, woman. We needed some red-haired genes."

I filled both their wineglasses.

"You don't think much of your grandfather, Jack."

"It's not just that Long Tom is a mean, moody, hard-eyed bastard. You run into herds of them every day if you're a lawyer. There's evil in his eyes."

"He's had a hard life, Jack," his wife admonished him, pushing him towards nice, I suppose.

"I know! I know! Bataan Death March! Wife dies young. His father a crook, a deadbeat, an adulterer, a bastard. Still . . ."

"He wants to hurt people," Marti took up the case. "I've only met him once. He looks me over like he's taking off my clothes, nothing subtle about it. But then I sense he wants to do something mean to me. I told my husband I'd never visit the man again."

"And I said right on!"

"Isn't he a nice man, Dermot?"

"I don't think, however," Jack became serious for a moment, "that he's put out a contract on my parents. I'm sure he hates their happiness and would like to make them suffer. But death in an explosion is too quick. A lingering death, maybe. A bomb, I don't think so."

"Just like the Japanese tortured his fellow soldiers."

"Maybe with his help."

Two good insights. These kids could do more than improvise comedy.

"Who then?"

"I've been saying he's stepped on some Mafiosi toes. The cops tell me they're not involved. They have their own contacts . . . so someone of the other mobs. The Puerto Ricans have their own drug gangs. The Russians, the Albanians, Serbians, White Sox fans . . ."

"Jack!"

"OK, scratch the last. They're like the Vatican. They couldn't organize a good conspiracy if their lives depended on it . . . My serious point is that someone is very angry at us. Trevor is going through our files looking for suspects. The cops say it's a Hispanic outfit from out of town. OK? Which Hispanic outfit? They don't seem to know?"

"It's a terrible feeling," Marti added. "You're always looking around to see if anyone is following you."

"Thank God — and you, Dermot — for Reliable Security. If it wasn't for them, Mom and Dad would be dead. But can they solve the mystery?"

Then I said something very foolish.

"If they can't, Nuala Anne will. She never fails."

That was a pretty blunt promise. I'd have to confess it to her.

I parted company with the young couple as they climbed into a cab to ride back downtown. I then walked over to the Cathedral to interview Father Rory, now on the staff. Kids were drifting out of the school. My friends the porter persons would be hovering at the door of the rectory. I took a deep breath. They were lovely young women but, after the riffing Currans I was not sure I was up to four sixteen-year-olds named Megan.

I pushed the doorbell button. I heard someone rush down the stairs.

Megan Kim threw open the door, the

most restrained of the Megans. The other three followed after her, Megan Flores, Megan Jones, and Megan Coogan — Blackie's multicultural team.

"Dermot!"

"How's Nuala?"

"How's the tiny terrorist?"

"Is Nuala pregnant again?"

"The Arch isn't in!"

"The Arch?"

"That's what we call Father Blackie now that he's an Archbishop."

"His robes are awful cute."

"The new priest is awfully cute too."

"He has charge of the young people. Of course he really works for Crystal. That's what he says."

"Father Rory?"

"It sounds like a girl's name."

Giggles all around.

"He's like awesomely cool!"

"Do you really want to see him?"

"Yes really."

I was shown into Blackie's office, a comfortable sitting room without desk or files or pictures of bishops or Popes.

Father Rory appeared in short order, dressed in a perfectly tailored black suit with a Roman collar vest. He shook hands with me briskly and sat down in a chair next to mine. He did not wear cuff links, which my brother George the Priest, once on the Cathedral staff, said were a sure sign of episcopal ambition.

"Technically this is the boss's room but he tells me to use it whenever I want. It's probably the only rectory office in the country like this."

"I'm told you are in charge of the young people!"

Rory Curran was about his father's height but must have been a throwback to another gene pool. His skin was pale and his thick, cropped black hair reached, it seemed, almost to his eyebrows. He might have been a pirate working for Gráinne O'Malley or an IRA gunman. His ready smile revealed flawless white teeth, unusual in our ethnic group. His features were sharp but pleasant. He seemed poised, utterly in control of himself. The perfect Vatican diplomat?

"In charge of that mob of teenage hope and enthusiasm?" he said with a short and amused laugh. "Even the Cardinal can't keep them in line and he has the sense not to try. What better manifestation of the exuberance of life to greet the Catholic people when they enter this foreboding old place?"

"Indeed."

"And there's the ineffable Crystal Lane? You have met her?"

"Mystic in residence."

"Indeed yes. I've never met one before."

"The Church needs more of them."

"My parents are somewhat upset about my assignment here. How wrong they were. I love it, I love every minute of it. The Arch, as they call Blackie, is one of the wisest men in the world. Once this mystery is out of the way, I hope to have the whole family over for supper to meet him — and the Cardinal if he's free."

"My brother George was here once."

"He was good enough to come over to welcome me into the neighborhood. I asked him if he could give me tips about the lay of the land. He said that the land doesn't 'lay' . . . Most of my contemporaries in the priesthood would get rid of the Megans and Crystal . . . and of Blackie and the Cardinal too. Give me a couple of more weeks here and they'll want to get rid of me too! The priesthood is exciting work."

"I've just come from a meeting with your brother Jack and his wife."

"Don't be confused by their gift of laughter and sense that the world is mad. They are two very bright people."

I noted the reference to Scaramouche.

"I confess that I wasn't sure for a few moments what was happening. It turned out that it was merely an improv with Oscar Wilde and G. K. Chesterton."

"A good description . . . Were they any help in your investigation?"

"I ask the questions and then report back to the Oracle of Carraroe, who sorts out the mystery."

"Blackie tells me I should take heart because she never fails."

"I make no guarantees."

"And herself?"

"She takes it for granted that she'll figure everything out."

"Interesting woman. Beautiful voice, not operatic, but in its own genre just about perfect . . . Can I help with some answers of my own?"

"It seems to us, Father . . ."

"Rory, Dermot, please."

The man was cool, smooth, polished, self-confident. Perfect diplomat. But perfect parish priest too, if a lot more formal than me brother.

"That with your parents, your family made a decisive turn."

"I had never thought of it that way until recently. On both sides the past was pretty bleak. Now suddenly its joyous. Mother and Father have made it that way, by great effort I would think. They are remarkable people. Someday I would like to know more about their stories."

"You've met your grandfather?"

"Long Tom, yes on several pilgrimages to Ocean Reef. As a boy I did not particularly like him. In fact I feared him. Then I came to realize that he is a lost soul, still fleeing from the Japanese in the Philippines. At first in my zeal as a seminarian I thought I would save him. Now I know it would require a priest of much greater maturity and wisdom than I now possess or may ever possess."

He lifted his shoulders in a gesture of resignation.

"And . . . ?"

"And I didn't like the way he looked at women. No one else seemed to note it. His appraisal would begin with a certain generosity and respect, then quickly morph into raw hunger. I warned my sister Marie Therese, a year older than I, not to be alone with him, and she asked if I thought she was crazy. However, I believe she took my point."

He paused for a moment.

"Morph" indeed. We never used that word on the West Side of Chicago though it has slipped into my poetry.

"If you asked me to guess, I have been told that Grandmother was an extraordinary woman and that he loved her deeply. It could be that he is angry at all women because she left him when she died . . . Irrational I know, but . . ."

This was one very bright young man. His parents had much of which to be proud.

"Not by any means impossible . . . You of course knew that your parents were flying to Italy?"

"It was my suggestion. They love to ski and they sounded like they needed to get away from Chicago. I had already made the reservation for us in Cortina. I wanted to tell them that I had informed Milord Cronin, as Blackie calls him, that I did not want to attend the College of Noble Ecclesiastics. I wanted parish work. I don't think I had gotten through to them when we received the call from the police. So I must assume that the bombers thought they would be in the house and some of us . . . In direct answer to your question, Marie Therese, to whom I am quite close, did send me an e-mail so that the rules of family communication would be honored. Mother has always been insistent on that."

"You have any ideas that might explain the crime?"

Again the shrug of resignation, very curial, I thought.

"None whatsoever. I understand the interest in the family. Yet I can't imagine anyone in the family ever conceptualizing such a plan. We love our mother and father too much. Mother is an extraordinary woman . . . When they arrived at Cortina, I realized that I was the proverbial third wheel and left them to themselves for the first day. The time together alone seemed to refresh them in an extraordinary fashion. I couldn't help but think to myself how clever God was to design sexual differentiation. I rejoiced with them in their love."

"Not the kind of people anyone would want to harm?"

"Not even my poor grandfather, who, however much he may have treated the rest of us, always seemed to talk about the firm with Father, in the most respectful and indeed praiseworthy manner."

I had not heard that before.

"So it would seem that the destruction of River House was designed to destroy them and not the rest of you?"

"Only if the bombers knew that they would be there and we wouldn't. But how would they have either fact at their command, unless they were watching all of us very closely?"

An acute observation.

"The Cardinal offered to say Mass for all of us privately in the side chapel here; Blackie would preach of course. Mr. Casey advised against it. He didn't want all of us in the same place at any time. So the Cardinal will say Mass for Mother and Father in their suite at the Four Seasons. Father Reide and I will assist. I would imagine that Blackie will stumble in, looking confused and unprepared, then preach brilliantly as he always does."

The young man had become a fan of the coadjutor just as quickly as my brother George had.

"That's about all, Rory." I rose and he rose with me. "I'm the spear-carrier and I'll bring all this material back to herself. Thanks for the conversation. Good luck in your work here."

"Thank you, Dermot." He shook hands firmly. "Pray for me and for all of us."

The four she-demons waited in the corridor along with Crystal Lane.

"I say she's really pregnant," Megan McCarthy insisted.

"I say she's not," Megan Flores responded, "and the others say maybe."

"What do you think, Crystal?"

"I think she's not yet but would like to be."

"As far as I know Crystal is correct."

"She always is," grumbled Megan Kim.

I took the L north, then walked home in a drizzle trying to become a downpour.

I encountered a domestic crisis as soon as I opened the door. The two older women in my family, Nuala and Nelliecoyne were glaring at each other in the middle of the room, the dogs watching anxiously, as they watched every family crisis. Danuta stood at the door, arms folded in imperial displeasure, frowning at the scene. Nuala was trying, as far as I could tell, to articulate the relationship between a lace veil and the still-incomplete white First Communion dress.

"Nelliecoyne, it's your fault. You have to stand still."

"Ma, I have been standing still."

My good wife was out of her frigging mind. As the Curran crisis continued she was trying to fix the dress for an event still two weeks off. How could she come home from a long session with John Curran, her nerves frayed, and hope to do anything but create a domestic crisis.

"If you want me to make your wedding dress, young woman, you have to stand still."

"First Communion, not wedding, Ma. Not yet."

Danuta laughed. I laughed. Nelliecoyne laughed. Nuala started to cry.

"Nuala Anne," said the little redhead, "chill out!"

"What did you say!"

A thundercloud, no, a massive weather system, appeared on my wife's face.

"I said, Nuala Anne, chill out. God doesn't care what kind of dress I wear the first time I approach the table. It's not worth getting frazzled about."

It was a verbatim repetition of something I had said a couple of weeks ago, not knowing that nosey little ears were listening.

The storm system wavered for a moment, then fell away. Bright sunshine appeared. With sun my wife's laughter returned. She and Nelliecoyne hugged one another and laughed together.

"Sure, child 'tis the first time you told your ma what to do, I'm sure it won't be the last."

"It's part of bonding, Ma," she said. This was also a quote from you know whom. Eventually herself would figure it out.

"I help, missus," Danuta said. "I sew real good."

"Much better than I do . . . And one thing always remember, Mary Anne Coyne. When a professional offers help and you're an amateur, always accept the help."

"Yes, Ma."

I slipped across the room and up the stairs to my study, hoping no one noticed me.

I began to work on a poem about priests, which had been kicking around in the back of my head. I managed four lines that were pretty good when me wife appeared with two goblets of the creature, straight up.

"If you don't want yours, won't I drink it meself," she said, collapsing on my couch.

"You didn't even take your gorgeous mint green suit off before you got yourself into that mess."

" 'Tis true, I'm a terrible shite hawk."

"Go take off your suit. I don't want you spilling the creature on your new suit. If you do, you'll blame me."

"And wouldn't it serve you right and yourself getting me into this detective shite!"

She removed her suit (and her panty hose), folded them neatly, then reclined on the couch, glass in hand.

"I don't want you ruining your mint green lingerie either."

"Go along with you, Dermot Michael Coyne, and your seducing remarks. I'm in no mood for focking. I'm a neurotic ninny."

"I don't like the adjective . . . Do you mind if I admire you?"

"You do that when I have all me clothes on . . . lock the door. I don't want the doggies coming and slobbering over me."

So I locked the door.

Glorious body or not, the poor woman looked terrible.

"I shouldn't have tried to mess with that Communion dress after blowing the interview this morning. I'm a real eejit altogether . . . And I know that Miss Nosey Parker caught that quote of yours about chilling out . . .'Tis all your fault that one of our children is spying on us."

" 'Tis not. The child is afraid we might be planning divorce."

"She's not!" Nuala sat up straight, spilling some of her whiskey on her bare belly.

"I'll lick that up if you want."

"Stay away from me, Dermot Michael Coyne."

"I was just going to give you this paper napkin."

"A likely story."

"Now drink your jar."

"Yes, sir."

She swallowed a large gulp of the Bushmills' Green, grimaced, then lay back on the couch and relaxed.

"Sure, it's a great medication now, isn't it? And what's this about divorce?"

"She asked me the other day about whether we were getting a divorce. Apparently the parents of some kid in her class are divorcing and that kid cries every day that she doesn't want a new mommy or a new daddy. She told Nelliecoyne that her mommy and daddy always fight and that's why she's getting a divorce. We fight a lot, so Nelliecoyne thinks we too might have to divorce."

"The poor children . . . Both of them."

Tears flowed down her face.

"We don't fight, do we, Dermot Michael?"

"That's what I told our Nellie. I explained that we banter and that's an Irish way of expressing love. I said I never would really argue with you because I'd lose."

"And she said?"

"She said, ' 'Tis true!' "

"Gobshites!"

"And I said that even if we were really angry we'd never get a divorce and she said is that because we're Catholics? And I said that too but we're too hopelessly in love with one another and always will be."

"And that satisfied her, did it now?"

"It did!"

" 'Tis true . . . Dermot, you can ogle me all you want!"

"I will but I don't need your permission . . . Now let's get to work."

I told her my story of my lunch at Pane Caldo. It perked her up considerably.

"Wicked little brats!" She laughed, as she destroyed the remnants of her jar of whiskey.

In Ireland any container whether it be a paper cup or a Waterford tumbler like Nuala had in her hand is always called a jar, so long as it contains a drop or a splasheen (or much more) of whiskey.

"But smart and I think honest. Poor Estelle. How much she had to suffer to be able to free them to have such fun."

"And John too."

"He had no choice — when she changed, he had to do the same."

" 'Tis true," I admitted. "Now tell me

what you picked up from himself."

"Gimme your jar!"

"Woman, I will not! You still have to do your exercises, take a shower, and have a nice nap — solo — before supper."

She sighed, sat up, and began to tell me about their long and discursive conversation.

She did it in remarkably succinct and coherent fashion.

"You're as good a spear-carrier as I am!" I complained.

"I am not!"

She lay back on the couch, by then a little dizzy from the drink taken. Each such movement contributed to my concupiscence. A good husband, however, knows how to wait.

"The question," she began, after a long and weary sigh, "is still what it was after those terrible dreams . . . Who are the spies?"

"Spies?"

"Someone is spying on Estelle and John. How else would the bombers know where their car was?"

"But the spy didn't know they had left for Italy?"

"Och, isn't that the problem? The one to whom the spy reports wants to kill them.

He provided the wrong information the night they blew up River House."

"That's a problem," I agreed.

"I keep thinking I know the answer, but can't quite find it . . . And now with the drink taken I can't think straight. But we have to figure it out or they'll have themselves another try."

She stood up, put on her mint green suit, and picked up her folded panty hose.

"Do I really have to exercise and meself with the drink taken?"

"Woman, you do! You haven't taken that much of the drink."

"I would have if you'd let me have your jar and itself half-full."

She paused at the door and turned around.

"I do love you, Dermot Michael Coyne, something terrible. You deserve someone better than me, but I won't let you go."

Then as she left the room, she paused again but didn't turn around.

"I should have let you lick the drink off me belly."

"I'll bring a jar to your boudoir tonight."

She didn't argue.

I turned to my notes to begin the task of putting them in order. It should not be the obligation of a poet to take responsibility for such matters.

I thought of the possibilities for the night and drained my own jar.

That didn't help.

So I called John Culhane to see what news he had.

"I'm worried, Dermot. We're hunting down the bombers. We think they're Cubans but from Texas. The one who put out the contract is still somewhere and still conniving."

— 26 —

In the days after the failure of the Rising, Bob Emmet was often on the move from the mountains down to Butterfield Lane in Rathfarham, then into the house at Harold Cross in Dublin.

This was madness. He should have stayed in the mountains. Some say he was burdened with guilt and wanted to be captured, so he could make a brilliant statement in the courtroom. Others said that he was romancing Sarah Curran. I think he was probably attempting to persuade her to flee with him to America. I think she wanted to go but was afraid of her father's wrath. If she had agreed, they'd most likely still be alive today — though the White Death could have taken her in America too. If she had asked me I would have urged her to leave. But she didn't ask me.

Bob was arrested in the house at Harold Cross on August 25, a place he had no business being at only a month after the

Rising; he was still wearing the fancy green uniform he had designed for the Rising. On his person they found letters about a planned escape and what appeared to be an unsigned love letter.

Bob went into panic when he was confronted with these letters and the letters from Sarah, which he had left at Harold Cross. They knew all about their romance.

He wrote a letter to Lord Wickham, the First Secretary, in which he proposed a deal. If the letters to Sarah were left out of evidence, he would confess his guilt during the trial. He surely knew that he would be convicted. He also had planned a statement from the dock which he thought would make him immortal in Ireland — and heaven knows it did.

Then some strange things happened. Major Sirr, the villain of '98, went to the Curran home in Rathfarham and confiscated Bobby's letters to Sarah. There were even then some questions about that raid. If Bob had agreed to plead guilty in effect, why were those letters needed? John Philpot Curran wrote a servile letter to Lord Hardwicke the Viceroy withdrawing from his role as Bobby's trial lawyer — a letter which caused great amusement at the Castle because now *they knew that they owned Curran like they owned other lawyers who had worked for the United Irishman.*

The legends say that Bob told his solicitor, Leonard McNally, about the letters at Sarah's house and the danger they might present. McNally, who was an informer, immediately told Lord Wickham, who sent Major Sirr to pick up the letters. Wickham's purpose was not to use the letters in the trial as he had already apparently promised Bob that he would keep Sarah's name out of the trial. It is said that Wickham wanted to gain greater control over Curran, who had been a constant annoyance to the Castle, and to have more solid proof against Bobby at the trial if Bobby changed his mind.

Even then I doubted this story. Wickham had the reputation at that time of being an honorable gentleman. It did not seem likely that he would retreat from an agreement, nor that he would doubt the word of another gentleman, which he had decided Robert Emmet was. In any event, Curran expelled Sarah from their home and sent her to the house of a friend, probably to convince the Castle of his fervent loyalty and his shame at the disloyalty of his daughter.

It all seemed strange to me when I began to hear the stories.

Down in Carlow, studying Latin texts, I heard only dribs and drabs of the story of Bob's capture at Harold Cross. What was the idiot doing there, I wondered. Chasing after Sarah when his life was in danger.

I was devastated by the inevitable death of a man who had been a close friend for the last ten years of our lives. The Latin words on the pages of the old books blurred before my eyes.

Not that there was anything in the books that would help me as a parish priest in County Wexford.

Should I go up to Dublin to see him? I knew they wouldn't let me in. Attend the trial to watch his performance? That he would route the Ascendancy and indeed the whole British Empire I had no doubt. On the other hand . . . I don't know what on the other hand. I wouldn't risk much by appearing at the trial. Father would get me in and he'd admire my loyalty. Yet that part of my life was over. I was no longer a messenger boy for the republicans. I had firmly embarked on another route, which would be difficult in County Wexford. They had hung Father Murphy and Father

Roache. The Yeomen were disbanded and hated.

I might have gone anyway. A letter I received on the 11th made up my mind.

Bob will go on trial on September 18. Please come. I need you.

Sarah.

I had no choice.

I went to the president of the college.

"Father," I said, "I realize that term has just begun. Yet I must go to Dublin for a few days."

"For what reason?" He took off his thick spectacles and looked up at me, his large pale blue eyes blinking.

"Personal reason."

"To attend a trial, I daresay."

"Yes, Father."

"I assume that you will go even if I do not give permission."

"I'm afraid that I would, Father."

"Hmm . . . I understand you knew the young man at Trinity College."

How did he know that?

"I also understand that you were not involved in any significant way in either of the Risings."

"No, Father, I was not."

"There is no danger that the English police might pick you up in Dublin?"

"They're not very competent these days, Father, even less informed about me than you are. Little danger, I would think."

"Well, then, son, I cannot prevent you from following your duty as a loyal friend. In fact, it may be possible to find you a horse for your trip."

"Thank you, Father."

He put his spectacles back on and returned to his work.

"Be careful, young man, be careful!"

"Yes, Father."

It was a dark cold miserable day to ride into Dublin. The horse was a pleasant and reliable one, what else would the president have. It was a smoother ride than the coach but wetter, though the roof of the coach leaked too. The drizzle was nasty; as Mother would say, the sky is in a bad mood today.

I was tired and wet when I arrived home. My parents were sitting in the drawing room in front of a warm fire with a plate of cold cuts and a consoling bottle of port.

"Can't say that I'm surprised to see you," said Father. "I have a ticket for the trial for you."

"Thank you, sir."

"I don't think Major Sirr will be looking for you. The trial is scripted, I gather. Your young friend will doubtless give a good account of himself. Would have made a fine lawyer."

"That poor young woman," Mother said sadly. "I hope she doesn't go to the execution, and herself losing her twin sister when she was eight and her mother deserting her when she was twelve."

"She probably will."

"She was interested in you before you went to the seminary, was she not?"

I could not suppress a chuckle. Mothers are all alike.

"Better to say, Mother, that I went to the seminary only when it was clear she lost interest in me."

"I must say that I have never been able to have high regard for John Philpot Curran," Father remarked. "However, I never thought of him as a poltroon . . . I assume that the president of the college gave you permission to be here?"

"Not exactly but he offered me the use of the horse."

"This has to stop," my father said, lighting his pipe. "Yet it will only stop when the English see that they have to leave."

"I quite agree, sir."

Thirty years later they have given us seats in their parliament in Westminster. Our men will be clever enough to make life difficult for them. How much longer will it take and how many dead young men and broken young women?

The trial the next day lasted twelve hours. It was, I thought, for an English trial of an Irish rebel, remarkably fair. They had no need, however, to indulge in trickery or deceit. Bob denied only that he was an agent of France. He stood on his feet in the dock, in full possession of himself. When he rebuked Lord Norbury, the judge, for his illegal jibes, he was calm and reasoned.

At the end, Bob asked for an adjournment till the next morning. He was obviously tired. He probably wanted to retreat to his cell and polish his talk.

The court refused his request, perhaps afraid that there would be an attempted rescue. The English also had reason to fear the final words of a man whose dignity and patience had won him the sympathy of everyone in the court.

Then Bob began his "speech from the dock" which has become a classic of Irish literature. I wrote it all down to give to Sarah the next morning.

I will cite here, only the most stirring passage at the end, taken word for word from my transcription of his words:

My Lords — You are impatient for the sacrifice . . . be yet patient! I have but a few more words to say — I am going to my cold and silent grave: my lamp of life is nearly extinguished: my race is run: the grave opens to receive me, and I sink into its bosom! I have but one request to ask at my departure from this world, it is the charity of its silence! — let no man write my epitaph, for as no man who knows my motives dare now vindicate them. Let them and me repose in obscurity and peace, and my tomb remain uninscribed, until other times, and other men, can do justice to my character; — when my country takes her place among the nations of the earth, then and not till then — let my epitaph be written — I have done.

Bob was moved to Kilmainham so he would have a room and a desk at which to write. He apparently spent the whole night writing, one to his brother Thomas, with a touching reference to Sarah, which the

English confiscated, one to Richard, with tender words for Sarah, which also was never sent, and one to me, which breaks my heart whenever I read it.

Dear John Peel,

Forgive me if I use the code name which we both have found amusing. There has been little to smile about this last full day of my life, but I smile as I remember the all-too-brief good times we had together at school and afterwards. I had hoped that our friendship would increase through long years of life in a free Ireland. That was not to be. I regret that our rising was ill timed and ill conceived. I regret even more that good men on both sides have died. I have received the Lord's Supper from one of our clerics and am completely at peace. There will be future conflicts, I am sure, and other good men will die too. Finally, someday, we shall succeed. Perhaps at that time I will be remembered as one who tried and failed.

My deepest regret is that I have failed Sarah, Dear God in heaven, please take care of her.

It was good to see you in court

today. I know you will pray for me, as you good Catholics do and must. I am grateful for that too. When you are saying Mass as a priest in years to come, I trust you will remember occasionally your school days chum.

With sincere respect,
Bob

Early the next morning I received a hand-delivered note.

They will bring Bob from Kilmainham tomorrow at 1:00. I would hope you can come to the house where I'm staying and join me in a closed carriage in which I will wait to wave good-bye to him on his last journey.

Fondly,
Sarah

I showed it to my parents at breakfast.
"You will go of course," said my father. "You have no choice really."
"Poor wonderful child." My mother began to cry.
"I hope that cad doesn't try to interfere."
"He won't, sir. It would reveal to everyone what a cruel man he is. When I return from the . . . the execution I will take my

horse and ride back to the college."

"By all accounts he gave a fine account of himself at the trial yesterday," Father said.

"Let me read the most powerful paragraph."

I read him the passage I had transcribed earlier.

"Indeed! How terrible to lose such a brilliant young man. However, I think I can safely say that he has not lost. He has beaten the English and will haunt them until someone does write that epitaph."

My father, as is usual, was right.

At 11:00 I rode up to the house in Rathfarnham where she was living. A closed coach waited in front of the house. I dismounted from my horse and handed the reins to a young groom. The door of the coach opened and I entered.

Sarah, who was all in black, moved her veil away as I sat next to her. Her pale face was dry and composed. She looked so very young and so very beautiful.

"Thank you very much for coming. I must wave good-bye to him and see the execution."

The carriage began to move.

"No, Sarah," I insisted, "you must not."

"Because of the love between us I must

. . . please do not try to dissuade me. I must . . . Now tell me about the trial."

I offered a version I had carefully prepared in my head at night, unable as I was to sleep. I read her the entire text of Bob's speech. She listened attentively, nodding several times. She was as self-possessed as Bob was.

I gave her my original transcript, which I had copied verbatim the previous evening.

"Ireland will never forget him," she said. "Thank you for this paper, I shall always treasure it."

We were not certain which route the sheriff would take from Kilmainham, so we waited at the head of Thomas Street, knowing that they would have to travel that way to come to the square in front of St. Catherine's Church, where Bob Emmet was to die.

Sarah threw open the covered window of the coach and peered out of it. She did not care who might see her.

Bob walked by us with calm dignity. He glanced at the coach, saw that beautiful face which he so much adored and the brave wave of her hand, and smiled and bowed his head twice.

"He saw you too. Isn't he wonderful?"

"Yes, Sarah. He is truly wonderful."

She tapped on the roof and the coachman eased us into the square. I cannot describe even today the details of his hanging and beheading. He remained utterly calm and serene. His last words from the scaffold, I would later learn, were "my friends, I die in peace — and with sentiments of universal love and kindness towards all men."

There were thousands crowded in the little square, the men all took off their hats out of respect. Bob tilted his head in acknowledgment. The crowd protected us from being too close to the ghastly scene. Sarah was not impatient to be closer than we were. The English soldiers and the Yeomen fingered their guns, afraid there might be a riot or a desperate attempt to save him.

Then they hung the finest Irishman of my generation and cut off his head, a remnant of the old custom of hanging, drawing, and quartering. Then the executioner held up his head. The crowd growled in rage. Sarah gasped and grabbed my hand. The soldiers seem frightened.

Sarah closed the window, drew her veil, and tapped on the roof. We journeyed in silence back to the house where she was staying.

At the door she pushed aside her veil. Her face was unmarked by tears. I feared she was close to collapse.

"My father says I must go to Cork. There as well as anywhere else. Thank you."

She brushed my forehead with her lips. As I rode away she opened the window, smiled, and waved at me.

I rode back to Carlow and arrived late at night. The light was on in the rooms of the president of the college.

I walked down the corridor and knocked. He asked me to enter.

"Of course you stayed for the execution." He sighed. "I would have expected nothing else. You are exhausted. I think we can excuse you from classes tomorrow."

I gave him my transcription of Bob's speech.

He read it quickly as he reads all things. Then he read the final paragraph aloud, as if to himself.

"Amazing!" he said. "And from a man no older than you!"

"In point of fact, two months younger, sir."

"You will never forget this day. And nei-ther will Ireland."

It took me a long time to recover. I could not sleep, I could not concentrate on the Latin texts, I was inattentive in class. My professors seemed to understand. Bob's head haunted my dreams as well as Sarah's smile.

It was not all over, however.

I returned to Dublin at end of term. Same old gray, grim, smelly, poverty- and germ-ridden city.

My parents and my little sisters were glad to see me. Mother gave me a letter addressed to me in a woman's hand that I remembered.

Could you possibly come by the graveyard of St. Michan Church on Thursday evening at half eight. We will say some prayers by his secret gravesite. I would like you to lead the prayers. We will expect you if we don't hear from you.

Fondly,
Sarah

I showed the letter to my parents.

"Of course you will go," Mother said.

"No harm in it," Father added. "As far as

the English are concerned, your young friend is forgotten, an unimportant footnote to the act of union."

At that time of year in Ireland, 8:30 is the deep of night. I had to pick my way through the fog to find St. Michan. A faint glow in the fog suggested a torch.

Three women stood around the grave, all in black. Sarah introduced me to Mary Anne Emmet Holmes who, I had heard, was pregnant and in ill health, and her daughter Kitty who was reputed to be suffering from nerves occasioned by Uncle Emmet's death.

"Will you lead the prayers please, Father?"

"Not for a few more months," I said lightly.

No laughter.

But no tears either.

Rosary in hand, I recited the Lord's Prayer, then the ten Aves. To my surprise they all knew the words of the "Hail Mary" even though as Protestants they ought not to know them.

At the end, I said a little prayer for Bob.

"Heavenly Father, we know that Your servant Robert is with You and that we shall all meet again in Your kingdom. If it is Your will, please tell him that we were

praying to You for him and that we all love him and will be with him in spirit all the days of our lives. Amen."

They all answered with enthusiastic "Amens."

Sarah took me aside briefly.

"I'm for Cork, the Penroses down there are old family friends. Father wants to get me out of Dublin before the English come to ask more questions. I'm happy to leave. Cork is as good as anyplace else."

"God go with you, Sarah."

"It is my fault. I killed him," she said. "He wanted me to go to America with him. I was afraid of Daddy. I made up my mind the day before the day they arrested him. He was in Rathfarnham to see me. If I had made up my mind a day or two earlier, he'd still be alive . . ."

"I'm sure God has forgiven you, Sarah. And certainly Bob has. Now you must try to forgive yourself."

"Yes," she agreed. "I will try."

"Promise me you'll try with all your strength."

She hesitated.

"I promise," she said at last. "I promise."

She hugged me very briefly, then they vanished into the darkness.

It was the last time I would ever see her

beautiful face. I see her often in my dreams, however.

"I did what I could," I said to Bob's grave.

There is little more to say. Under the kind care of the Penroses, Sarah recovered her vitality and her will to live. She had become famous and was greatly admired all through Ireland. She attracted the respectful interest of Captain Henry Sturgeon, nephew of the Marquis of Rockingham. They were married in Cork in November 1805, two years after his death and a year and a half after my ordination. She left with him and his regiment for England, then for Messina while the war with Bonaparte went on.

Her letters to her friends indicated that she was very happy in the marriage and even happier when she conceived her first child. The babe was born on the ship returning to England in the midst of a terrible storm and died shortly thereafter. Sarah followed him into the grave two years later, of the White Death, I believe. She was only twenty-five.

Requiescat in pace.

— 27 —

"The man had an intense religious experience, didn't he?" Nuala asked with a tone of awe in her voice. She was standing behind me, bathing me in the smell of spring.

John Coltrane's *Love Supreme* was blaring on our stereo system which plays in most of our house, unless you turn off a specific room at the controls in the kitchen. Why in the kitchen? Because me wife wanted it there so she could make sure the noise wouldn't bother the children. Since she believes that music is good for me, the speakers in my room are on all the time, unless I walk down to the kitchen and turn them off. Nuala also believed that music should be enjoyed at full volume and, since she was just discovering jazz, the "Trane's" music was shaking the walls of our house.

Both the final movement of *Love Supreme* and my wife's alluring scent were distracting me. I turned around from my desk to look at her. She was dressed in a flowery spring dress which clung lightly to her body. She also wore a large white hat. Yet a third distraction, or fourth counting the hat.

"You look and smell ravishing this morning, Nuala Anne," I said. "Where are you going so early in the day?"

"Sure won't I walk by Millennium Park and turn heads in me new spring dress which I bought at a sinful discount!"

"You should wear a sign saying that the markdown was 75 percent — and how often do I tell you that they mark down dresses because no one buys them?"

"Sure, this wouldn't look right on everyone" — she spun around to create the swirl the dress was designed to produce — "but doesn't it have my name on it altogether?"

"It certainly does!"

"Actually, I'm going to the studio to listen to the first mix on me new record."

Herself was a perfectionist on her recordings. These sessions on *Nuala Anne Sings Gospel* would go on for a long time.

Nuala Anne was in a spring mood, brought on perhaps by the glorious late-April weather, though she never needed external forces to put her into moods.

"We're making no progress in this case," I said.

YOU'RE AN ASSHOLE FOR BEING

GRUMPY IN THE PRESENCE OF THAT
SPRING VISION.

If I want to be grumpy, I'll be grumpy.

"Sure we are, Dermot Michael. Aren't
the pieces beginning to fit together?"

Nothing would interfere with her spring
effervescence.

"Is that scent you're wearing called seduction?"

"Am I needing spring scent to seduce
you, Dermot Michael Coyne, when I want
to?"

"I concede the point."

The "Trane's" desperate appeal to God
from the whole human race faded away.
The woman was in a teasing mood, not especially erotic, just troublemaking.

"And haven't I solved the other mystery
already, not that it was terrible difficult?"

"What mystery?"

"Sure isn't there a grand mystery in that
second to last chapter you gave me yesterday? And here's the envelope with me
solution. Maybe it'll cheer you up!"

We have rules about reading these old
Irish manuscripts. I read a section first,
then give it to my wife, who naturally has
made the rules. Then, after we both have
read the penultimate chapter, she seals an
envelope with her solution to whatever

mystery there might be. Then I read the last chapter to see how the story ends. I open the envelope to see that her analysis was correct.

"Don't open it till you read the last chapter."

She bent over and kissed my lips with a passion that sent flames through my bloodstream, my nervous system, and my digestive tract. Also other parts of me.

"I love you something awful, Dermot Michael Coyne. I don't deserve you, but I'm never letting you go. See you in bed tonight."

"I wasn't planning to leave," I gasped.

"Tonight I may just do my Rite of Spring Dance," she promised as she flounced out of my study. My study indeed. I hoped she'd not mess with the stereo before she left the house. However, in a couple of minutes, Stravinsky music reverberated against my eardrums.

My virtuous wife had been a singer, an actress, and a dancer when she was an accounting major at TCD (Trinity College Dublin). She has experimented with choreography since she came to America, but only privately. "I'll have something to do to earn my keep when I lose my voice."

Her Rite of Spring is an overwhelmingly

erotic, though never lewd, event, loosely based on Stravinsky, with veils and scarves and diaphanous gowns and such things. She does it for her husband but only when the spring mood takes over completely. The Spring Goddess does not die at the end but falls ravenously on her poor husband. I tell her that, alas, she can never do it in public. She sniffs and says that we'll have to see about that. Quite apart from my obvious and multiple prejudices in the matter, it is very good choreography.

She was being her usual provoking self when she warned me ten hours in advance. The images of promise would torment me all day. It was worth waiting for nevertheless.

Indeed, as the Arch would say.

Late in the afternoon my Nuala Anne arrived in my study (de facto our study because I was not welcome in her office). Our bright spring flower was wilted.

"Och, Dermot Michael, don't I want to go back to my original vocation?"

"Contemplative nun?"

"Accountant, you amadon!"

She collapsed on the couch, which was now hers by right of expropriation.

"Hard day at the factory?"

"Why do I have to be such a frigging perfectionist?"

"Because you are you . . . The mixing was terrible?"

"I'd die of humiliation if anyone ever heard it outside the studio. It was awful, terrible, disgraceful."

"And no one but you would have noticed." She pondered.

" 'Tis mostly true . . . The techs are good at what they do, but . . ."

"You have to urge them to be better . . . Read these dossiers which Marie Therese prepared for us and I forgot about in all the confusion. She's a researcher so she did research in a database that lists at-large sociopaths."

She glanced at each of the documents, as is her custom, then read them each carefully, concentrating all her faculties, normal and fey, on the details.

"Well we found one of our spies, didn't we now? What are we to do about this Paul Barnabas McGovern?"

"Cindy will subpoena him and leak the subpoena to the media with the details of all the people he reported to Homeland Security, yourself included. That will be the end of his life as a spy."

"Won't that be a blessing still. You see what I mean about spies! What does Marie Therese know about us!"

"My life is an open book. She remarked about your remarkably generous contributions to charity!"

"The bitch!" she shouted. "The frigging bitch! She has no right to know about those things!"

"Not even your husband knows about them."

"Dermot! I wasn't hiding anything from you" — she became plaintive — "I reckoned you had better things to worry about. Honest. I'll give you all the details as soon as I can pull them together. Honest, I will . . ."

"To quote our favorite First Communion candidate, Nuala Anne, chill out!"

She laughed and relaxed.

"Still nothing. I'm proud that you give a lot of money away. It's God's business and no one else's."

"Save for them snoops who put together them friggin' databases . . . You called the information to Commander Culhane?"

"I did indeed. He thought the three suspects sounded very interesting."

"Well, we don't have to do anything about them. The cops can handle them. I'm worried about the evil whose name we don't know yet. Maybe it's one of them three sociopaths. I kind of doubt it.

There's still bad things out there . . ."

Bad dings!

If she said there were, indeed there were.

"We have to save them, Dermot Michael. They're nice folks, kind of conservative, but they have the right to lead out their lives and we've promised to help them."

"You need a nap, Nuala Anne."

"Do I ever, I think I'll go down and crawl in with the little one. She likes to wake up and find me next to her . . . I won't exercise because there'll be plenty of that tonight, won't there now?"

"Only if you want to dance in honor of spring."

"Won't I have to, or I'll lose my spring spirit altogether!"

"I'll be happy to cooperate in that worthy cause!"

"Will you unzip me dress, Dermot Michael?"

"I will."

This was unnecessary ritual, required only because Nuala wanted to excite me. Nothing wrong with that.

"Dermot, did I tell you this morning that you're the most brilliant husband in all the world?" she said as I unzipped the flower print garment.

"Woman, you did!"

I kissed her back gently. Her shoulders slumped.

"And did I tell you that you deserved a better wife than me?"

"I don't remember, but probably because you tell me that every day."

I caressed the back of her neck gently.

" 'Tis true."

" 'Tis not . . . Now off with you woman to your nap with the tiny one."

I pushed her rear end gently.

"And, Dermot Michael, read the last chapter of Father's story and see if I'm right about the mystery."

"Woman, I will."

OTHERWISE, TONIGHT'S DANCE MIGHT NOT HAPPEN.

She wouldn't dare.

— 28 —

There is more I must say.

The wars on the Continent kept me away from Rome. My first assignment was to work in the bishop's office in Wexford. I was his whole staff. I learned a lot about the Church in Ireland, its glory and its shame, its hardworking priests and its lazy troublemaking drunks. I was glad that I had set my mind against ever becoming a bishop. I'm not sure that I'll succeed in this resolution, however.

After the failure of the '98, the revolutionary spirit faded in Ireland, save for folks like the Whiteboys out in the countryside and they were as much bandits as patriots. Daniel O'Connell and his Catholic Committee were arguing that power should be taken piece by piece in political efforts. I went up to Dublin occasionally to officiate at my sisters' weddings and visit my parents, who were aging gracefully. Each time I would walk over to St. Michan's and talk to Bobby. And pray for him too. I wondered who cared for the grave. The three women who were with me that night in 1803 were dead. But "Bold Robert Emmet," as he was already being called in the ballads, had lots of friends in Dublin.

My poor old bishop died. The new man promptly made me rector of the Cathedral, which added to my responsibilities and took away none. He promised me that after five years he would give me a parish in the country. It took ten years and my present parish is only a half hour's canter from Wexford. That's the way of it.

The revolution in Wexford was dead, but not the pain and anger over the massacres. Protestants were moving to Dublin for fear of the next time. Catholics were treasuring resentment for the next time.

I denounced this foolish hatred from the Cathedral pulpit and later from my parish altar. Most people knew that I was a friend of Bob Emmet and stood there, with my hat off in respect when he was hanged and beheaded. So they cut me some slack. No messages or threats from the Whiteboys, only an occasional hate-filled frown.

"Tell me, Father," one elderly man asked, "if you were here in the '98, would you have been with Father Murphy?"

"I don't know."

He nodded, satisfied with my ambiva-
lent answer.

I see Sarah often in my dreams. She always smiles at me. I don't believe in
dreams. Not much anyway. Sometimes I
think I see her walking towards me in a
white dress in the green fields of Wexford,
the most beautiful fields in the world. She
always disappears when she is near me. I
don't believe in ghosts either, not much
anyway.

One early-summer day as I was reading
the morning paper in my parents' house,
my father appeared in the drawing room,
a bemused smile on his face.

"There is a man over at the Royal
Hibernian Hotel who would like to have a
drink with you at the bar there this afternoon. I told him I would pass on the invitation."

"And his name is?"

"Lord William Wickham. He wants to talk
to you about Bob. There's no reason to
fear him. He's elderly now, though in good
health, better, I think, than when he was
First Secretary. It's entirely up to you, but I
think there's some secret he wants to tell
you. Coming from him, a secret about Bob

406

Emmet might be worth noting down."

"I will see him of course."

There was no missing Lord Wickham in the bar at the Royal Hibernian. His hair was snow-white and his movements as he rose a little hesitant, but he was still the same man who tried his best to heal the grief and pain of the Rising.

"It's good to see you again, Father," he said, shaking hands and trying not to seem feeble. "Parish life in the country seems to agree with you."

"I'm not sure Wexford Town is exactly country, milord, but I certainly am happy down there."

He signaled the waiter. He ordered whiskey, I ordered sherry, an interesting reversal of what one might have expected.

"Are the wounds healed down there?" he asked anxiously.

"That depends, sir, on what one means," I replied carefully. "There is little taste in Wexford for more bloodshed. They've had enough for another generation or two. The pain remains for those who suffered loss. The memories remain. They will surely be passed on to generations not yet born. In the long run, I fear, there will be more violence until . . . until *someone is able to write Bob's epitaph."*

"You mean until England leaves Ireland?"

"I say that without any enmity towards you, sir. You asked about healing. It will take a long, long time."

"I understand, Father. I understand."

Silently we lifted our glasses to one another.

"I wish to show you two documents, Father." His fingers trembled as he passed them across the table. "I have transcripts for you of both. It is not generally realized that as he was leaving Kilmainham to begin his walk to St. Catherine's Church, Robert Emmet begged leave to return to write one last letter. It was to me. Consider this letter:

Sir, had I been permitted to proceeded with my vindication, it was my intention, not only to have acknowledged the delicacy with which I feel with gratitude, that I have been personally treated; but also to have done the most public justice to the mildness of the present administration of this country, and at the same time to have acquitted them . . . of any charge of remissness in not having previously detected a conspiracy, which from its closeness, I know it was impossible to have done.

"That was the kind of man he was, Father. A man of honor, bravery, and deep humanity. I carry this letter with me at all times to remind myself how strong human dignity can be under the greatest pressure."

"Thank you, sir," I said, my voice catching.

"Shortly after his death I resigned though it took some time before it was accepted, this is a passage in that letter. I believe it has been removed from the archives at Dublin Castle. I wanted someone to have it who would keep alive the memory of Robert Emmet's character. He is becoming a symbol of Irish nationalism. The man must not be lost in the symbol."

No consideration upon earth would induce me to remain after having maturely reflected on the contents of this letter . . . in what honors or other earthly advantages could I find compensation for what I must suffer were I again compelled by my official duty to prosecute to death men capable of thinking and acting as Emmet has done in his last moments for making an effort to liberate their country from grievances the existence of many of which none can deny of which I have myself acknowledged to be unjust, oppressive, and unchristian. I well know that the manner in which I have suffered myself to be affected by this letter will be attributed to a sort of morbid sensibility, rather than to its real cause, but no one can be capable of forming a right judgment on my motives who has not like myself been condemned by his official duty to dip his hands in the blood of his fellow countrymen, in execution of a portion of the laws and institutions of his country of which, in his conscience he cannot approve.

I tried to control my emotions.
"This is most touching, sir. I promise you that it will always be read, as proof of what kind of man Bob was and what kind of man you are."
"In the long space of years, Father, this letter has been my constant companion. I show it to my friends, especially those who are prejudiced against Ireland. I tell

such friends how light the strongest of such feelings of prejudice must appear when compared with those Emmet so nobly overcame even at his last hour, on his very march to the scaffold."

England had sent many good men to Ireland, then had listened to the recommendations of the worst instead of the best. If George III had not vetoed Lord Cornwallis's plea for Catholic emancipation, Catholics would have been sitting in the Westminster parliament for thirty years now. If Dan O'Connell is right, this will drain a lot of anger out of Ireland.

"I have a revelation for you, Father, that needs to be preserved. Leonard McNally, Mr. Emmet's solicitor was indeed an informer. The police knew too much about him. However, he did not betray to us the existence of Miss Sarah Curran's letters to us. Her own father did."

"What!" I exclaimed.

"Even if McNally had told us about the letters, we would not have tried to possess them. Mr. Emmet had already agreed with us that he would not deny most of the charges, save for that of being an agent of France, if we agreed to leave Miss Curran out of the trial. We had made that compact. However, her father, who had found *the letters while searching her room, feared that the police might come and confiscate them and thus put him at great disadvantage with the Castle. So he informed Major Sirr of the existence of the letters and he insisted that he must obtain them. The whole incident was a charade between Sirr and Curran. Thus Curran was able to cast the poor child out of his house with a great show of loyalty to the Crown. I'm afraid that he doomed both Emmet and his daughter."*

I was dumbfounded. I knew that Joseph Philpot Curran was a cruel man. I had not realized how cruel.

"If he had not been so violent on the subject," I said slowly, "Sarah would have agreed to emigrate to America with him and they might still be alive. We don't know that for sure . . ."

"Yet the truth must be told."

"I assure you milord, it will be told."

The first one I told was my father. He was not surprised.

"I always knew that Philpot was filth. With your permission, I will note this story in my journal."

I rode back to Wexford with heart at ease.

Sarah smiled more benignly at me in my

dreams for some time after that experi-
ence.

*However, as I have said, I don't believe
in dreams. Usually.*

29

I closed the folder with the nameless priest's story.

I had seen quotes from Emmet's letter to Lord Wickham and the latter's letter of resignation. That part of the truth had been told. There was debate among the writers about Philpot Curran's part in the confiscation of his daughter's letters. When I publish this remarkable manuscript, the debate would be closed.

With a sigh, I reached over to the desk in which Nuala Anne had placed her sealed envelope. I opened it and was not in the least surprised to find the following note, in green ink:

Darling, wonderful Dermot,

It's as plain as the nose on your lovely face, Dermot Michael Coyne, that Curran was a complete gobshite and that he and not Leonard McNally was the informer. Obviously, since our priesteen has already hinted from hindsight that not all was quite what it seemed. In the final chapter, I expect he'll say so with some evidence. I'll have to read the whole chapter now that you're finished with it to see how it all emerges.

I hate meself for being right all the time, but I can't help it now, can I?

Your humble and always obedient wife,
Nuala Anne

Provoking bitch! I congratulated her, of course. One has to be a good sport in these matters. Drat her.

However, the Spring Dance was better this year, overwhelming but never lewd or vulgar or even dirty. Nuala Anne couldn't be any of those things even if she tried.

The next morning John Culhane called me.

"Those were great leads, Dermot. If whoever did the research wants to do work for the CPD, we'd sign her on, but I don't think we could match her salary."

"I didn't say it was a woman, did I?"

"Nope and it may not be. But women are better at this work than we are. It's a wonder the CPD survived as long as it did without women researchers. They're much more thorough."

"But there's nothing in the leads?"

"We checked them all out. Paul Barnabas is quite incapable of any more than writing letters and denouncing people to Homeland Security. I think that they will disown him when your sister finds out about this. Mr. McNeill is not taken seriously by anyone on the South Side and has to keep a low profile or some of those who are taken seriously will make his life very difficult if not impossible. Ms. Livermore still wants vengeance but her partner is on his very good behavior at the insistence of the gangs. We are convinced that the bombers are Hispanic, perhaps Dominican, but they are very different people than he would be able to contact."

"Thanks for looking into it, John."

"They were good leads."

Nuala joined me at the breakfast table, in a chaste sweat suit, and poured herself a cup of tea. We looked at each other shyly. Had last night really happened?

"I hope I wasn't too dirty, Dermot love."

"Woman, you couldn't be dirty if you wanted to. It was a marvelous choreography of married love."

"Is that what it was?" She giggled.

"Among other things."

We both remained silent, proud of ourselves and yet embarrassed by our memories. We were good dancers it had turned out.

"John Culhane called to say he had looked into the cases Marie Therese researched for us and that, while they were all good ideas, those people were not involved. He also said that the actual bombers are probably Dominicans from New York."

"Dominicans like Thomas Aquinas?" She gave me a piece of soda bread slathered in butter and raspberry jam.

"Dominicans like Sammy Sosa."

"Oh, poor dear man."

We sipped our tea.

"I forgot to mention that Blackie wants me to sing gospel songs over at the church for Johnnie Pete's Baptism on Saturday."

"Across the street?"

"Don't herself and Peter Murphy think it appropriate?"

"Does the pastor know about it?"

"I assume so."

"He's not going to like our crowd taking over his church."

"Poor dear man will have to learn to get used to it, won't he now? I'd better go down to the music room and practice a little."

WHAT DO YOU WANT TO BET SHE CONCEIVED LAST NIGHT.

It would be just like her.

I went over my notes again. I could find nothing in them that shed any light on the exploding River House or the almost exploding automobile. In the first case, it would appear that the bombers either had erroneous information or intended to kill the inhabitants. In the second case they had intended to kill the people in the Lincoln Continental and anyone else who might have happened to be around. Did they then intend to kill in the first explosion? That seemed likely, didn't it? So the information was erroneous. They thought that at least some people, mostly likely John and Estelle, would be in the house, didn't they? They knew for sure where the Lincoln Continental would be. Had their spies become more competent or had the ante gone up? Warn them first by blowing up the house, then, after they've suffered the purgatory of waiting and wondering, blow up their car and them? Having failed in that, what would they do next?

My wife returned to the study, small harp in hand.

"May I sing 'Down by the River' for you?" she asked shyly. "I'm not sure I have it right, I mean for a Baptism in a Catholic church?"

"Marie Phinoulah Annagh, you have carte blanche to sing anything you want for me from this day forward for the rest of your life!"

It was very different from the way she had sung it the first time at the recording studio. She had toned down the enthusiasm a little and toned up the sacramental reverence. It was still gospel music, but maybe Catholic gospel.

"They'll love it!"

"You sure?"

"Certain."

She nodded dubiously.

"You got a minute? I want to run through some reflections about the Curran case."

She nodded solemnly and sat down, harp resting in her lap.

I went through my notes.

"This has gone on too long, Dermot Michael. It has to stop. Those poor innocent people have suffered too much. It has to stop."

"And how will it stop?"

"I don't know, Dermot love, but it will. It all has to do with the spies, don't you see? We have to find the spies, don't we?"

"Sure."

She frowned as if reaching for something.

"I don't know who the spy is, but I can't quite see . . . No matter how hard I try . . . I half think it is in the family, just like poor Sarah Curran . . . I don't see yet . . . But I will . . . The clouds are very dark and" — she shivered — "they're closing in . . ."

I waited. She slumped and became very sad.

"Those poor people . . . I have to go back and practice my song . . . Are you sure I'm going in the right direction?"

"Catholic gospel?"

She grinned, the clouds banished temporarily. "Don't you have the right of it, Dermot Michael?"

The Mass late on Saturday morning was a festive event. The multiple divisions of the Ryan-Murphy clan showed up in force, all three generations of them. The Archbishop said the Mass, uh, presided over the Eucharist, assisted by Father Rory, whose job description apparently included making sure Blackie was properly dressed. Cardinal Cronin presided from the throne — in this instance a chair at the side of the altar. The pastor scurried around looking anxious and unhappy.

"My white dress, I think?" Nuala had said as we woke up on Saturday morning.

"Green suit," I had replied. "Stands for spring and hope. We're filled with hope today."

She had thought about it.

"You're right, Dermot Michael, as always. Green it is."

"With green lingerie."

"I don't need your advice on my lingerie, Mr. Coyne."

"You'll get it anyway."

Nuala, blushing from compliments about her green suit, gathered all the children around and taught them how to sing refrains from "Down by the River," "Amazing Grace," and "Balm in Gilead." Herself is wonderful with little groups of kids. She can turn them into a presentable choir in five minutes.

The liturgy began with "Down by the River" sung by herself as Catholic gospel, enthusiastically answered by the choir.

Cindasue turned to me and whispered, "Fust time I'm a-knowing that this hyar Church shunuff be a hard-shell Baptist church."

"Catholic Baptist," I responded.

Blackie preached about the waters of Lake Michigan — "A gift of God for which

421

we Chicagoans are not nearly thankful nor for the protection offered on the Lake by the always prepared United States Coast Guard." He described the joy of plunging into the Lake on a hot, humid summer day and coming out revived and refreshed. Baptism was an experience of new life, a promise of life without end. Heaven must be built on a place like Lake Michigan without lake effect snowstorms. Water means life. New life, old life renewed, promise of life eternal. Baptism an Easter Sacrament, Easter a baptismal feast. Sacrament of resurrection.

He was good, no doubt about it.

The Coast Guard was nothing if not visible. Cindasue wore her white dress uniform as did her commanding officer, whose name I never quite caught, a Coast Guard captain equally in white. Katiesue, clinging nervously to our tiny one's hand, was also in a white uniform, and the peacefully sleeping Johnpete was wearing a little Coast Guard jacket.

The Ryans, who adored their little Appalachian in-law, thought it was wonderful. My opinion, for what it was worth (not much), was that from anyone but Cindasue it might be tacky. From her it was classy.

At the beginning of Baptism, Blackie asked each of the children to come up and touch the head of John Peter to welcome him into the Church. "You first, Katiesue."

With considerable shyness and some fear, big sister approached little brother, clasping the hand of Socra Marie, who characteristically was not at all timid.

"You can touch his head too, Socra Marie, now that you're up here."

This permission merely legitimated what our daughter had every intention of doing. Nuala smiled proudly. At the promises I was afraid for a moment that Cindasue would respond "shunuff." I think the presence of "that thar Cardinal man" intimidated her just a little.

Blackie asked the kids whether they thought John Peter would cry when he poured water on him. They all thought he would. Blackie was willing to bet that he wouldn't.

After the water was poured — Johnpete continued to sleep peacefully — the impromptu choir sang "Amazing Grace." Nuala did her own top-of-soprano riff at the end. At Communion, they sang, "There Is a Balm in Gilead" and, at the end of Mass, Nuala and her faithful choir had the walls of Jericho come tumbling down.

Cindasue received Communion of course, like she always did. She was as she had often explained a "hard-shell" Catholic. Neither Blackie nor the Cardinal man batted an eye. There was a fix in somewhere.

There were many compliments after Mass to the parents, to the sleeping babe who refused to be wakened by admiration of the women of the Ryan-Murphy clan, to the Yewnited States Coast Guard, to the choir, to the bishop, to the Cardinal, and to Nuala for her green dress. Arguably, as the Bishop would say, she received the most favorable notices.

I would claim credit later.

"Any developments?" Rory Curran asked me.

"Herself says the pieces are coming together."

"I hope so . . . The family is very anxious. Jack and Marti are going up to their little house at Twin Lakes tomorrow morning, just for a day away from it all. They say that they are certainly not the targets. Everyone else would like to do the same, but are afraid."

"By next weekend," I promised, "it should be all right."

None of the Currans had any reason to

trust me. But they trusted John Culhane's endorsement of Nuala.

"This is not fair," I told myself. "Nuala should not have to tolerate all this pressure. I'm going to have to put a stop to it."

LOTS OF LUCK, BUSTER!

Point taken.

"What was the young priest talking to you about?" she asked me as we walked down the street to the Murphy A-frame, our kids in front of us.

"He's worried about the family. They're going stir-crazy. Jack and Marti are driving up to Twin Lakes tomorrow morning."

"Where's Twin Lakes?"

"Right on the Wisconsin-Illinois border, just west of Kenosha, a lot closer than Dorr County."

"Why not the Dunes?"

"They live up in Lakeview — Balmoral. They just have to drive over to the Edens, take it to I-94 and get off at Wisconsin 30. Short trip. Why do you ask?"

"Curious . . . Och, Dermot aren't young people reckless these days?"

"They're not much younger than you are, Nuala."

"Sure, they don't have kids, do they? So they're still young and they think they'll live forever. When you have kids, you friggin' know better."

"You're right as always, Nuala."

"Right as sometimes . . . I just want to know where they are."

"Why would they be targets?"

"Isn't he John P. Curran?"

"He is?"

"These people are like coyotes. If they can detach one animal from the pack, they go after that one."

My wife had never seen a coyote all her life, save perhaps on television.

She seemed happy enough at the Murphys' party, smaller than their earlier one and sang lullabies to Johnpete, who smiled up at her adoringly. Katiesue and Socra Marie watched very carefully; no one was going to hurt their little protégé.

There were also many more compliments on Nuala's mint green suit.

"Daddy" — Socra Marie hugged my leg — "can we have a baby like Johnpete?"

"We might someday."

"Then I won't be the baby anymore! Cool!"

Nuala heard the conversation and just rolled her eyes.

We already have three kids. They're healthy and happy and lots of fun — also lots of work. Why does she want another one so badly?

STOP THINKING LIKE A FATHER. BESIDES YOU HAVEN'T THE COURAGE TO SAY THAT TO HER.

Shut up.

We were both dead tired and went to bed early. No lovemaking that night.

I slept immediately and deeply.

Sometime in the middle of the night I heard my wife screaming into the phone. It was far away I thought and certainly a dream.

"Lakeview Balmoral is where they live . . . How do I know they're not there? That's a dumb question, John. I called them . . . I assume they'll go up Edens to 94 and then to Wisconsin 30 . . . And I want those telephone records today . . . Yes, in the morning . . . Wake up and listen to me, John . . . I told you it's a matter of life and death and tell that eejit at Area Six that when I call for you in the middle of the night it is always a matter of life and death and he shouldn't try to put me down . . . Yes, their lives are in mortal danger . . . You should be after knowing better to ask me whether I'm sure . . . Do they have garda in Wisconsin . . . State Police? Well, alert them too . . . I suppose they're most likely to be waiting on Wisconsin 30, not the interstate, but I don't know that . . . I just know they're in deep trouble . . . Call me as soon as you find out . . . Apologize to your wife for me . . . I wouldn't have awakened you if it wasn't deadly serious . . . She at least knew who Nuala Anne was . . . Not like that asshole at Area Six."

"Are you awake, Dermot love?"

"Woman, I am!

I rolled over and tried to sit up.

"You heard what I said?"

"You gave Commander Culhane his marching orders, didn't you?"

"That focking eejit who answered his phone didn't know who I was . . . Can you imagine anyone over there who hasn't heard of me?"

"New man in town?"

"Still."

"The younger Currans are in danger?"

"Terrible, mortal danger. It's going to be close. And it'll be all my fault for not seeing the threat all along."

"They left awful early for their few hours in Wisconsin."

"Wasn't I after telling you that they're kids! No sensible adult with children leaves that early for a trip on Sunday morning. What's the rush?"

"When did they leave?"

"How should I know? I called them when I woke up. It was three-thirty. It may already be too late."

"Your instincts wouldn't have bothered you if they had left long before."

"I don't trust my instincts on matters of time. Back in the Stone Age they didn't have clocks. Get up, Dermot, we have to pray for them."

She flipped on the lights.

She was wearing one of her most frilly gowns, which means that I'm correct that there's no correlation between the gown and sexual interest.

So we knelt at the side of our bed until first light broke in the sky, saying the Rosary over and over again.

Then my wife relaxed.

"They're all right, Dermot, we can go back to sleep."

Which I tried to do.

I didn't argue. She was a wonderful wife. But why did she have to be fey, especially in the middle of the night. And how did she know that Jack and Marti were safe?

Then the phone rang again.

"Yes, John, I know . . . I just know that's all . . . State Police intercepted them north of Mundelein . . . The cops are taking the

429

Curran car north in hopes of trapping the bomber? Fair play to them . . . And Wisconsin police will patrol Highway 30 . . . Brilliant . . . Thanks for the call, John . . . Oh, don't hang up . . . One more thing . . . Tell them to watch out for roadside bombs . . . I'm very serious.

"Before you even ask, Dermot Michael Coyne, I don't know why I thought of a roadside bomb. I just did."

"Are you sure?"

"Not completely . . . Now go to sleep, you poor dear man."

I don't know when, but later, the sky alight with the grayness just before sunrise, the phone rang again.

"Yes, John? Did they really! Thanks be to God and all the Holy Saints and Angels . . . Four Dominicans planting a roadside bomb on a deserted stretch of Wisconsin 30! . . . How are you going to explain that to the Wisconsin State Police!"

I didn't want to hear any more. I was married to a witch, a very dangerous witch!

"You heard that, Dermot love?"

She was crying with relief. And happiness.

I put my arm around her.

"You're quite incredible, Nuala Anne

McGrail, and yourself saving six lives this morning!"

"Six?"

"Figure four Wisconsin cops in the car."

On a daffy assignment in the early light of Sunday morning there was probably only two cops in the car at the most.

"Didn't they capture these four perpetrators in the very act of planting a roadside bomb. The cops are all pleased with themselves. Only some of the people at Area Six know how it went down. Commander Culhane looks like a genius."

"Good for him."

"Go to sleep, Dermot Luv, I'll get the kids up and feed them. Isn't that Fiona bumping the door to remind me that's it's time for Ma to get to work? You'll need a good night's sleep . . . We have a long day ahead of us."

I'm not sure I liked that promise, but I was too tired to care.

30

We were in Mike Casey's personal limo, a Mercedes 300SL equipped with every known electronic gimmick, and ourselves about to solve the mystery, as Nuala herself had put it.

We had met at our house at eleven — John Culhane, Mike Casey, Nuala, and myself. The dogs were in attendance. Fiona would not be denied admission once she smelled a cop in house. Maeve had to come along. Ethne had readily agreed to take charge of the kids for the day. His eyes wide with affection and desire, Damian agreed to help her.

Nuala had proposed her plan. John was reluctant. Mike sympathetic. The three of them argued it out — I was, as usual at these times, odd man out. John finally agreed that Nuala had to be right. She'd saved a whole bunch of lives last night, who was he to argue with her instincts? There could be no doubt about her solution. The telephone records were on the coffee table with the key dates circled.

I had called Jack. He knew that the Dominicans had been caught but was astonished by the events.

"Both of us are still trembling, Dermot! Then we heard about the roadside bomb and we trembled even more . . . What's happening?"

"It's almost over, Jack, almost over. Your family is safe. Have you talked to them?"

"We didn't call them because we didn't know what to say . . ."

"Good! Don't call them. By tomorrow afternoon we will have a full report."

"Marti is on the other line. She wants to say thanks too, Dermot."

"I bet your wife saved our lives. Tell her thanks too."

I had passed on the message to my wife.

"And herself pregnant too!"

The two cops were astonished.

"And herself probably not knowing it."

Neither John nor Mike had asked a question. I had given that up long ago.

So Commander Culhane went home to catch up on his sleep and the rest of us went forth on our mission.

"This is a little dicey, Nuala Anne. I hope it works."

"Sure, there's not a doubt in the world like."

We discussed the various roles we would play. Rather my wife the actress told the other two of us what to say and what she would say. I was not allotted much of a role — which was fine with me.

YOU KNEW SHE WAS DAFT WHEN YOU MARRIED HER.

I didn't expect this.

IF YOU HAD ANY SENSE YOU WOULD HAVE.

We pulled up to the house. Mike Casey knocked on the door.

Trevor Curran admitted us. Mike introduced himself and us, though Trevor seemed to recognize me.

"I want to be clear before we begin the conversation," he said formally. "I understand that this is not a criminal investigation and that you are not here in any way as officers of the law."

"Mr. Curran," Mike replied with equal formality, "we are all bound by contract to protect the Curran family, I by an explicit written contract, these young people by an implicit one."

"Very well, come in and sit down."

"I must say also that if we cannot resolve this problem today, police officers will come in a day or two with a formal warrant."

Annette, taut and stiff, in a light blue Easter dress, glared at us.

"I will not talk to these people, Trevor. Father Charles has advised me not to."

"And I, as your husband, order you to."

Did Trevor know what was coming, perhaps only vaguely?

We all sat down.

Nuala began. She spoke so gently and so sorrowfully that I could hardly hear her.

"Annette, we know that you have been spying on the rest of your family at your husband's grandfather's request for some time. We have the phone records of your conversations with him on the day River House exploded, on the day the bomb was found in the car at the Four Seasons, and yesterday, when you told him that Jack and Marti were driving up to Twin Lakes this morning."

"No, no, none of that's true. I did only what Father Charles told me to do . . ."

"By the grace of God," Nuala continued, gently implacable, "no one has been killed, though I'm thinking the angels had to be working over time. John and Estelle were not in the house at the time because they had flown to Italy and you didn't know that when you told your husband's grandfather they would be in the house. Mr. Casey's agents found the bomb on the car before it exploded and some Wisconsin State Police found the criminals planting a roadside bomb on Wisconsin Highway 30 before it could destroy Jack and Marti."

"You can't prove it! I didn't do any of it!"

She eased into hysteria. We let her make the trip.

"Yes, we can prove it, Annette. We don't want to hurt you or your family but we know you spied on them."

"You have the phone records?" her husband asked.

I walked over with the excerpts on which Nuala had marked the appropriate calls between the Ocean Reef number and Annette's cell phone. Trevor glanced at them, shut his eyes, and shook his head.

I was supposed to note that the numbers were of her cell phone and Long Tom's apartment. It wasn't necessary.

"Father Charles told me that everything I did was all right. He praised me for my courage. I am not ashamed. Besides, they all hate me, they make fun of me, they despise my children! They all should die!"

"If that be the case, Father Charles will be liable to indictment as an accessory to multiple attempts at murder," Mike the Cop said firmly, "should this information become public. You should consider that you engaged, however unintentionally, in the attempted murder of four people, all of them your in-laws or their spouses."

"I hate them, I hate them, I'm going to talk to Father Charles and he'll tell me that I've done the right thing."

She fled from the room screaming.

Trevor opened his eyes.

"What would you people have me do?"

It was my turn.

"We presume you will seek psychiatric help for your wife."

"Naturally, I will have no choice but to institutionalize her for some time . . . I should have seen this coming. I will withdraw my children from that school. They will be delighted . . ."

He rubbed his hand across his forehead.

"She didn't use to be that way . . . Father Charles took control of her life. I should have stopped that relationship. It is truly my fault."

"These things happen gradually," I was extemporizing. "One doesn't notice the change, then there are serious problems. I'm sure that with proper therapy and medication, she will recover."

Me wife, the director, nodded in approval.

"Yes," he said thoughtfully, "I suppose you're right, Dermot. She always was a perfectionist — four kids, keeping the house in order, she became a prisoner of her obsessions . . . I know an excellent institution. I have some influence there. I'll see that she's placed in their care tomorrow. I will see also that Father Charles has no further contact with her. I will threaten his organization with legal action . . ."

"That's wise. Legal action will not be necessary against them, however. The people at Opus are good people and they mean well. Sometimes neurotic relationships happen there as in other institutions. They are not the villains portrayed in the Da Vinci Code. I'm sure a measured discussion will be enough."

"Thank you, Dermot, you are a very wise man."

I shut up because I knew that if I said any more, I would be in deep trouble. Two unscripted paragraphs were all right, but a third . . . !

"And now, Mr. Casey, what about the Chicago Police Department, over which you presided with so much dignity and humanity."

The play was going as planned.

"I spoke with the police and the State's Attorney this morning. They have great respect for the Curran family and they wish to avoid any more suffering for you. The testimony of the Dominican mob the Wisconsin police arrested this morning will be enough to settle this case. If you call Commander Culhane at Area Six and tell him that you and a lawyer would like to talk to him on Tuesday morning, he will provide all the privacy arrangements you need. You will have to do nothing more than tell Commander Culhane and the State's Attorney who will be with him what you have learned about your wife's phone conversations with your grandfather. They agree that no useful purpose would be served at this time for that part of the story to become public."

"I have to trust you, don't I, Superintendent?"

"Yes, sir."

"Whom better to trust . . . I must thank you all very much." His voice wavered. "You've been very helpful, very considerate. You, Ms. McGrail, I am sure, are responsible for saving the lives of my parents . . . Thank you."

"You're welcome," said my woebegone wife.

"I do love her," he said, choking back tears. "I will stand by her . . . Now I must see to her. Would you be so kind as to show yourselves to the door."

We did.

"Well done, everyone," herself said. "Youse both was brilliant."

Still, we drove back to Southport Avenue in silence.

Mike called John Culhane and filled him in.

"What about Long Tom?" I asked.

"We'll have some of our friends in Florida keep a close eye on him. My information is that his health is failing rapidly."

"He did a lot of bad stuff for a man who is failing rapidly."

"If the cops get anything out of the Dominicans, we can have him arrested, but we'll have to see what the situation is."

Back in our house, I hugged me wife.

"Congratulations, Nuala Anne, you were the one who was brilliant."

"I'm not quite finished yet, Dermot. Let's go up to our study."

So it was "ours"!

"Pick up the other phone, Dermot love."

I did. She punched in a number.

"Tom Curran," a voice growled.

"Tom Curran, I'm Nuala Anne McGrail.

I'm your nemesis. I'm the one who has frustrated all your plots. I will continue to do so. If you keep it up, I'll arrest you and bring you to Chicago for trial. That will kill you, something you barely escaped in the islands so long ago — and I won't say how you escaped either. If I were in your position, Tom Curran, I'd call a priest and confess all my sins while I still have time. Don't waste your last chance. Good-bye, Long Tom."

She hung up gently, then bent over and wept bitterly.

I sat next to her and put my arm around her.

"Well done, Marie Phinoulah Annagh. You just saved that man."

"I hope so, Dermot. I hope so. Poor old bastard."

31

"Without going into the details," my wife began in the Four Seasons suite, "I was pretty sure that someone in the family was behind the attempted murders. 'Tis almost always someone in the family. I couldn't see any of you wanting to murder your parents, whom you all dearly love, each in your own way. That left Long Tom. But how could he know your movements so perfectly? But wait a moment, he didn't know about your flight to Rome. How could he have missed that? Finally, it dawned on me that one family member didn't know about the flight."

"Trevor!" John gasped. "That's why he's not here? He wasn't in when I made my call. So I called Deirdre . . . and the circuit was completed!"

"No one told me to call Trevor," Marie Therese said. "I sent an e-mail to Rory . . . I didn't know . . ."

"So who then was the spy? Trevor? That would be absurd."

"Annette," Estelle gasped.

"It took me the longest time to figure it out and there it was right in front of me face. So we checked her cell phone records. There were the calls back and forth which fit perfectly with the three attempts. Nothing supernatural about that."

Yeah, sure!

Jack caught my eye and winked that he knew better.

"Annette is in a mental institution now and her prognosis with good therapy and medication is promising," I said. "And Trevor has sundered their ties with Opus. He also agrees that Father Charles is not typical of the group."

"They place too much emphasis on blind obedience," Rory observed. "That's not a good idea."

"Will she be indicted?" Deirdre asked anxiously.

"I shouldn't think that will be necessary. The police have the actual bombers."

"Dad?" Estelle said.

"He had an extraordinarily malevolent influence on your daughter-in-law," Mike Casey replied. "He is, however, a sick old man. We will keep a close watch on him. If he has any more contacts with professional killers, we will have him arrested. I don't think that will be necessary."

"He's my father," John finally spoke. "I guess he hates me. That hurts. That the hate was so terrible . . . is even harder to bear."

"He also loved you, John," Nuala Anne told him. "He never was able to conquer the ambivalence, poor dear man. And it's over . . . Rory, you have a friend or a class-mate in or near Ocean Reef?"

"Why yes, I do. He's friend, FBI, Foreign Born Irish. A very clever guy."

"Call him and tell him that he should go see your grandfather."

"As soon as I get back to the rectory."

John then announced that they were going to buy a big old house in Lincoln Park, not too far from the old place and we would be neighbors and that soon they would have another dinner.

Everyone cheered.

As Rory shook hands with me, he whispered, "I'm getting to know about mystics over at the Cathedral, Dermot. I know one when I see one."

I just laughed. Smart young man.

Back on Southport Avenue, we toasted each other in very expensive Irish whiskey, just a splasheen in each glass.

"We did it," Nuala said with a triumphant smile.

"You did it, Nuala Anne, my Irish Crystal wife!" I said.

"We're a team, Dermot love, and that's that . . . Speaking of which, do you know what your daughter said to me before she left for school this morning?"

"Ah, it must be bad if she's my daughter again. Socra Marie?"

"No, that little spy, Nelliecoyne. She asked me what we were going to name our little boy baby."

"And you told her?"

"I told her that we had no such plans and she shouldn't listen to the wild things her little sister said. She was very disappointed."

"Then you're not pregnant?"

"I'm not, Dermot, and I always know when I'm pregnant. And you're the first one I tell."

That was that.

Rory called the next day around noon. I was back working on my poetry and also trying to figure out how to turn the priesteen's manuscript into a story.

"Well, my friend, Father Enright, went to see Granddad last night. He called me to tell me that he had made a very good confession. Then he called me this morning just a few minutes ago to report that, when he arrived at the apartment this morning to bring him Communion, he was dying. Yet he gobbled down the host and kissed the crucifix, then sat up, stretched out his arms, and cried, 'Elizabeth, take me home with you!' "

"Extraordinary!"

"Sure is. I'm going to call the family now. We'll probably fly down there. He wanted to be buried near Ocean Reef. I wanted Nuala to know. Tell her for me that I said thanks."

"I certainly will."

32

The only crisis on First Communion day was not over the dress — which, with Danuta's assistance, was wondrous. It was over why Nelliecoyne's mother was not singing as she had at Johnpete's baptism.

"I'd love to, dear, but that wouldn't be fair to the other children whose mothers can't do anything special at First Communion."

She rolled her eyes at me.

Nelliecoyne accepted the explanation. Sometime soon we'd have to explain to her about the pastor.

Nonetheless, the ceremony was lovely. Our daughter was the perfect model of the reverent, solemn seven-year-old, though she grinned at my camera.

The pastor preached for a half hour on the evils of abortion.

Nuala filled several handkerchiefs with tears.

Then at breakfast on Wednesday morning, Nuala said brightly over our tea and soda bread, "You probably ought to know, Dermot Michael Coyne, that you're going to have a son. He'll be full-term and it will be an easy pregnancy and I vote that we call him Patrick Joseph after me grandfather and I'm not going to put on a lot of weight."

I cheered, leaped out of my chair, and hugged her.

"How do you know! Are you sick?"

"Certainly not! I don't need to be sick to know!"

"Do you know all the other details? You never did before."

"I knew that Socra Marie would be early. I didn't know how early. I didn't want to worry you. But there's nothing to worry about this time."

"I'm so happy," I said.

LIAR.

No way.

"And your grandfather was called Patjo, as I remember?"

" 'Tis true!"

"I like that."

Not that I had any choice.

— Afterword —

The description of the Risings of '98 and '03 in the narrative of the nameless priesteen, as Nuala calls him, are historically accurate with some details elided (but none changed) for narrative pace. The priesteen is a fictional observer, hence he has no name. Since he didn't exist, he never fell in love with Sarah Curran.

Readers wishing more details might consult *Citizen Lord* by Stella Tillyard, *Cornwallis* by Franklin and Mary Wickwire, *Wolf Tone* by Marianne Elliot, *Robert Emmet and the Rebellion of 1798* and *Robert Emmet and the Rising of 1803* both by Ruan O'Donnell, and *Robert Emmet* by Marianne Elliot. The toast from Charles Cornwallis to George Washington is taken from *Washington's Crossing* by David Hackett Fischer, page 362.

The O'Donnell books are rich in detail, indeed too rich by half, and hence very difficult reading. Ms. Elliot's two books are a study in contrasts. The former is straight historiography, though she does in her introduction identify Wolf Tone with the Provisional IRA of which he was surely not a member. In her book on Emmet, she engages in a debunking exercise. She aims at the "Emmet" myth, which she claims has produced subsequent republican violence from Young Ireland of 1848 to the Provos of the present.

I make no case for the IRA, but I wish writers like Ms. Elliot would also denounce wars of liberation in other countries. If Gerry Adams is a terrorist, then so is Nelson Mandela. Other peoples in the world have the right to turn to violence to defeat colonialism. The Irish somehow do not. Ms. Elliot reveals that she is part of the Ascendancy school of Irish historiography in a passing comment that Lord Cornwallis was too lenient in his repression of the remnants of '98. One must assume that she meant that he should have hung more Irish. In this perspective the Irish are always to blame for the problems in the country and the English never.

It would appear that the most effective strategy for ridding Ireland from colonial rule was, as Nuala Anne says, fight, then negotiate like Michael Collins did.

The many deaths of infants, children,

and young adults (including Nuala's friend Mollie Malone) in the Irish segment of my story was not unusual for the time and place or indeed for any time in human history up until the middle of the nineteenth century, when sanitation measures and water purification in much of Western Europe improved.

No one has written Robert Emmet's epitaph yet. Ruan O'Donnell suggests that now is the time. Marianne Elliot says that he has become such a patron saint of the IRA that it should never be written, a curious form of historical argument if there ever was one. The Irish government is not eager to erect a monument because of the situation in the North.

Ireland has indeed taken its place in the family of nations. Yet should anyone write the epitaph while a quarter of Ireland is still an English colony?

The most fundamental question is why England had the right to conquer Ireland, then colonize it. Ms. Elliot clearly assumes that it did. Others will want to disagree.

I agree, however, with Nuala Anne (heaven help me if I do not) that if England had not suspended its 1912 promise of Home Rule to Ireland at the start of the Great War, then there never would have been the Easter Rising and the subsequent Anglo-Irish war and probably not the endless succession of "troubles" over the North. They should have waited, it will be said. England would have honored its promise in the 1920s. England always honors its promises.

Yeah?

Tucson
Palm Sunday 2005